STRIFE

Hidden Book Four

COLLEEN VANDERLINDEN

Strife: Hidden Book Four
Colleen Vanderlinden

Published in the United States
by Building Block Studios LLC

ISBN 0692220623
ISBN-13 978-0692220627

http://www.colleenvanderlinden.com/hidden
http://www.buildingblockstudios.com

DEDICATION

As always,
to my amazing husband and
partner in crime, Roger

CONTENTS

ACKNOWLEDGMENTS

Thank you to my husband and my crazy awesome kids. You guys are the absolute best, and I am so lucky to have you!

Thanks to my lovely in-laws, Peggy and Roger, for their support and enthusiasm.

Thank you to Will Vanderlinden for proofreading help with a touch of humor.

Many thanks to the lovely Elizabeth Hunter. The advice you've given me, as well as the much-needed pep talks, have been such a help to this newbie indie author. Thank you!

I was extremely lucky to have an amazing group of beta readers for Strife. You ladies absolutely rock, and I know for a fact that this is a stronger book because of your input. Huge thanks and many hugs to Susan Cambra, Shawna Cerda, Jolissa Cooke, Ginger Garff, Jennifer G., Katie Knudsen, Sarah Leenart, Kathie Littlemore, Jayna Longstreet, Katherine Helen Peters, and Rachel Scott. Let's do it again sometime, shall we?

Thank you to everyone who has followed Molly's story up to this point. Every writer dreams of the day when their words will actually be read by someone, of the day when they hear the words "I was up all night reading this!" You guys have helped make that dream a reality for this particular writer, and I cannot thank you enough.

Colleen Vanderlinden
Detroit
June, 2014

CHAPTER ONE

My name is Molly Brooks.

Vigilante.

Godslayer.

Oathbreaker.

Daughter of the Lord of the Dead.

The Angel.

What a joke.

I now lead a team of supernaturals who chose me when I'd split from my old team. The people of my city consider me a legend, a god. A hero.

You want to know what I am?

I'm someone who's afraid to go to sleep at night. I'm someone who scrubs my hands so often I make them bleed. I'm someone who re-lives every single one of my deaths, over and over and over again.

I'm a powerful being who can't use my powers without ending up in agony.

I'm afraid of myself. The darkness inside me grows, and I am losing hope that I'm strong enough to contain it. If I lose control, if I unleash whatever this is that is inside me, everyone I've ever loved will suffer for it.

One, in particular, more than others.

And the easy solution would be to get rid of the problem: me. Except that unfortunately, I can't die.

As in, plenty have tried to make that happen. But I just keep fucking coming back.

Lucky me.

I drove the route I'd driven dozens of times from my house to the loft where Nain and his team lived. Every block that closed the distance between me and the people who lived there made my stomach clench a little more.

My hands gripped the steering wheel, hard enough to snap it if I'd unleash my powers just a little. As it was, the stress was stirring my powers, heightening them, and it was starting to hurt. Eunomia reached over and put her cool hand over mine on the steering wheel.

"Relax, my friend," she said softly.

"Better to be on edge than relaxed, considering. Don't you think?" I asked her. I glanced over at her, then into the rear-view mirror. The rest of my friends, my team, sat in the back seat. Levitt, Hephaestus, and Shanti. The imps had gone ahead; they'd meet us there. My team knew about the problems I was having. They knew that the moment I relaxed, the darkness inside me threatened to take over. They knew how close I was to giving in to it, to becoming the thing I feared most. They fought beside me. They watched out for me. And maybe most importantly, they watched me, always prepared for that moment when whatever was inside me took over for good. And they knew that when that moment came, their job was to try to put me down.

Yes. I trust my best friends to try to destroy me. Doesn't everyone?

We'd gotten to know each other better than I could have imagined over the past few weeks. We lived together, worked together, fought together. My house, which had seemed so big during all the years I'd lived there alone, felt cozy now. Granted, it was a crazy combination of gods, demons, vampires, and imps, but it was mine.

They knew my weaknesses. My problems. The promises I made to myself. We were more than a team. We were a family and I trusted them with my life, as they trusted me with theirs. Considering how many powerful beings I had gunning for me, I thought their trust was misplaced. They ignored me when I said stuff like that.

They knew, better than anyone, that I was not as tough as most of the world believed. They knew I still tried to scrub unseen blood and gore off of my body. They knew I had nightmares, when I managed to let myself sleep. They knew that in my weakest moments, I cursed my life for the things I couldn't have.

"This is exactly why you should have talked to the fuckin' shifter on the phone all those times he called. Now you're goin' in with all this pent-up shit. Not healthy, queenie," Hephaestus said from the back seat.

"Well, that's why you guys are here, right?" I said, glancing at him in the rear-view mirror. "Keep an eye on me. Make an excuse to leave if it seems like I'm going to lose it. But I can't keep putting Nain off about this meeting, considering we're all trying to hunt Strife down and she's here because of me."

Strife.

I'd trapped her in my realm back when I'd initially destroyed the gateway between here and the Nether, cutting off this world from the world of the immortals. She was not my biggest fan. I'd killed one of her closest friends, Enyo, the goddess of war. And I'd trapped her other pal, Ares, the god of war, in a talisman that added to my power. She'd been doing her best to cause chaos, even going as far as using Brennan's infant son (another thing I tried not to think about too often) to harm those I cared about.

And we'd all been hunting her, but she was wily. We hadn't even gotten close.

So I'd finally given in and agreed to meet with Nain and his team.

I hadn't seen Brennan since the night we'd decided to stop seeing each other. So I'm a coward. But it hurt too much, and I had enough on my mind. I knew it was for the best. It didn't make it any easier.

Sometimes, love doesn't conquer all. That's a bunch of bullshit.

I pulled into the parking garage and we all got out of the car. My team, for better or worse, had adopted my uniform as their own: black cargo pants, black shirts. The imps were there already, waiting for me as they'd said they would. And it wasn't just them. My parents, Hades and Tisiphone, stood by the elevator. Hades leaned against the wall, arms folded over his chest. My father never looked worried about anything. Though, I guess if you were the Lord of the Dead and ruler of the afterlife, you wouldn't be worried about much, either. Tisiphone, as always, looked like she was on guard, ready to kick ass.

"What are you two doing here?" I asked them as my team and I walked toward the elevator. "Not that I'm not happy to see you," I added. My mother gave me a small hug, murmuring a hello, and my father studied me.

"There's a reason you've been avoiding this. We're here in case we're needed." I hadn't been thrilled about telling my parents about the issues I was having, but E had insisted and I had to admit it was smart. If I lost my mind, they were two of the few beings who had any decent chance of getting me under control.

I nodded. My parents, as always, were also dressed in black. "Go team death," I muttered under my breath as I pulled the gate up and we all got onto the elevator.

"We need a secret handshake," Shanti said. Then she hit the button to take us up to the loft. I took a deep breath. My stomach was turning. It wasn't seeing the team, or even Nain, necessarily. I was fine with that. I'd had lunch with Ada and Stone the previous week, seen Nain around town, and while things with my ex always had a weird undercurrent of tension, I was fine. It was Brennan. I loved him. At least, I thought I did. I was hurt over what he'd done, and the more I thought about all of it, the harder it was to just let it go. Maybe I wasn't as mature and understanding as I thought I should be. But the fact of the matter was that the more I thought about it, the less likely it could ever be that I'd be fine with Brennan, with seeing his son every day and knowing how he'd come to be.

Great. I was more like my stepmother than I'd ever realized.

I could admit that I missed him. I'd loved the way he'd taken care of me, the way every one of my whims had been met. I missed the way he made love to me.

But I was starting to believe, deep down, that maybe it just wasn't enough. And that was without the darkness rising within me. Because as much as I missed the good things, the time apart had given me plenty of time to think. And I was starting to think that maybe there are just some things you can't come back from.

When I had my blackouts, I had visions of murdering him, brutally, in ways that made me sick. And even though I'm hurt, I know I'd never do any of those things to him. It was this...thing. Whatever it was that was inside me. It was even more bloodthirsty than I was, and it wanted to hurt everyone I cared about. Especially him, because he was mine. I'd claimed him, and I cared about him. It hated him. It regarded him with loathing and jealousy. I knew that without knowing how, and that alone scared the shit out of me.

I'd tried to talk Nain out of this dozens of times. But my ex-husband was not the most accommodating man. And he'd finally just growled that I needed to get the fuck over it, that I was being weak.

And he knows me well enough to know which buttons to push. The weakness button is almost guaranteed to make me move my ass.

So there we were. I just wanted to get through the meeting without crying. Or, you know...killing anybody. Either or.

"I'm going to say as little as possible. Maybe this will be quick and painless," I said to them as the elevator creaked up to the main living area.

We poured out of the elevator, and I lifted my hand to knock on the heavy mahogany door that led into the loft. When I'd lived here, I'd just walked in. But this wasn't my home anymore, and I wasn't going to let myself fall into my old habits now.

Any of my old habits.

I was relieved when it was Ada who answered the door. She smiled when she saw me, pulled me into a huge hug, and I hugged her back. "Good to see you again, baby girl," she said softly, and I gave her another squeeze. She greeted the rest of my team, and they greeted her politely, Shanti and Levitt hugging her when they stepped into the loft.

I could feel him. Our connection was still alive, and I could practically feel every breath he took. I could feel his eyes on me; need, raw anger flowing from him like lava. It was agony. I took a breath, and we followed Ada into the dining room, my team trailing behind me. Nain, Brennan, Stone, and Chief Jones were all sitting at the dining room table. Brennan's son, Sean, played quietly in a playpen nearby.

Nain stood, eyes on me. Then he glanced at my team.

"Didn't know you traveled with an entourage now, Molls," he said, deep voice practically making the floor vibrate.

"Yeah, well. You know me. There's nothing I like more than feeling important. Hence: entourage."

He studied me for a minute, and I kept my eyes on him. He knew at least a little bit of what was happening with me. I'd confessed it to him before I'd moved out, warned him he might have to try to put me down. Told him how to do it. And we'd worked together a few times over the past few weeks. He'd seen, close up, how hard I fought against the darkness. How close I was to losing it.

"You look good," he said, and I felt the usual from him: anger, desire. Mixed together. It was our signature blend. Always had been.

I just nodded, not really in the mood for making nice. Please, let's just get this over with, I thought to myself. Then Chief Jones shook my hand, said a few words in greeting, and Stone wrapped me up in a huge bear hug.

Brennan stayed where he was. He seemed unable to stop looking at me, and I did my best to avoid looking at him. But I failed, as usual, and when I looked at him, our eyes met.

"Hey," he said quietly.

I nodded at him then looked away, unable to trust my voice. Jesus, I just wanted to make it through this so I could go home and bury my face in my pillow and scream. I sat down, and my team arrayed themselves behind me. They stood, Levitt and Shanti at attention, hands folded behind their backs. My parents and Hephaestus stood with their arms crossed, watching everything. Especially me. And Eunomia took the seat beside me. My right hand. She was able to read me better than most, and I needed her now because I couldn't trust myself.

Gods. He was sitting right the hell there. Not even six feet away from me and everything sane in me, the part of me that had claimed him, bonded him to me, screamed in desperation, needing to be closer to him. And the thing inside rose, wanted to see him bleed. And I sat there, and tried to ignore the fact that my heart broke a little more every single time I saw him, remembering that no matter how much he'd claimed to love me, it hadn't been that hard for him to warm someone else's bed.

I tamped it down. I'd made my decision for a reason, and I'd stick to it no matter how good he smelled or how much I'd missed his touch. And there was something I had to do, something I'd known for a while I'd have to do, and I kept putting it off. Today was the day. I just had to get through this first.

"Okay," I said. "I'm here. Let's get this over with."

Nain nodded, took his seat after I was settled in mine. "Strife. You know more than any of us do about her. What can you tell us?"

I took a breath, forced myself to focus. "She's a spirit daemon. Not quite as powerful as immortals like my parents."

"Or like you," Nain put in, and I hesitated, nodded.

"But powerful enough in her own way. She works with witches, especially, tells them how to do spells they'd never be able to do on their own. She incites chaos, and the more she causes, the stronger she becomes. It feeds her, kind of the same way anger and pain strengthens us," I said this last part more to Nain, and he nodded. "She's pissed. She was friends with a couple of immortals I ended. She wants revenge on me and she knows enough to know that taking her shit out on this city is a decent way to get back at me."

"So is that all there is to her game? Just cause chaos?" Jones asked.

I shrugged. "My guess is she's biding her time. Building her strength. Probably rebuilding her team, since I destroyed her old one."

"And there's another one, right?" Jones asked, shaking his head.

"Yeah. The spirit of terror. They're likely working together. What's better than fear and chaos, right?"

"Shit," Jones said, sitting back. He'd heard some of this before, but he still wasn't any happier about it. I knew he blamed me for the troubles his city had to deal with. He wasn't exactly wrong.

Eunomia leaned toward me and I tilted my head toward her. "Do you need a break?" she asked softly.

"I'm fine," I said. The truth. The longer I sat there, the easier it became to quiet the thing inside me, even with Brennan sitting right there. Good. It would make it that much easier to do what I knew I had to do before I left.

"So what's the plan, Molls?" Nain asked. I looked back up at him.

"We're doing the same thing you guys are doing. Trying to find even the smallest lead to her. So far, we've come up with jack. It's like she doesn't exist, except for the fact that we're still seeing her mark show up in places. Graffiti in alleyways, carved into trees. At least not in any bodies lately. Unless you guys have found something like that," I finished.

Nain shook his head. "No, we've seen the same thing you have. She seems to have let up on the killing. That makes me feel like some bad shit is on the horizon."

I nodded. "Me too. I wish I knew more. I've asked my parents," I said, gesturing back toward Hades and Tisiphone, "and they have said pretty much what we already know: she's likely lying in wait. She's good at hiding, sticking to the shadows, working her angle without anyone knowing she's doing it."

"What about getting rid of her?" Nain asked. "Can she be killed? Or is this another one of those things only you can do?"

I turned to my father. "Do you want to explain this one?"

Hades nodded. "The spirit daemons can't actually be killed. Think of it this way: they're the physical entity, an avatar, if you will, of the emotions of humanity. They exist because mortals feel these things. So unless mortals stop causing chaos, or stop feeling angry, or honest, or whatever it is, that's the only way a spirit daemon can truly cease to be."

"Great," Jones groaned. "So what does that mean for us?"

"It's not as bad as you think, shifter," Hades said. "It's complicated. As I said, these are avatars of the different spirits. You can destroy the avatar, the physical manifestation of the spirit. Eventually, it will just develop a new avatar. They never really go away."

"So she's just going to pop up in a new body later?" Stone asked.

"Yes, and no," Hades answered. "Strife will have a new body, but that new being won't be the same as this one. The next avatar will have its own memories, its own agenda. It will have its own loves and hates."

"So the next avatar of Strife won't want to destroy my city over a grudge?" Jones asked, and my father and I both nodded. "You're sure?" Jones asked, looking right at my father. I had to give it to the chief: dude had guts. Most beings wouldn't even think of challenging my father.

"Yes. We've done it before."

"So this isn't something Molls has to do on her own, then?" Nain said, repeating his initial question.

"No, it isn't," Tisiphone said. "We can kill her. It's likely a very strong mortal could even kill the avatar, though I don't recommend trying. She'll only get more powerful the longer she's here."

"I don't want any of you facing off against her, thinking you're gonna be a hero," I said, looking straight at Nain. "Just because you'll 'probably' be able to kill her doesn't mean you should try. She's mine," I finished, and I heard the snarl in my voice. I took a deep breath, tamping down the rage beginning to rise within me again.

"How do the avatars get reborn, or whatever?" Nain asked my father. "Does it work the same way it did with me and Molly when we came back?"

I felt a wave of irritation roll off of Brennan, and glanced over at him. He was looking at the table top, avoiding my eyes.

Hades nodded. "Pretty much."

"Here's a question: has anyone figured out yet what the hell is going on with Molly?" Brennan asked, finally speaking up. He was still looking at the table. The room went silent.

"We are not discussing me," I said. My team had tensed around me. Anger rolled off of them. They were loyal, protective. And the one thing we'd all agreed on was that the fewer people who knew about my issues, the better.

"So, no, then," Brennan said.

"We're not talking about it," Nain growled. On the same page as me for once. I liked the chief. I loved Ada and Stone. But they were not in my inner circle, and the chief especially already had issues with me.

Chief Jones opened his mouth.

"Don't bother, mortal," Hades said, and Jones closed his mouth, irritated.

Nain shot another glare in Brennan's direction, then he looked at me. "What do you need from us? How can we help you find this bitch?"

I shook my head. "I wish I knew. If I had even the slightest idea of how to find her, I'd be tracking her ass down now. The only thing we've come up with is to try to watch the news and the chief's reports more closely, try to find patterns. Higher rates of crimes concentrated in a particular area. People will feel her presence, even if she's not trying. Things should be rougher in any area she's settled in."

"And if she hasn't settled anywhere, then we have nothing," Jones said.

"Right," I agreed. "I'm sorry. It's all I have for you."

We sat for a while longer, sharing the few, almost worthless things we knew. Jones agreed to pull some reports together and send them over to Nain and I, and I hoped we'd find something that way. Jones left pretty quickly after. I glanced over at Brennan, who was still sitting there simmering.

"I need to talk to you a minute," I said.

He nodded. Need, mixed with irritation. I'd felt it, every time Nain and I had exchanged a word during the meeting. One more reason to do this, now.

We walked to the far corner of the loft, to two chairs in the corner of the living room, near the windows. He reached out to touch me, and I flinched back. Anger washed over me again.

"What? I can't touch you?"

"I need to be able to focus," I said, watching him.

"Apparently answering phone calls is too much to ask. Or does that make it too hard to focus as well?" He asked this last with a bit of a sneer in his voice that I didn't like. I knew he was hurt, frustrated. I got it. But I'd tried the best I could to make it clear that I was trying to keep him safe.

"I have been trying to get my head straight. It hasn't been easy," I said in a low voice. "So yes. I haven't been answering the phone—"

"You answer when he calls you," he interrupted.

I stared at him. "Really? Are we back to this?"

"It kind of seems like we are. Especially when he came home the other night and I could smell you all over him."

"Then you also smelled the fucking werewolves we fought off together. And you know what? I don't have to explain myself to you. I'm doing the best I can, and you're not helping."

"Right. How often do you talk to Nain on the phone again?"

I didn't answer.

"I know how often. It's at least once a day."

"About work shit, Brennan," I said, shaking my head.

"What else am I supposed to think, when you answer his calls but can't be bothered to answer mine?"

"You're supposed to think of what I've told you, and understand that this is time I need." I glared at him until he finally looked away. He was making this easier every second. "Listen. I'm trying to get a handle on this thing. And it's hard. It's getting harder all the time. I think it would help me a lot if you broke your bond to me."

He snorted. "Right."

"Brennan. I'm not messing around here .."

"You want it broken so I won't know when you're with someone else," he said, obviously looking toward where Nain stood talking to my father on the other side of the loft, near the kitchen.

My jaw dropped open. Of all the things he could have said, that was about the last thing I'd expected. "Are you serious? Messing around is the last thing on my mind. That's more your territory, isn't it?"

Probably not the nicest thing to say. But now I was pissed and slightly in agreement with the thing inside me that wanted to kill him.

"And clearly you're not over that, huh?" Brennan asked.

I watched him. Anger rolled off him. The need was almost nonexistent, now. "Yeah. Silly me, having a hard time dealing with the fact that the man who swore up and down that I was the love of his life knew I was alive and chose to sleep with someone else. Crazy, right? Especially considering that you're sitting here pissed at me for *talking* to Nain."

"You were gone for two years when I had my thing with her. I was pretty sure you weren't coming back. I was pissed off and weak and thinking that maybe it was time to move on. Maybe it's time now."

"We've been over this. And I--"

He held up his hand, glared at me. "No. You know what? Fine."

"Fine, what?"

"Fine, I'll break it. It's a nightmare being bonded to you, you know that? Almost constant pain because you won't stop fighting and using your powers. And I can't even be by your side to make sure you're okay."

The thing was raging, and I fought it back as hard as I could. I closed my eyes, opened them again when I felt in control.

"Do you think I wanted this? Do you honestly think I wanted to come home from the goddamn Nether and find everything in my life upside down and then have whatever this is making me insane? I didn't fucking ask for this, Bren."

"Whatever. Let's just do this and then you can have all the space you need to figure out what it is you want."

I shook my head. "It has zero to do with what I want, and everything to do with the shit I'm forced to deal with. Again." I wanted to hit him. I wanted to cry. I wanted to tell him I was an idiot and beg him to take me back so I wouldn't have to feel so alone. I wouldn't do any of them, though.

He closed his eyes for a minute, anger still coursing through him. And I felt the warm, bright bond between us darken, his part of it, gone.

"Your turn," he muttered.

I closed my eyes. Mine was more complicated. I'd claimed him as mine. When an immortal does that to a mortal, it means something. It's not done lightly. You give them a little bit of your strength. It makes them stronger, less likely to get sick or injured. It was the reason the Guardians hadn't managed to kill him when they'd had him. It makes it so you always know, in general, where they are, and you can always find your way back to them. It makes it so their soul is deeply entwined with your own.

So it took some time for me to untangle us, to separate myself, my soul, from his. Finally, I felt the connection slither away, as if I'd let go of a helium balloon and watched it float off into the sky.

There was emptiness there now.

I clamped down the sadness, the sense of mourning that filled me. Later. I'd deal with it later. I opened my eyes. "Done."

"Great." He sat there for a moment, not looking at me. "I hope this does what you wanted it to."

"I think our bond was maybe why whatever this is has such a crazy reaction to you. It's the best guess I have. I'm sorry. And if you honestly think that screwing around with anyone is any part of my motivation, then you don't know me as well as you think you do. Maybe you need some time, too."

"Yeah. Well. I've had time. A couple months. A few years, before that. Maybe this was for the best. Now I can stop needing you to feel complete." He sat in silence, not looking at me. I could see that he was biting the inside of his cheek, a habit of his when he was irritated; the kind of thing you'd only notice if you lived with someone day after day.

"Bren... " I said, my heart breaking, his sadness overwhelming my own.

"I'm starting to figure myself out. This whole thing has made me take a good look at myself. And you know what I need?" he asked me, and I just watched him. "I need somebody to need me. And you don't need me. Not the way I need you to. I was so mad at you after you were gone. You threw us away, and I bet you didn't give it a second thought."

"I didn't know I would get trapped, Brennan."

"Yeah." He seemed like he wanted to say something else, but he stayed silent for several long seconds. "You've changed."

"Actually I haven't. Not all that much. I am what I am, Bren. I'm not going to stop fighting and settle down and be some kind of demure little woman."

He rolled his eyes. "I know. I feel like I put everything into us and you never even bothered trying to meet me halfway."

"Don't you get it? I don't want that. I don't want anyone's entire life to be about me. Do you have any idea how much pressure that is?"

He shook his head. "It's all about you. I think you two deserve one another."

"I cannot even believe you're reducing this to a you versus Nain thing."

"Yeah, well. You're free now. I hope it's all you hoped it would be." He met my eyes one more time, anger and sadness in his slate-blue gaze. And then he got up and walked away. Picked Sean up out of the playpen and left the loft.

I stood up and walked over to my team, all of whom were watching me closely.

"Okay. Let's go," I said to them, needing to get out, away, by myself. We walked out without another word. The drive back home was silent.

When we got home, we pulled into the driveway to find my parents sitting on the front porch steps. The imps were arrayed around the block surrounding my house, and the dogs stalked back and forth in the fenced portion of my back yard, doing their guard dog thing. It had been nice being back in my own house, using my stuff, surrounded by the crazy vintage shit I collected. I loved hearing my dogs bark at squirrels and imps in my yard. I was looking forward to spring, to seeing the huge lilac hedge at the back of my yard in full bloom.

Assuming the world didn't end before then, of course.

We all got out of the car. Shanti said something about needing to feed, and Levitt followed her into the house, need flowing from him. I tried not to think too much about the fact that the two of them had been together. She was over it; he very much was not.

I had my own relationship problems.

Heph went into the house. He'd be leaving for his patrol with Levitt soon, and Shanti would have to go back to Queen Rayna's; she'd taken the night off to accompany me for the meeting with Nain, which meant a lot to me. That left me in the front yard with my parents and Eunomia.

"Are you all right?" Tisiphone asked me. I crossed my arms over my chest. Nodded. "The shifter was quite angry when he left," she said.

"He was. I made him break his bond to me. We'll see if it helps with this," I said, gesturing toward my head. Didn't need to explain what "this" was. They knew. I glanced over at my father. "What were you and Nain talking about back at the loft?"

"He was trying to learn as much as he could about Strife," Hades said. "And I was trying to keep him from killing the shifter."

"What?"

"Your emotions were a mess while you were talking to Brennan," Tisiphone said, reaching out and taking my hand.

"And you are terrible at hiding your feelings. You don't need to be able to sense emotions to know exactly what you are feeling sometimes, my friend," Eunomia said. "You looked like you wanted to cry or kill someone, and maybe both. Whatever he said hurt you It didn't sit well with the demon."

"Or with me," Hades muttered. In daddy dearest mode. It was cute, in its way, if the possibility of my dad smiting and/or torturing whoever had hurt me wasn't a very real one. He wasn't a huge fan of Brennan in general since the whole cheating incident.

I shook my head. "It hurt. But it made it a little easier to tell him to break the bond, so... it doesn't matter."

"When you hear back from the police chief, let me know," Hades said, and I nodded. "I'll be checking around Seven and Kelly tonight. That area is a mess."

"It usually kind of is. But it's definitely worse lately," I agreed.

A few minutes later, they left, my mom hugging me before she winked out of sight. She'd rematerialize elsewhere. It was a handy skill to have, and I missed being able to do it.

That left me and Eunomia standing in my front yard. I sat on the wooden front steps, and she sat beside me. I looked down at the step below where I sat. The porch was in bad need of a paint job, gray paint peeling from the stair treads. Another task to take care of once the weather warmed up in spring.

"What did he say to you, Mollis?" E asked me.

"Oh. What didn't he say? He basically accused me of messing around with Nain. Flat out said he thinks I wanted our bond broken so I could screw around without having to worry about him sensing it. Said he was kind of ready to be rid of me." Saying it was even more difficult than remembering it. I leaned forward, rested my face in my hands, tried to force the tears back. "He was so cold, E. I did that to him."

She put her arm around my shoulders. "You didn't. Yes, he's hurt. He's angry. But if he honestly believes those things of you, then I think he never deserved someone like you in the first place," she said softly. "He was speaking out of anger. You know this."

I nodded, face still in my hands. I kind of hated how often my team saw me cry. How often they saw me fall apart, after I'd taken care of whatever needed to be taken care of. It used to be, I'd fall apart in private. There was no privacy anymore and my control was shit. But they were with me, and as much as I hated them seeing my weakness, it felt good to be surrounded by people who genuinely cared about me, who didn't want a damn thing from me other than to fight by my side.

Shanti came out then and sat on the other side of me on the step. "Fuck Brennan," she muttered, which was her most common refrain when it came to him. "You're amazing. If he thinks anything other than that, then he's too stupid to live."

I shook my head. We sat in silence, E with her arm around my shoulders, Shanti resting her head against mine. The warmth coming from both of them soothed my ragged nerves, just a little. The thing had been raging, fighting me for control since I'd walked into the loft, and I was exhausted. My frazzled emotions only seemed to excite it more.

"I kind of adore you two. You know that, right?" I asked, finally raising my head.

"Obviously," Eunomia said.

"You have exceptional taste in friends," Shanti agreed, and I laughed. Shanti stood up. "I have to get back."

I stood up too. "Okay. Be careful, kiddo."

She hugged me tightly, and I hugged her back. "Always am," she said. "See you soon. Call me whenever you want to, okay?"

I nodded, gave her another quick squeeze, then E and I watched as she walked over to her sporty little red car. She honked the horn as she drove away and I felt the same thing I felt every time I watched her leave: worry.

"Stop being such a mother hen," E said, smiling. "She's scarier than most things out there."

"I know. I just hate the idea of her working with people we don't know. I need to pay a visit to the queen soon."

E nodded, and we walked up the front steps and into the house. We followed the sound of Heph and Levitt's deep voices, leading us to their favorite place: the kitchen.

As the two beings in the house who ate the most (seriously, they were kind of gross, with the amount of food they could demolish in one sitting) they usually ended up cooking. E never had a very big appetite and I forgot about eating most of the time. Coffee, though, was something else, and I noticed that one of them had started a fresh pot.

"Thank you, Heph," I said as I poured a big cup, adding plenty of cream and sugar.

"Anytime, queenie," he answered, patting my shoulder as he walked past.

Levitt was cooking four steaks that were large enough to fill a plate each, and there was boxed macaroni and cheese already sitting ready in another pot.

"Did you want to eat? I can put another steak on," Levitt asked us, and I shook my head, as did E. We exchanged a look.

"Don't leave the dishes the way you did last time," E said.

"The imps had no problem doing them," Heph said.

"The imps are not our maids," I said, crossing my arms.

"We should get paper plates next time we go to the store," Levitt said to Heph, and Heph nodded his agreement. E rolled her eyes and headed up to the room she was staying in, across from mine. Levitt and Heph shared the other bedroom, which had once been my office, but now held two twin beds and a couple of dressers, as well as a large-screen TV that Heph found in the garbage and fixed. I really didn't want to know what the demon and the immortal watched on it.

Shanti had a special room in a corner of the basement, which Heph and Levitt had built. It was actually really nice: finished walls painted a soothing green (Shanti's favorite color), laminate floors. There was a television in there too, and a clock radio. No windows. The dogs adored Shanti, and if she was around, both Kurt and Courtney could usually be found sleeping outside her bedroom door until she woke up. It was only partially because she brought them treats every time she came home.

I left the kitchen, headed up to my room and closed the door. I flopped down onto my bed, stared up at the ceiling for a while. I loved my room: quiet, peaceful. All of my vintage McCoy planters were lined up on a plant stand and a couple were on each nightstand. I'd replaced the succulents in a few of them, but for the most part, they still sat empty. As I laid there, I let myself think about my Brennan mess. I let my heart ache, because I was starting to recognize that keeping everything bottled up took a lot of effort and energy I didn't have. Unfortunately, letting myself feel also excited the darkness in me, made it harder to hang on to control.

I'd hurt Brennan. And he was right about so many things, the biggest of which was that I did just run into situations without thinking. I hadn't thought about Brennan until they'd told me he'd been taken. Didn't give him a thought when time came to close the gate. Of course, after that, I'd thought about him a lot.

What the hell was wrong with me? Why couldn't I just be a normal person? Why did I have to go looking for trouble all the time?

I thought he was being a little selfish too, though. How many times, how many ways could I possibly say "hey, this thing in me wants to kill you and it puts me in agony every time you're around?" But no. All he saw was that I was avoiding him and not Nain. Never mind the fact that Nain and I were doing what I thought of as an exceptionally good job of being professional and mature with one another, considering. He was being well behaved, and I appreciated the fact that I didn't have to constantly be on guard when we needed to work together on something. He was still crude and impatient. Still bossy as hell. But he took orders as well as he gave them and he'd stopped talking about anything other than work stuff with me for the most part. It made my life easier, in at least one small way. I still felt the usual from him: hunger, desire, ever-present demonic rage. But even that was comforting in its way; at least it hadn't changed.

My phone buzzed, and I dug it out of my pocket, hoping and not hoping that it was Brennan. It wasn't. It was a text from Chief Jones.

Hey Angel. Coffee tomorrow morning ok? Nain said to check w/you.

Oh, this could be good. Hopefully the chief's reports had turned something up.

I texted him back that coffee was fine. We agreed to meet at Farmer's Restaurant in Eastern Market. On a Wednesday morning, we could count on it not being crazy busy, and it was close to where all three of us lived.

I considered sleep; changed my mind. I got up instead, opened my window and flew out into the night. There was always someone I could be helping, and I owed it to them to be out there whenever I could be.

.

CHAPTER TWO

I drove to Eastern Market. Parking was easy, mid-week. The market was closed and we'd missed the early morning coffee and breakfast rush. I parked, then walked the short distance to the restaurant to meet with Jones and Nain. I looked fully human for once: no glowing eyes, no wings. Enchantments were damn useful sometimes. I'd forced myself to put on something other than my usual all black. Jeans and a soft gray sweater that Ada had given me, altered to accommodate my wings. Black leather boots from Shanti, who I now knew had a bit of a shoe obsession. E had approved saying that I didn't look like a corpse. Ah, friends.

I walked into the restaurant, and it was like déjà vu. I'd done this same dance the day after I'd met Nain, come to this same restaurant to meet him. I could clearly remember, like it was yesterday, standing in that exact spot, scanning the restaurant to see if he'd already arrived. And, just as before, he caught my eye, stood when he saw me.

I gestured toward the waitress that was coming to seat me that I was meeting someone, and she smiled, nodded. I reached the table and looked up at my ex-husband.

It should be illegal for your ex to look that good. He was wearing jeans and a dark blue button-down, sleeves rolled up, giving a nice glimpse of his muscled forearms.

Remember what an asshole he is. Remember what an asshole he is. Don't look at his eyes. Whatever you do, for the love of Hades, don't look at his hands. Reminders on auto-loop, trying to make myself focus on what I needed to.

Freaking nostalgia, messing with my head.

"Molls," he said in greeting.

"Hey," I said, shrugging my coat off.

"Jones said he's bringing his daughter," Nain said, and I nodded. I sat on one side of the booth, scooted toward the wall, and Nain followed, sitting beside me, leaving the other side of the table open for the chief and his daughter. The booth felt tiny all of a sudden, and I took a deep breath. The waitress came over and I ordered a coffee. She brought it, refilled Nain's already-empty cup.

"Memories, huh?" he asked after a while.

"Yeah," I said.

"You're not gonna blast my ass across the overpass when we leave like you did last time, are you?" he asked.

I smiled a little. "Just don't piss me off, and you won't have to worry about it."

We sat in awkward silence for a few minutes, and I stared at my menu without seeing it.

"Any improvement with what's going on with you?" he asked after a while, mercifully changing the subject. As much as I hated this one, it was better than taking a little side-trip down memory lane.

"No. I'm still blacking out. So far, I'm not doing any damage when it happens, but it scares the hell out of me."

"You seemed to be in control yesterday," he said.

"Barely. It was raging. By the time I got home I was completely exhausted. I could absolutely kill you for making me do that."

"I know. Think about it, though. How are you going to learn to control it if you stay away from your biggest trigger?"

I didn't answer. I wondered how much he knew about what had happened the day before. "We broke up," I said, not even really knowing why I was telling him that.

"I know. He told me."

"So I think hanging out with him is kind of out of the question right now. It's probably for the best."

"Either way, you can't keep hiding from the shit that scares you. And it can be him, or me, or whatever else is out there that makes you want to run away. But you're giving up control by letting your fear win."

"You sound like my father," I muttered. "And what happens if I lose control and kill him or someone else in the process of trying to control myself? Do you see what I'm saying?"

"Yeah. I see what you're saying and I call bullshit. You're a strong woman, Molly. When, in your entire life, have you ever tucked your tail between your legs and ran? If you're so worried, don't be alone with him."

"In your totally objective opinion," I muttered. "Let's just drop it."

He didn't answer. Then: "where the fuck is Jones already?"

Finally, the chief and his daughter arrived. They both sat, and Jones began the introductions. "Angel, this is my daughter, Jamie," he said, and I reached across and shook her hand. She smiled at me. Very pretty, tall, thin. Her hair was cut close to her head, dyed bright pink. Diamond stud in her nose, bright against her warm milk chocolate skin. She wore jeans, a black t-shirt that claimed "rock is dead." Scruffy old Chucks on her feet. Strong as hell, too, like her father.

I smiled back at her. "Nice to meet you," I said. They got settled, and we all ordered. "So aside from wanting to spend more time with my lovely daughter," Jones said, getting down to business, "the reason Jamie is here is because even though I tried to get her to take the straight and narrow path her old man took, joining the force, she likes to do things the way you-all do them."

"The effective way, you mean?" Nain asked, and Jamie laughed.

"The vigilante way," Jones said.

"Effective. Right," Nain said, and the chief shook his head.

"Anyway. She's been working with the coalition of shifters that formed when the Angel was in charge of things," Jones said.

"That was really more Brennan's doing than mine," I said.

"Brennan organized it. I know I joined up because I wanted to help you, though," Jamie said, looking at me. "You're a damn legend. I can't even believe I'm sitting here with you."

"She's looked up to you since she was fifteen," Jones said, shaking his head, almost apologetically.

"Obviously," she said. Then Jamie leaned on the table, eyes on me. "You probably don't remember this, but you saved this girl and her boyfriend from a pack of weres a few years back. They were parked on Belle Isle during the full moon, which was freaking stupid."

I thought back. Nodded, slowly. "I remember that. Once they were safe all the girl did was beg me not to tell her mother."

Jones and Nain laughed, and so did Jamie. "Right! That was my cousin, Amari. You never did tell her mama, either. But she told me about it and swore it was the Angel, and her boyfriend did, too. And I already wanted to be you, but that sealed it."

I met her eyes. "You don't want to be me," I said softly. "Trust me."

Nain pressed his knee against mine under the table, a brief touch that comforted me more than I would have expected it to.

"Maybe not. But I know I want to do the right thing. I know I want to fight for those who can't. I know I want to be of use," Jamie said, still holding my gaze. Strong. I felt for her. She believed wholeheartedly in it. Dedication, stubbornness. I nodded.

"Those are good reasons," I said, and she smiled.

We ate for a few minutes, chatting about general stuff, a stop Jones had made the night before. Voices low, in our little corner of the restaurant, so the Normals wouldn't hear.

Once we finished eating, we all had a refill on our coffee. "I pulled those reports you wanted," the chief said to me, and I nodded. He handed a folder of papers over to me, and I flipped it open, Nain leaning over to see as well.

"I think we may have a couple of solid leads. The area around Seven and Kelly is a damned war zone lately," he said.

I nodded. "My father was working in that neighborhood last night, for the same reason." Anxiety from he chief, the same as it was every time I mentioned one of the immortals. That was not a revelation that had sat well with our friendly local police chief. "And it would almost make sense. I took out her old team in that area."

"Do you really think she'd stay then?" Nain asked, and I shrugged.

"Besides that, we've had an increase in weirdness downtown, which is bad for many reasons."

"What kind of weirdness?" I asked him.

He looked thoughtful. "Nothing we can even put an official report in about, really. People getting scared all of a sudden. Cases of mass panic. We had to go down to one of those big offices yesterday because everyone in it was just totally freaking out, terrified, and none of them knew why. It's the damnedest thing I've ever seen."

"That would be Terror, I guess," I said. "Are you seeing that anywhere else?"

He shook his head. "Not yet, anyway."

"How long has that been going on?" I asked.

"That's just the last two weeks. Quiet before that," the Chief said. "The mess in the Seven and Kelly area has been going on a lot longer. Over a year and a half, at least."

I looked over the report. It listed the address, the crime, the number of victims. Lots of assault, way too many murders in that neighborhood. The thing was, that was often considered the deadliest zip code in the state already, so in some ways the violence could just be an escalation of what was already happening. The downtown craziness was totally new, and unheard of. Downtown was generally one of the safest places in the city to be.

"Where do you want to start, Molls?" Nain asked, looking over the report with me.

"Seven and Kelly is a bigger mess," I said, and he nodded in agreement. "Even if she's not there, this shit has to stop and my team isn't enough."

I sensed anxiety from the chief, and I looked up at him. "What's wrong?" I asked him.

"Those are just the official reports. It gets worse, Angel."

I took a deep breath. The thing inside me was quiet for the moment, which was a relief. But I had the creepy feeling that it wasn't because it was calm, as much as because it was listening.

Holy crap was I getting paranoid or what?

"Okay. Let's have it, then."

The chief met my eyes, then Nain's. "Wondering if maybe you already noticed this. Have you seen more violence between supers lately?"

"Yeah," we answered, in unison. Something we'd talked about briefly in between saving people and trying to figure out where Strife was.

"Yeah," the chief echoed. "Us too. The shifter team that Jamie is on noticed the same thing."

"It seems organized," Jamie said, and I glanced over at her. I'd had the same thought, but had dismissed it as my usual paranoia.

"It's not just me then," I said. "They're working in teams, it almost seems like."

"Right," she said, nodding. "We're used to seeing groups of banished shifters, or weres, or warlocks or whatever."

"Yeah. Always sticking to their own kind," I said. "But now I keep hearing about groups of mixed supers causing trouble. Weres and shifters working together."

"Unheard of, right? Other than your team, I mean," she said, and Nain and I nodded. Supernaturals are not very trusting in general. They tend to stick with their own kind, and avoid Normals as much as possible. Not because Normals are a physical danger to them, exactly, but more because we're all doing our best to keep our presence a secret. If the Normals knew for a fact that we walked among them, it would be panic and chaos. Of course, there were rumors. People who swore up and down that they'd seen a man change into a wolf, or a red demon in the streets. People who swore they saw a woman with glowing eyes at the scene of a massacre or two. But nothing could ever be proven and we did our best to make damn sure it stayed that way. During the war between the immortals, when chaos had spilled over into my realm, there were some supers who decided to stop hiding what they were. It kind of became Jones' and Nain's main duty to find them and get them under control however they could.

If they were organizing in groups, that was bad. And the new groups we were seeing weren't helping old ladies cross the street or cleaning up litter. They were fighting other supers.

I flipped to the final packet of papers in the chief's report. Incidents, over the past week, of supernaturals being attacked in their homes or out on the streets.

"If they're really organizing, this is going to be a fucking mess," Nain said, voice low. He was still scanning the report. We'd been on several calls ourselves, with the same general attributes.

"Why, though?" I asked.

Jones shrugged. "Maybe they saw a taste of what they can do during the chaos we had here."

"Could Strife be doing this?" Nain asked me.

"Maybe. I mean, we know for a fact she can affect us, because of what she did to Sean." Brennan's infant son, who she'd had one of her witches put a spell on so he'd cause problems between members of our team. "It's possible."

"If she's using supers, then we have a whole new shitstorm to deal with," Nain said.

"Yeah."

Jones took a deep breath, shook his head a little. Worry, anger, irritation radiated from him. "So what are you going to do about this?" he said, looking directly at me. I felt Nain tense beside me, anger coming off of him in waves. He did not like it when other men had an attitude with me. That was his job, mostly.

Relax, I thought at him.

He didn't answer, but I did feel his anger draw down just a little, though he continued to glare at Jones.

"If they're organizing then we need to be more organized, too. We've got a good start. Most of the supers who aren't out there causing trouble know to check with Nain or I before they do something. They come to us first, which is the way I wanted it."

Jones nodded.

"Proof that you're a hell of a lot smarter than me," Nain muttered beside me.

I shook my head. "And the shifter coalition also reports to me or Brennan, which has been a huge help. I think we need to work even more closely together. If we had, we would have figured this out right away, instead of just really coming to the realization now. We need to be more unified in this, especially if Strife is involved."

"So what's our next move?" Jones asked.

"Time for me to go meet with our new vampire queen."

Nain and Jones both stared at me. "We've tried that," Nain said.

"She's really private," Jones said, agreeing.

"Well, so am I. But we're all making sacrifices now, aren't we? She'll see me."

Jones just watched me. "How?"

Nain snorted. "It's better not to ask."

We parted ways shortly after, Nain insisting on walking me to my car.

"You know nobody's gonna mug me or anything, right?" I asked him as we walked.

"They'd be fucking stupid to try," he answered.

"Trying to watch and make sure I don't black out?"

He didn't answer for a minute. "Yeah," he finally said. "Really I just want to say hi to Bash and Dahael. They're with you, right?"

"Of course."

We reached my car. Bash and Dahael were sitting in the back seat. Who needed a car alarm when you had demonic imps? Dahael opened the driver's side door from the inside, and Nain held it open for me.

"Imps," he said in greeting.

"Demon," they both said, Dahael settling back into the seat.

I looked up at my ex-husband, feeling, as always, completely dwarfed standing near him. I let myself feel the hunger and demonic anger coming from him, and as screwy as it was, it kind of soothed me. "I'll call you after I talk to Rayna," I said, thinking about my upcoming meeting with Detroit's vampire queen.

He nodded. "Let me know if you need anything. I'll get Brennan and the leaders of the shifter coalition together to go over how things are going to be now."

"Think there'll be any problems? Should I be there?"

He looked down at me. "No. All I have to do is tell them the Angel said to do it, and they'll jump."

"You are so full of shit," I said, ducking into my car.

"You know I'm right," he said. Then he closed the door behind me, stood there watching as I pulled away and out of the parking lot.

"Demon missed you," Bash said.

"Still an asshole, though," Dahael said, and I laughed. Soon, I was laughing so hard tears were coming from my eyes, and I sensed satisfaction from my imps. Making me laugh was not the easiest thing in the world to do, especially since I'd been back from the Nether.

The imps and I spent the day checking into a few places for Strife. I didn't really have much hope we'd find her, but that didn't mean I was going to give up on looking. Besides, sitting around didn't work out all that well for me lately. Either the thing inside me got restless, which made me feel like I could barely stand being in my own skin anymore. Or I ended up thinking about Brennan or Nain. When I thought about Brennan, I felt angry and sad and lonely and guilty and like I'd thrown away something most women would have held on to a hell of a lot tighter.

Well. I mean, maybe they would have held on if not for the whole "hey honey, here's my son!" thing.

And Nain... it was really best for everyone if I didn't think about my ex at all. Nain was something I couldn't deal with right now. Not on a personal level, at least. His emotions toward me were still for the most part a jumbled, chaotic mix of love, desire, anger, and guilt. He'd never been an easy man to read. I had a general sense of him, and in different situations, I could feel when he had a spike of a certain emotion over the others. It's kind of a demon thing, I think. Most demons' emotional lives are chaos. Maybe that's where all the rage comes from.

Anyway, with Nain, I get this sense that he's trying really hard sometimes not to feel anything. And then he loses his grip, and his emotions come through loud and clear. The most common emotion from my ex lately was a searing hunger, the kind I'd felt from him in those weeks when we were just starting up together, lifetimes ago. It had been irresistible to me then. And I was finding it just as hard to resist it now.

I've been through some shit. Feeling wanted, the way only a demon can want, is a nice little stroke to the ego. And Nain's particular brand of desire/hunger is like being caught in an inferno.

And I feel guilty and angry at myself for wanting it, and I know there's not a chance in hell I'm capable of having him in my life again that way. I'm just not strong enough to handle everything that comes with him.

So… yeah.

That's why I was out with the imps, checking up on leads that I knew would amount to nothing. We focused on the Seven and Kelly area for most of the day and into night. After breaking up my fourth fight, I glanced toward Dahael (imps are invisible to Normals, which is why they're so damn effective). "Yeah. I'd say Strife's been around."

"Indeed, Mistress," she agreed. "Can practically feel her taint here."

I nodded. As we walked, I opened myself, letting myself feel the emotions and hear the thoughts around us. It still wasn't something I liked doing. Now, it reminded me too much of having the immortals all bonded to me, their thoughts a constant cacophony in my mind. I sifted through the thoughts and emotions as we walked, able to disregard most of them almost immediately. Normal, everyday things. I was focusing so hard on a particularly screwy tangle of emotions that I didn't notice the group of women approaching at my right until they were practically right on top of me, and Dahael hissed "Mistress!" I glanced over just in time to see one of them raise a gun, and then my stomach exploded in one fiery shot. She shot again, hitting my shoulder, and I grunted.

I've been shot before. Several times. It's still not my favorite sensation. My stomach was bleeding, burning, my body immediately working to heal the damage. I gritted my teeth against it, against the way the pain and loss of blood made me start trembling.

"Don't move," I roared, ripping into their minds and making them obey. They froze. It was almost comical, like pausing a video or something. "Drop the guns, right now," I said, quieter but still with a definite snarl in my voice. All four women dropped their guns, and the imps went and quickly retrieved them. They'd destroy them. We were barely putting a dent in the number of guns on the street, but we tried.

I stared at the women, trying not to wince as my stomach and shoulder repaired themselves. All four of them were young, barely out of their teens. They had that crazed, hungry look that wasn't uncommon among addicts. If they'd been robbing me, I would have written them off as junkies desperate for money so they could get their fix. But this was different. They weren't trying to rob me. They'd tried to kill me. Even in this neighborhood, that wasn't par for the course.

"Mistress," Dahael said, and I glanced toward her. She gestured toward her nose, and I raised my hand to mine. When I pulled it away, it was smeared with blood. I was already in pain from the gunshots, then healing, then using my powers to force my way into their minds. And I wasn't done yet.

I studied them. One of them, the one who had shot me, was struggling against my influence, trying to gain control of her mind again. "Don't bother," I muttered at her. "You can speak if you want to though."

"How the hell are you still standing? I shot you twice."

"I don't know. Maybe you have shitty aim," I said, crossing my arms, letting her see very clearly the way the flesh of my stomach was knitting itself back together, shredded organs growing new parts to replace damaged ones. She stared. "Or maybe you messed with the wrong person. Why did you do that?"

She was still staring at my stomach.

"Hey!" I said, trying to get her attention, and she forced her eyes up to mine. I dropped the enchantment on them, let her see the way they glowed, and I felt absolute terror from her. And it was everything I needed. It fed my demon, gave me energy I was sorely lacking due to loss of blood and the amount of power it takes to heal myself. "Why?" I asked again, more forcefully. Not a question as much as an order to answer.

"I don't know," she said, staring at me.

"So, what? You were just walking along, carrying your guns, and said, 'hey! Let's murder that one!'?"

She looked at least as confused as she was afraid. "The guns were to protect ourselves," she said.

"From what?"

"Shit is crazy around here. Worse now than ever. Some asshole pulled her," she said glancing toward one of the other young women, "into a house and nearly raped her before she was able to escape. And that ain't new, either, but it's happening more. People acting like wild animals out here."

"So you don't know why you shot me?" As they'd been standing there, they'd lost the hungry, insane look that had initially made me mark them as junkies. Now they just looked like four terrified, confused young women.

She shook her head, fear rolling off of her. I took a deep breath, steeling myself against the pain, and I entered her mind. I bit my lip as anguish roared through me, punishment for using my powers. I sifted through her thoughts, saw that in general, she was a good person who'd made a few mistakes. That what she'd said about how bad it was in this neighborhood was true, and had been true for quite a while. That she was afraid. Didn't have a history of being a violent person. She was disgusted and afraid of what she'd done to me. She was terrified of me, of my glowing eyes and ability to repair myself.

I nearly missed it. I was about to pull out of her mind when I felt it. There was a dark, tumultuous, cloudy feel, barely there, like the mere trace of perfume that's left when a woman walks out of a room. It was dissipating, even as I felt it, studied it. And I felt one thing from it: chaos.

I should have felt sorry for the woman, but I was excited to have my first real sense of Strife in someone other than a supernatural. And I was starting to put it together; what it looked like when she affected a Normal.

I stayed in her mind. "I don't suppose you have come across any strangers lately? People who didn't seem like they belonged here?"

She shook her head, but an image flashed across her mind, for just a second: a stately-looking woman, with skin the color of porcelain and white-blond hair plaited in one long, thick braid over her shoulder. Eyes that glowed a deep purple. A smile, the kind that made you want to do whatever she said, just so she'd smile at you like that again. Power. Different from mine, but very much there.

Fuck yeah! My first view of the skin Strife was wearing. Finally. It was worth getting shot for.

"Who was that woman?" I asked.

"Who?" she asked, confusion rolling off of her.

"Did you see a woman with glowing eyes like mine? But purple?"

She shook her head, even more confused now. "Uh. You're bleeding. A lot."

I pulled out of her mind, trying not to puke from the pain of using my powers. My nose was gushing blood now, and I felt the skin of my neck and chest cracking, splitting, as if the pain of holding my power was too much for my body to bear. And I felt the thing inside me, smug, enjoying my pain. I closed my eyes, released them from my hold on them. I could feel the moment they realized they were free. Relief. An insane amount of fear of me. Good.

"You never fucking saw me. Understand?" I growled, and all four of them nodded. I gestured that they should take off, and they did, walking as quickly as they could away from me while still looking dignified and unafraid. I didn't hold that against them. They'd clearly been in this neighborhood a long time. Letting anyone see your fear here was practically a death sentence. So you keep your head down, and you act cool, and you never let anyone see how bad you want to panic, how bad you want to run. You do that, and there'll be someone ready to take you down.

I grew up here. I know. I'd been chased by boys and girls alike, beaten up in alleys and backyards, until I learned how to act like a badass. Until I beat up my first few bullies. Until I made it clear, when I was twelve years old, that I was the one they should be afraid of.

Of course, I didn't understand back then why I could hurt them so easily. All I knew was that they started leaving me in peace.

I made my way back toward my car, where Bash was sitting, along with a couple of the other imps. I'd started trying to learn all of their names. The two male imps he was sitting with were Elsog and Vadin. "Anything?" Bashiok asked as he stood and thumped his fist to his chest. The other two imps followed suit.

"I have an idea of who we're looking for now," I said, and Bash pumped his fist into the air. I'd had them working nonstop trying to find something, anything, and they were getting frustrated as well. Without a physical description of Strife or what it looked like when she affected someone, they'd been taking guesses and hoping they worked out. So far, everything had been a dead end. I described the woman I'd seen in the young woman's head, as well as what it looks like when Strife had someone under her influence. All four imps listened, focused. Four pairs of glowing orange eyes looked up at me as I finished talking.

"Demon needs to know this," Bash said, and I nodded.

"I'll call him later. I'll have to fill him in on what happens with the vamp queen anyway."

"Really going to see her, Mistress?" Dahael said, ears drooping a little.

"Yes. I have to. Besides, I want to see who Shanti's working for. I've put this off too long."

"Already been a long crazy day," she said, taking my hand gently in her gnarled ones. "Rest. Exhaust yourself, that thing takes over," she said, and I knew she was referring to the darkness, sitting smug inside me, enjoying the pain I was still in after using my powers.

"Just this one last thing. And then I will go home and rest," I promised her.

"And eat food like a normal person," she said, putting her hands on her hips.

I smiled. "Don't push it."

CHAPTER THREE

By the time it was dark, I'd rescued two Normals from a house fire and broken up a handful of fights on my way from Seven and Kelly to Palmer Woods, which was where the vampire queen lived. I'd also managed to stop hurting from using my powers, which was a bonus. It was taking longer to recover after using them, and no matter how many times I promised myself I wouldn't, I ended up using them anyway. Part of it was habit; I'd been using my mind control powers since I was seventeen. Part of it was laziness. I could make someone tell me what I wanted to know without using them, but that took a lot of threatening and sometimes a lot of punching and it was just so much easier to take what I wanted by using my powers.

I am well aware of how evil that sounds.

That has been pretty much everyone's fear from the beginning. I know it stressed the hell out of Nain, especially early on. What would happen if I went bad? What damage could I cause if I ever decided to use my abilities for my own gain instead of for protecting others?

And I know, even when I use my powers for noble purposes, that I'm walking a thin line between good and evil. Part of me believes that the things I do are never right, that it's not okay to violate someone's mind, to force my way in and take what I want. And there's guilt there, for sure. But I try to weigh it against the lives I'm potentially saving by learning what I do. Most of the time, the balance tips toward "well, I don't hate myself for this."

And sometimes, I forget to feel guilty about what I'm doing. That scares me more than anything else. I'm reaching the point where control and violence have become commonplace, and the woman I was before I met Nain, the one who never killed, the one who turned criminals over to the police like a good little vigilante... well. She's mostly gone now. Too many deaths and too much darkness. And there's really no going back. Not now.

I shook my head in irritation as I drove through the streets of Palmer Woods, looking for the mansion where the vampires lived. I was becoming melancholy in my old age.

As I maneuvered the Barracuda through the streets of well-kept homes and clipped hedges, I thought about what I actually knew about vampires. Not a whole lot, actually. The vampires I'd come up against, the ones who caused trouble in the city, were always loners. I'd never dealt with a nest or family or whatever the hell they call themselves of vampires. And there's not a lot that makes me personally afraid anymore, but the idea of walking into a house full of strong vampires is one of them. I'd been very stupid and over-confident early on, flush with the beginnings of understanding my powers, and charged into a vampire's house, where I'd nearly been drained to death. I can still feel the slowing of my heart, the sluggishness that comes from feeling your life drain slowly from your body. And this was one of those situations in which using my powers would be a terrible, awful idea. I bleed every time I use even a little bit of power. And from what I understand, my blood is kind of awesome, as far as vampires are concerned. So starting to bleed in a house full of vampires would be a really dumb thing to do.

No powers, I reminded myself for the fortieth time as I pulled up the long, winding driveway toward the sprawling Tudor, its gray stone facade lit with floodlights. My first thought was to wonder how the hell the vampire queen had gotten the money to afford something like this, and then I reminded myself that Nain was a multi-millionaire, just from being around for so damn long. Three hundred years worth of saving adds up, I guess. And while he didn't actually work a traditional job anymore, he'd told me that early on he worked factory jobs and things like that until he could afford a place to live, and he'd bought the loft back when it really was industrial mostly with an eye to reselling it for more money later on.

So basically, Nain had been one of those real-estate flippers before there was even a thing. He bought property in Midtown and Downtown, waited until property prices rose, then he sold everything off, a little at a time. He ended up holding onto the loft because he liked it. As far as I knew, he still had a few buildings in Midtown he was holding onto.

And why am I thinking about my ex-husband right now? I chided myself. I got out of the car and looked around. I was surprised there weren't any guards around. Of course, it could just be that I didn't see them. I could definitely feel plenty of vampires around. A little shiver went up my spine and I started regretting deciding to visit. I could have put it off longer.

I shoved the thought away, squared my shoulders, and knocked on the massive front doors. They were dark wood, heavily varnished. The whole house was impressive, but also definitely gave off some horror movie vibes.

A moment later, the door opened, and I looked up into the face of what I could immediately feel was a very powerful vampire. He was maybe a little shorter than Nain, so six-two or so. Built like a bull; broad shoulders, thick neck. His head was shaved, and his skin was a golden honey color that did a good job of hiding the whole undead bloodsucker thing. He had light grayish-green eyes, a strong, square jaw.

"Angel," he said, and his voice was low and smooth.

"I'm sorry for coming unannounced. But I really need to speak to Queen Rayna."

He looked me over. "You should have called ahead. The queen is busy this evening. As I'm sure you can understand."

"And you are?"

"Ronan. I'm her head of security."

"Well, Ronan. There's a whole lot of shit going on, and I need to talk to her. We can do this the easy way, where you just show me in and I spend ten minutes of her time getting her up to speed. Or we can do it the hard way, where I rematerialize in your nice little house and find her myself. If I do that, I'm gonna be in a bad mood and somebody might get hurt."

He watched me. "Never took you for a thug, Angel."

"I only am when it really matters."

His face was expressionless. "She really is busy tonight."

"I really don't care. I've left her alone all this time. Nain has left her alone all this time. Both he and chief Jones have been stupidly accepting of this whole 'Queen Rayna is very private' bullshit while she's taken control. I am not Nain, and I'm sure the hell not Jones. Patience and understanding are not two of my strong points."

We stood, measuring each other up. I poked at his mind a little, found his mental shields very strong. I approved. Too many supernaturals left their mental state up to chance, relying on brute force instead.

So says she who smashes first. Anyway.

"Could you really get in here like that?" he finally asked, and I nodded.

"I'd rather not. I respect what Queen Rayna has done for the city. She's taken a huge burden off of our teams by handling the vampire problems. And I can even respect that she needed to go it alone early on so she wouldn't look weak in front of your people. I get it. But she's in control now, and it's time for her to get to know her counterparts in this city. It makes a hell of a lot more sense for all of us to work together than it is to not know what everyone else is doing."

He smirked. "As if you all don't have people watching us."

"As if you don't have us under surveillance as well."

He just watched me. There was no point in denying it. Even if Nain and I hadn't spotted them ourselves, Shanti had let us know they were there. "Shanti tells you things, I guess?"

"Shanti doesn't tell me nearly as much as I'd like to know. And I have refrained from pressing her because I know she values her position in your organization."

"She is very disciplined. I understand she owes a lot of that to your team."

"And to herself. She's a strong woman."

"May I ask who trained her? She is extremely well-trained for someone her age," Ronan said.

"The credit for that goes to Brennan," I said.

"The shifter on the demon's team?" I nodded.

"And where did he learn to fight like that? The number of weapons she's more than capable with is astounding. Her fighting style is enviable," Ronan pressed.

"All I know about that is that he traveled extensively for several years in his twenties and he's said that he developed an interest in martial arts and other forms of combat during that time. He's always learning something new, it seems like," I said, shrugging.

"The Nain Rouge was lucky he decided to return here then and rejoin his team," he said.

"We all are," I said, trying to maintain my patience. Small talk is not my strong point, but I was determined not to act like a jerk. Diplomacy is not really my thing, but sometimes it had to be.

"Ronan, there's shit going on that we're going to need to work together on. I don't doubt you've noticed that things out there are getting worse."

After a slight hesitation, he nodded.

"Okay. Well, I know why they're worse. And I know who's doing it. And for us all to be safe, and keep innocents safe, it only makes sense that we're on the same page. She can spare fifteen minutes for that, I'm sure."

"She does not want to look like she's under your thumb," he said quietly. "This is all new. Her position is still tenuous."

"I understand that. And she will be treated as a partner and ally. And if you know anything at all about me, you know I am devoted to my allies."

"I do. Come on in," he said, waving me inside. I stopped myself from sighing in relief. That would look weak. I walked past Ronan and into the foyer. The white marble flooring reflected the light from the ornate chandelier above, and dark wood accented the stairway banisters and trim of the room. The house had kind of a medieval feel to it that almost made me laugh. It was like being in some kind of cheesy vampire movie, except that the vampire in question looked more like a cover model for *Muscle & Fitness* magazine and less like Dracula. He walked through an archway to the left, and I followed him. I dropped my mental shields so I could pick up any thoughts around me. Especially any thoughts related to drinking from me.

Fine. Vampires give me the heebie-jeebies. Whatever. The only one who didn't was Shanti. It was something I was working on.

As I followed Ronan through a formal sitting room and then down a long hallway, I tried to pay close attention to the interior of the house. I was glad Ronan hadn't called my bluff earlier. I could have probably made my way into the foyer behind him, but because I'd never been inside the queen's home, I had almost zero chance of getting into one of the rooms. I had to see a place before I could rematerialize there. Details mattered. I focused on the woodwork, the leaded glass windows, the heavy chandeliers and sconces on the walls. The ice-slick marble floors throughout this part of the house. If I ever needed to make my way in, now I could.

Not that I planned on it. But you never know.

Finally, Ronan reached a set of double doors and knocked. I heard a quiet voice say "come in," and Ronan gestured for me to wait a second. I nodded, even though I was starting to feel antsy again. All of this being nice was testing my patience, and the thing inside was starting to become restless as well. As if I needed more to worry about.

Ronan came back and waved me in. The room I entered was a vast improvement on the rest of the house. It had the same white walls and heavy woodwork, but the floor in here was a dark wood, and an area rug softened that. There were a couple of sofas, layered with pillows and throws, and a coffee table stacked with books. A fire crackled cheerfully in the large stone fireplace with its heavy wood mantle. Standing near it was a powerful vampire. I could feel it immediately. More powerful than Ronan, but not by a ton. I glanced between the two of them. She had the same skin tone the same grayish-green eyes. She had a bit of squareness to her jaw as well, but while it made Ronan look like more of a brute, it just made her look strong. Her long dark hair flowed down her back in waves, and she wore jeans and a Detroit Red Wings t-shirt. Which was totally not what I was expecting royalty to be wearing, but vampires are just different.

"Angel, it's a pleasure to meet you. I'm Rayna," she said, holding out her hand to me. I took it, nodded.

"It's nice to meet you as well. Thanks for seeing me."

She smiled. "Honestly, I was surprised you didn't come before now."

I didn't really know what to say to that, so I just nodded. "I won't take up much of your time. There is a situation I thought you should know about, and I'm here to ask your assistance."

She watched me. "We don't believe in involving ourselves with other supernaturals."

"Why?"

"It never works out well in the end."

I just watched her, and she shook her head. "You're not a naive woman, from what I hear. You know how they all see us. Parasites. Bloodsuckers. There isn't a being alive who trusts us, because everyone believes that the second they let their guard down, we're going to drain them or turn them. You know it's true."

I didn't deny it. Couldn't. I'd called vampires the same things, more than once.

"I think you and your people are doing a good job of starting to dispel some of those notions. You've done a great job of getting rogue vampires off the street, and it's saved me a ton of work."

She nodded. "It's easier for us to deal with our kind. We understand them better, even the ones that are beyond reason."

"The ones that are beyond reason are always the worst ones for us to track down."

"That's because there's often no logic to their actions. Our ability to track one another makes it easier for us than it would be for you, even as powerful as you are."

"Well, as I said I appreciate it. There is another danger out there, and I think you should know about it whether you agree to work with us or not."

She nodded. "Please, sit. Can we get you anything?"

"No thanks." I settled myself onto one of the sofas, and she sat on the one opposite me, on the other side of the coffee table. She was watching me intently, and I could see it for what it was. She was trying to learn more about me, as both a possible ally and as a possible threat. It's nothing personal. I was doing the same thing. Examining her power level, watching her face, monitoring her emotions for signs of threat or deceit. "So, I mentioned to Ronan when I arrived that things are getting worse, and I asked if you'd noticed, and he said you had."

She nodded.

"I know what's causing it. I know why." I paused. "How much has Shanti told you about me?"

"Hardly anything at all, other than that you're scary powerful and that she adores you. That you saved her life and if it ever came to choosing between serving you or serving me, there was no question where her loyalties would be."

I smiled. "She's very straightforward."

Rayna laughed. "That she is. It's refreshing to deal with someone like her."

I nodded. "Okay." I took a breath. "How much do you know about Greek mythology?"

She was watching me closely. "Why?"

I shook my head and started talking, giving her the very, very abbreviated version of what I was and why we were having so much trouble lately. I told her what Strife looks like, what it looks like when she has someone under her influence. I told her where we were seeing the most trouble, and that finding her was my number one priority, and that I hoped she'd help as much as she could.

She sat in silence for several long moments after I stopped talking. "And this being, Strife, can she be killed?"

"As far as we know, she can. She is extremely powerful, so I wouldn't recommend it. It's probably going to have to be me or someone else in my family. Have you seen signs of her?"

She nodded. "Seven and Kelly, as you say. East English Village, too. I'd do some checking there, because we've had a few vampires out of control in that area, and now that you're telling me this, they were exhibiting similar behaviors to what you've seen. Acting very much not like themselves."

"I will check it out. Thank you."

She took a deep breath, and I felt worry, mixed with determination from her. "As for the rest. I apologize, but I am going to have to stick to my guns on this one. We avoid others for a reason. And now you're talking about things like gods and spirits and I have enough on my plate without contributing my people to a fight that has nothing to do with us."

"You just said Strife has affected some of your people as well. She's targeting supernaturals, knowing how much damage and chaos we can cause. I'm pretty sure that should concern you."

"And I will handle my people my way. I do not need to involve them in your teams and coalitions. The shifters are fine with taking orders and teaming up. We don't do that, and I told you why earlier."

I clamped my jaw down to prevent something stupid from popping out of my mouth. I wanted to threaten. I considered trying to make her do what I wanted. But even I know that's the kind of thing that can come back and bite you in the ass when you least expect it.

"I think that's a short-sighted view of things, but that's just me," I said, standing up. "Thank you for your time, as well as for sharing that information about East English Village."

She stood up as well. "Thank you for understanding."

"Oh, I don't. I think you're making a mistake. I just hope your people don't suffer for it."

I felt anger wash over me, and her posture changed. "Is that a threat, Angel?"

I met her eyes. "I don't make threats, your majesty. Ask anyone."

And I headed toward the door, where Ronan was waiting just outside. I knew he'd heard every word. Vampire hearing. He escorted me wordlessly to the door, opened it for me.

"If I see anything, I'll have Shanti relay the information to you," he said quietly as I stepped past him.

"Your queen is not going to be happy about that, Ronan," I warned.

"Maybe not. That's my problem. Not yours."

I gave him a terse nod and headed to my car. Dahael unlocked the door from the inside and I climbed in and started the engine.

"Well that was frustrating," I said as I drove down the driveway.

"Vampires," Bash said.

"Vampires," I agreed as I steered the car toward home, looking forward to a hot bath, coffee, and maybe a movie.

I walked into my house, sighing in relief and tossed my car keys onto the kitchen counter. The house was mercifully silent. Levitt and Heph were out on patrol, and E was asleep, having done the morning patrol with some of the shifters earlier that day. I considered eating, started rooting through the cabinets. Nothing looked good.

I heard a car pull up in the driveway, and I closed my eyes and focused. And then I suppressed a groan. Brennan.

I walked through the house and out onto the porch. I watched as he got out of his car and headed up toward the porch. He stood on the front walk, and I stood up on the porch, and we watched one another.

"I know I'm not supposed to be here," he finally said. "But I needed to see you."

"Why?"

"We can't leave things the way they ended yesterday, Molly," he said, and I nodded. I sat on the top step and he came and sat down next to me. Close, but not touching. Not the way we would have sat, what felt like lifetimes ago.

I waited for him to talk. He was clasping his hands in front of him, his forearms resting on his knees. He looked over at me, met my eyes.

"I was mad yesterday," he said.

"I know," I said, and he smiled a little.

"You're a hard woman to let go of."

I felt like I was about to cry already, and he'd barely even started.

"But we both know it's time. It's past time. I was just determined to hold on to you, to try to fix things between us. But at some point you have to be able to recognize when something's broken beyond repair."

I wiped the tears away from my eyes. "It's not because of Sean," I said. "I would have stayed. We would have worked it out. It's because I'm so messed up now, I barely even know who I am anymore."

He shook his head. "We would have tried. We wouldn't have made it, honey. What I said yesterday about needing someone who needs me was the truth. I want to take care of someone. I want to feel needed. And maybe that's my gigantic male ego, but that's what makes me happy. Maybe it's a shifter thing. My dad was the same way. And my mom was a powerful woman, but she needed him. They needed each other, and it just worked. We never had that. I tried to believe we did, but every time you ran off into danger, I realized we didn't."

I looked down. "You're an amazing man, Bren."

"You're an amazing woman. But we're not right for one another. The harder I try to hold on to you, the bigger of an asshole I become. I started our relationship competing with Nain. I tried to make myself into the man I thought you wanted. I tried to give you everything he

50

didn't. But the fact of the matter is, you don't want that, and I just kept crossing further and further into 'dude, you are pathetic' territory. I don't want you to hate me. And I have some growing up to do, I think."

"I don't think it's possible for me to hate you," I said. Then I met his eyes. "You got me through some of the worst times of my life, Brennan. Thinking of you gave me the courage to fight my way back from death, over and over again."

He took a deep breath, looked away from me, and I could feel that he was trying to get his emotions under control. "I'm glad. And I'm grateful for what we had. But we need to be honest about some things here."

"Such as?"

He smiled a little. "You kept a lot of yourself from me, and I kept just as much from you. There was so much I wanted to tell you, and I never did it. I was a coward. And there were other things, too. I was desperate to hold on to you and made an ass of myself. And we jumped into something neither of us was ready for. What was the last thing we argued about, the night before you died?"

I just watched him. I remembered. Just didn't want to answer.

"We argued because you were still wearing your wedding ring. We argued because you wouldn't let anyone touch Nain's room, and I asked if we were keeping it a shrine."

I nodded, looked away.

"And then that last day, I took off before you woke up, because I knew you well enough to know you didn't want any part of me, not on the anniversary of his death. Not when we both knew that, all things being equal, when you had the chance to choose, you chose him. He was what you wanted and he was gone. And then you were gone and he was back," he said, shaking his head.

"I am so sorry I hurt you, Bren. I never wanted to," I said.

He faced me, took my hands in his, and the feel of his warm skin against mine did it. I lost it, started crying. The finality of it all hit me, and I couldn't hold it back any more.

"Don't do that," he said. "You know I hate seeing you upset."

I laughed a little, tried to calm down.

We sat there, our hands clasped. The thing inside me raged, and I hated it a little more.

"You are an amazing, brave, giving woman. And the fact that you loved me isn't something I take lightly. It's impossible for me not to love you. I don't want to lose you as a friend. I am here. I will always be here, and if you ever need me, I'll come. But this part of our life together is over. Isn't it?"

I nodded, even as my heart broke. It had been over for a long time, and part of the reason I'd avoided him, aside from the thing inside me, was because I didn't want to deal with that. But that was selfish, too. He needed to move on, and he couldn't if he still thought I was hanging on to him.

I squeezed his hands. "You're the best, Bren. Thank you for being mine, even for a little while," I said and the tears started flowing again.

"Oh, hell," he said. He let got of my hands and pulled me into his arms, and we held each other for a few minutes. I breathed him in, knowing this was the end.

"You should go," I said after a few minutes, pulling away from him. "I need some time here."

He cupped my face in his hands and kissed my forehead. "Take care of yourself," he murmured before he pulled away.

"You too."

And then I watched as he got into his car and drove away. I sat on the porch for a long time afterward, thinking. I was sad, but I was relieved, too. We didn't hate each other. I wasn't naive. Things would be awkward for a while. Someday, maybe we'd get to a comfortable place again.

Eventually I got up and went inside. I locked up and went up to my room after calling good night to Bash and Dahael, who were watching some classic Bugs Bunny cartoon. Once I got there, I didn't even bother showering or changing. I fell onto my bed and stared at the celling, wondering what I could possibly mess up next.

CHAPTER FOUR

Everything was darkness and emptiness. Silence and cold. There was not a thing here worth saving.

Certainly, nothing worth breaking an oath for.

This city was a glorified trash heap, and the people in it no better, deserving of the place they called home.

I rise over the city. Block after block of emptiness, the stench of exhaust and fast food filling the air. I watch as Detroit's East Side disappears beneath me. I am flying so fast everything is a blur, places I know and love almost unrecognizable from this height and speed. I see it all through a haze and it leaves me feeling both confused and nauseous. I am afraid, and I don't know why.

I stop still in the air, and through the haze, I see a neighborhood not unlike my own: mostly empty, except for a sad looking house or two. It is off of a busier street, and storefronts line that, mostly abandoned as well. I feel myself hurtling toward it, feel disdain, disgust. Not my own. The darkness has made its opinion known, and it has nothing but hatred for the city I call home.

I know I'm dreaming. I know I'm seeing my home through its eyes, and that it doesn't see things the same way I do. It's choosing to show me how it sees things. And the way it sees things is terrifying. It wants to lay waste to everything it sees. It knows that, to the west, there's a building in which the people I care about reside, where the two men who have been everything to me at one time or another, lie sleeping. Maybe another day, it thought, taunting me as I watched, unable to do a single thing as I was forced to follow, flying over the neighborhood, looking down on it.

The thing was thinking that this was as good a place to start as any. And it laughed, and I watched my hands extend in front of me and shoot flames, and I heard it laugh as the storefronts exploded, as fire engulfed the contents inside a small resale shop.

And it laughed and threw more flames, and flew in closer to examine her work; satisfaction, glee rolling off of her. I could smell the smoke. I could hear the flames crackling, the buildings creaking as their structure started to fail.

This, little Fury, is only the beginning. And then it ended, as if a curtain fell, and I was plunged into darkness again.

CHAPTER FIVE

A loud pounding noise startled me awake, and I sat up, staring around, trying to get my bearings.

"Molly," a deep voice said outside my room.

I groaned. What the hell was he doing here?

"What?" I said, and the bedroom door opened. Nain stalked through, stared down at me. Now I was really glad I'd slept in my clothes. A barrage of emotions washed over me from him, but the most prominent was fear, and that was enough to make me want to puke. Nain was never afraid. Ever. The only time he had been was when he was sure I was nothing more than a normal demon and I'd die at Astaroth's hands. His sapphire eyes flicked over me.

"What's going on?" I asked. And then something terrible occurred to me. "Oh, god. Everyone's okay aren't they?"

He met my eyes. "Yeah. Everyone's fine. They're here."

"Why?" I asked, focusing. I could sense them. Everyone, for sure. Levitt, Heph, E, Ada, Stone, my parents. Brennan and Sean.

Fuck.

"What's going on, Nain?" I asked, and I could hear the tremor in my own voice.

"Did you go out last night?" he asked.

I shook my head. "I got home from my meeting with the vampire queen around midnight. Why?"

He looked uncertain. Angry. Worried.

"Nain?"

"Come downstairs, Molls."

"Tell me."

He shook his head. "Just come." He took my hand, pulled me up out of bed and led me downstairs.

My living room was packed, and everyone was staring at the television. Well, they were until I stepped into the room, then everyone turned to stare at me.

"What the hell is…" I said, trailing off as I glanced toward the television. I was vaguely aware of Nain's hand on my back, drawing me closer to the television so I could see better. I didn't want to.

It was on channel seven. They'd broken into whatever they'd been broadcasting. Jumpy, dark video. Fire.

And a winged, flying figure, cackling and throwing fire into storefronts along Hayes. I'd recognize the wings, the skinny, scrawny frame anywhere.

I saw them every time I looked in the mirror.

I put my hands over my face, stared at the television as the video showed her, me, throw another fire blast into a storefront, and the building erupted in flames, and I/she laughed.

"Oh god," I said, felt my knees buckle, and then Nain was there, catching me, holding me up. I couldn't stop staring at the screen. They played the video again, and I listened as the very obviously shaken female newscaster spoke.

"For those of you just joining us, we've obtained this amateur video from the site of the fires we reported along Hayes earlier this morning. I… I don't know how to explain what I'm seeing. I've watched it almost a dozen times now, and I can't make myself believe this. We've verified that this was raw video, shot directly from the phone of a passer-by as this happened. It appears to be a winged woman..." She trailed off, and the rest of the video played out in silence.

Nain's arm was still around me, hand on my waist, holding me up and comforting me at the same time. I stared as the video started again. They had Jones on the line, and he said he was as confused as everyone else, and that the Detroit Police Department was looking into it. We watched the video as they looped it again, now talking about whether it was staged or not. The consensus seemed to be: how?

Then there was a knock at my front door, and Ada went to answer it. Jones and Jamie walked in, and he was staring at me.

"What the hell, Angel?" he said. "Tell me you have an evil doppelganger out there. Give me something."

I didn't answer, stared at the screen again. I heard Nain give him a very general explanation: something had happened to me in the Nether, and I'd had what seemed like a malicious spirit or something inside me now since I'd come home. That I'd been fighting it for control. That this was what happened when it won.

E came up to me, took my hand.

"And what am I supposed to do with that? Is it going to take control again?"

"I hope not," I said, finally looking at him. Didn't know what else to tell him. Heard from his frenzied, frightened, angry thoughts that he was considering arresting me. And if I heard it, Nain heard it, too.

"You do that, and we are going to have a big fucking problem with one another. You don't want me for an enemy," Nain told him, and when I glanced up at him, his eyes were glowing red.

Time to maybe make it clear what he was dealing with.

58

"Even if you could arrest me, you saw what happened at the jail when I got you and Nain out. There's not a cell in existence that can hold me," I told him. He stared at me, and I felt fear. He seemed deflated. "And here's another thing. You can't kill me. Nothing can kill me. Someone might be lucky enough to get a killing shot in. I'll come back. Over and over and over again. I've done it already."

He was staring at me. His daughter was watching me with a mix of fear and awe on her face. Nain still stood beside me, large hand on my waist. I pushed his hand away, though I hated to admit that I felt better with it there.

"Was anybody hurt?" I asked Jones.

He shook his head. "Most of those storefronts were abandoned. DFD got the fire out quick enough."

"Why would it do that?" Ada asked, watching me with concern, as if the thing inside would take control at any moment and kill them all.

I shrugged. "I think maybe it was trying to make a point," I said.

"Which was?" Jones asked.

"That when it gains control, I won't even know it's happening. And that it can do pretty much whatever it wants."

Fear rolled over me, from just about everyone in the room. Except Nain, who was just pissed off. Soon, everyone was talking, in small groups, stealing occasional glimpses at the television, which was still playing the video. Brennan got up from the chair he was sitting in, handed Sean to Ada. He approached me, and Nain stepped away.

"I have to get him home. It'll be okay," he said, reaching over and hugging me gently. I hugged him back. "Is that my fault? Did I do that?" he whispered close to my ear.

"No. I was tired and stressed out. It's my fault," I said.

He watched me for a second. "It'll be okay," he repeated. "I'll see you around, okay?"

I nodded then stood there trying to wrap my brain around what was happening. It was overwhelming, terrifying. I had to get away from all of these people. So many emotions pressing on me was about the last thing I needed just then. Everyone walking on eggshells as if I'd lose control at any second was just the icing on the cake. I left the room without another word and walked through the kitchen and out the back door.

I went into my backyard, started pacing back and forth, trying to quiet the darkness inside me, trying to stop the way I felt wrong in my own skin, trying to stop hating the fact that I existed at all. Cursed the fact that I would be alive forever, and I'd have to keep dealing with shit like this.

I kept pacing. It was one of those things. I'd always had a lot of nervous energy. Pacing wasn't uncommon. But now, being back and having whatever this was inside me messing with me, I found myself doing it more, almost unable to stop once I got started. And when I was stressed out, which was more and more common, I got into this almost unstoppable pacing pattern, as if my body couldn't handle the insanity happening inside it, needed some way to try to let off some steam.

I heard cars pull out of the driveway. I focused for a moment, realized that the only ones left were Nain and my parents. I heard the back door open, and glanced that way to see Nain and my parents standing on the back porch, watching me as I paced between my garage and the end of my yard.

I knew how insane it looked. A lot of the time, it helped me get under control. I had enough power flowing through me just then that I could have destroyed just about anything. And that was the problem. I didn't want to go out when I was like this. Too much danger of losing control, of an innocent getting hurt if I couldn't hold it together.

I was full, nearly overflowing with power. It had grown

steadily since I'd seen myself on television, fed by my anger, my fear, my pain. I was so full, it hurt. I clenched my teeth, glanced around for something to let it out on, away from everyone. Nain and my parents continued to watch me.

There was a large Norway maple across the street, and I focused on it, snarled and unleashed the overflow of power. It hit the tree full blast, and the tree gave a loud, sickening screech as it split, fell over. It landed in the empty lot, one of several.

It hurt to have the power, it hurt just as much to release it. I bent double, trying to get my breath, trying to wait the pain out. Nain walked over to me, crouched in front of me. He stayed, watching me as it felt like I was being ripped apart from the inside. I looked up and met his eyes.

"That tree was a fucking asshole. It had it coming," he said, very seriously, and I couldn't help it. I laughed, just a little, shoving him away from me as I stood up. I heard my parents walk back into the house, closing the back door behind them, leaving Nain and me alone in the yard. I stepped away from him, holding my head, trying to massage away the headache. Trade one pain for another. Kind of the story of my life.

I headed toward the back porch and plopped down on one of the steps. Nain sat next to me, and I felt a mixture of relief and irritation that he was staying.

"Do you need anything?"

I shook my head, stared down at my feet as I willed the pain to stop.

"Did you have any idea that was happening last night?" Voice a low rumble, rage flowing from him.

I took a deep breath. "No. I had a nightmare, like I was flying through the city, seeing everything through the darkness, watching it set fire to shit. Maybe it was making me watch. I don't know," I said, shaking my head.

"What do you think set it off?" he asked. "Was it that

shit with Brennan the other day?"

I shook my head. "It wasn't just that," I said. "It was everything. Everything we went over with Jones yesterday, meeting with the vamp queen, who refuses to join us, by the way. Brennan, you, the stress of never being alone. Just... everything. I'm exhausted," I said, and I hated the weakness in my voice. Waved it away. "Not that it matters."

"It matters," he said. "We need to find a way to fix this. You can't keep going on this way."

The back door opened, and we both turned and watched my parents walk through. "We may have an idea," Tisiphone said.

CHAPTER SIX

"What?" I asked, standing up. Nain stood up as well, stayed beside me.

"We think you should have Asclepias look at you," Hades said.

"No. Not a chance in hell," I said, kicking at the edge of the bottom step.

"Who's Asclepias?" Nain asked.

"Healer god," Hades said. "One who joined our side during the war and also came and healed the shifters from the plague sent by the Nosoi."

"An Aether healer immortal," I said, emphasizing the "Aether" part and looking at Nain.

He got it, nodded once and crossed his arms over his chest. He had about as high of an opinion of the immortals as I did, after seeing more than a little of what they'd done to me when I'd opened my mind to him.

"An Aether god who doesn't care at all for politics, Mollis," Tisiphone chided, and I almost laughed, hearing her mom voice.

"Yeah? So he says. Everyone has a price. Everyone has a point at which they decide someone isn't worth saving. Not a chance in hell am I letting any of them know what's going on with me."

"Did you see yourself on television today? It's kind of obvious something's wrong with you," Hades said, glaring at me. "Do you really think none of them saw it? Aphrodite is in town trying to see Hephaestus. Apollo is around too, because his sister is here. Trust me: they know."

"But they don't know that whole story and I'm sure the hell not letting them learn more than they already know," I said, glaring right back at my father. "Are you nuts? Why in the hell would you trust any of them, ever? Especially knowing what I am and what I can do to them?"

I glanced at my mother, who was looking like she was ready to beg me, then glanced back at my father and Nain just in time to see them exchanging a look.

"Molls. Just let the fucking healer god look at you," Nain said after a few moments.

"Did he tell you to say that?" I demanded.

He gave me one of his typical Nain glares. "Have you ever known me to give a shit about what anyone tells me? I don't care about what he wants," he said. "But this is something you need. And if he betrays you, then you end him, because you can."

I felt the horror from both of my parents at his last statement. They both genuinely liked Asclepias. I did too. Didn't mean I trusted him.

"Do this thing. You can't fix it until you know. And I'll be here and I swear I'll watch him, every second."

I met his eyes.

Just do it, Molls. If he blabs about what's happening with you, I'll help you hunt his ass down. But this isn't solving itself and if they think he can help, you should see what he says. Nain's voice in my mind.

I hate this, I thought at him.

I know. But you know as well as I do that we have to figure this out to prevent it from happening again. It could have been a lot worse. Next time it might be.

I watched him for a moment, looked away. "Fine," I said, shaking my head. "Bring him here."

My mother went to find Asclepias and Nain, my dad, and I went into the house. I made a pot of coffee and we ended up sitting around my kitchen table drinking out of my vintage FireKing coffee cups. It felt surreal, especially since my father was drinking out of the Snoopy one and Nain was using the same one he'd used the morning he'd died, the dark orange one. I looked down at the Formica tabletop. The thing inside me seemed smug, almost pleased. It wasn't raging, which I guessed was a good thing, though it had apparently gotten all of its rage out the night before.

Hades and Nain talked about damage control. About how it was a good thing many beings hadn't seen me in my true, winged, form. Nain seemed perfectly fine with the idea of destroying anyone who decided to publicly connect me to the video.

"Don't," I said, still looking down at the table top.

"If they talk, if they cause trouble for you, I'm gonna shut them up. We can't be soft about this."

"I agree with the demon."

"Of course you do," I said, glancing up at my father. "But I don't. Hunting down anyone who talks isn't going to help. It's only going to make people wonder if maybe those who talked were right. We're not the mob."

They were both silent, irritated. Demonic/Nether anger coming at me from both directions.

"Set the testosterone aside for a minute and think," I said, transferring my gaze to Nain. "You want to make me look guilty? Do you want to make it obvious I did this, or do you want to help me fix it?"

"You didn't do this, though," Nain said.

"And how many people would believe I was possessed or whatever the hell it is? Come on," I said, getting up to pour more coffee for myself.

I heard Nain huff out a breath in irritation. "Fine."

"But if this becomes a bigger problem, then we do things the demon's way," Hades said.

"You just want to hurt someone," I said to my father, and he nodded in agreement.

"Of course I do. I'm the Lord of the Nether. And you're my daughter, and despite your noble words you want the same thing."

"Well. We don't always get what we want. There'll be plenty of time for me to hurt people later."

It was then that there was a distinctive "crack" and my mother and Asclepias appeared near my back door. The dogs started barking. They were used to the imps. It was all of the immortals materializing out of nowhere that freaked them out now.

I greeted the healer immortal, and he shook my hand warmly. He looked the same: flowing white beard and hair, pale blue robes, kind eyes.

"Ah, Mollis. Pleasure to see you again my dear," he said, taking my hand.

"Thank you for coming."

"Your mother says you are having some issues. I saw the news reports. She showed them to me before we came over here."

I nodded. "It started in the Nether when I was dying and coming back, and it's just gotten steadily worse since I've been back here. It seems to be affected by my moods, my energy level, my former boyfriend…"

"The shifter?" Asclepias asked, and I felt a stab of irritation from Nain.

"Yes. The one you healed for me."

"I remember it well," he said, nodding. "Very odd that it would focus on a specific person."

"I know. And he's the only one. On the other hand, it's calmer when I'm around my parents, my aunt, Eunomia, Nain," I said, gesturing at Nain, who was still sitting at the table, watching us.

Asclepias studied him for a moment. "Demon. Very powerful one. Have you shared blood with him?"

I nodded. "We were bonded, but then he died, and then I died, and our bond is dead," I said, hating having to explain all of my personal things to a stranger.

"Yet I can still feel you in him."

"And can you feel him in me?" I asked, curious. The healer god focused for a moment and nodded.

"Yes."

"How?"

He shrugged, smiled. "Your bond may be broken but it isn't dead, my dear."

I felt satisfaction from Nain, resisted the urge to flip him the bird.

"Getting back to the subject," my mother said. I nodded in agreement.

"Right, of course," Asclepias said. "So you say this started in the Nether?"

"Yes. I really started noticing it after I released all of you from my bonds," I explained, and he nodded. "And it's just gotten worse, stronger, since then."

"And has this happened before?"

I shook my head. "I've had blackouts but my imps have said that all I've done during those periods was drive or walk around. This is the first time it's been violent."

He watched me. Seemed uncomfortable. "I have to ask, my dear. Please don't kill me. Are you sure this isn't you?"

I felt anger from Nain, my parents. I held my hand up, motioning for all of them to calm the hell down. "It's not me," I said, meeting his eyes.

He nodded. "All right. Let's see what we're dealing with here. It's best if you lie down and relax a little."

"I don't know how to relax," I told him, leading them into the living room. Asclepias laughed.

"Well. Try your best then," he said, still chuckling.

I really hoped I wouldn't have to kill him.

I settled back onto the sofa. My parents stood at one end, near my feet. Nain crouched near the end where my head was, alert, already watching Asclepias for any sign of bullshit.

"All right. Close your eyes. Try to relax. Try not to think, as impossible as that sounds. I'm going to try to sense for any energy signature within you."

"Wouldn't any of the immortals have been able to do this?" I asked him, opening my eyes again.

"No, dear. If there's some kind of possession or something like that, it will be subtle. And you are a raging torrent of power. Very hard to decipher anything in you. It was quite difficult to feel your bond to the demon, here. Now please settle down."

I took a deep breath, closed my eyes again.

Soon I felt a warmth pervading my body, my mind. Not like when Nain was in my head listening to me. Just a quiet, warm energy that I immediately recognized as that of the healer god. It went on for quite a while, and I did my best to stay still and calm. Being still in general wasn't something I was good at and in these particular circumstances, it was even harder. I tried not to let myself feel the emotions of the other people in the room with me, but Nain's worry and anger and my parents' watchful concern still came through, no matter how hard I tried to block it out. I wanted to sense for Asclepias, see if I could get any indication that he'd betray me, but I waited. I could sense for that after he did his thing.

Finally I felt the warmth recede. It felt like an eternity.

"All right, Mollis," Asclepias said, and I opened my eyes and sat up. Nain sat beside me, still keeping his eyes on Asclepias.

"So?" Nain asked. I watched Asclepias. He looked visibly shaken. His forehead was furrowed, and his eyes had a sadness in them that caused my stomach to sink in dread.

"What did you say happened when you resurrected, Mollis?" Asclepias asked me.

"Which time?"

"They buried you, yes?"

"Yes. And then the Nether kind of bonded with me. It saved me."

He sat back on his heels, deflated.

"What?" I asked him softly.

"The Nether did more than bond with you. The Nether inserted itself into your very being. You are currently sharing a mind, a body, a soul, with the Nether itself."

"That makes no sense," I said, even as I thought "oh, shit." "Why is it getting worse, then?"

"Without knowing for sure, all I have are theories. But I'd bet that this is what happened." He paused, took a breath. "The Nether took up residence within you, giving you enough of its power to escape your grave. Just a bit of it, just enough to own a piece of you."

"Enough to try to keep her in the Nether?" my father asked.

Asclepias nodded, slowly. "That would make sense. Yes. Did it fight you when you left?"

I nodded.

"Okay. So it probably wasn't happy when you did that."

"To say the least," I said, agreeing. "But why is it worse now?"

"When you bonded all of us, it caused damage to you."

"Told you," Hades said.

"What?" Nain asked, and I glanced over at him.

"I'll explain later."

"Yes, you will," he said, anger, worry rolling off of him.

"So when that damage occurred, it left a void in your soul. And with more space to grow, more of the Nether made its way into you, drawn by the parts that were already there. And then you got here, and you have a lot of the Nether in you, and it's fighting you for control."

"She," I said absentmindedly.

"Pardon?" Asclepias asked.

"The Nether is a she," I said.

The immortals all stared at me, waves of apprehension flowing over me. "You're right. Nether is a 'she,'" Asclepias said quietly. "It has been eons since I've felt her, alive, the way I can feel her now. But I wouldn't mistake that presence for any other." The healer god shook his head. "I met her once, shortly after I came into being. I must admit, I never even considered the possibility that I'd meet her again."

"Is this why the Nether, the realm, is weakening?" Hades asked, and Asclepias nodded.

"I would say so. This explains quite a bit. As it grows in power in her, it weakens the realm. My guess is that once it gets total control of Mollis, the Nether will die completely."

"Oh, fuck," my father said, plopping down into one of the chairs.

"If that happens, Tartarus will fail. Everything will be overrun by the monsters within it," Tisiphone said.

"Oh, fuck," I said, repeating my father's words.

"Can you think of a reason it's focusing on your former mate, though?" Asclepias asked, watching me. "That part makes no sense to me."

I nodded. "I think maybe she's jealous of him."

"Why?" Nain asked me.

"I thought about him a lot when I was buried there, when it bonded with me. And he was the thing I thought about the most, especially when things got bad. He was my primary motivation in coming home. So maybe it blames

70

him for me breaking my oath to it, even though I never promised to stay. It decided that part for me."

I expected Nain to be irritated, angry, even, over hearing about Brennan. Instead, he reached over and took my hand. There was an undercurrent of anger, jealousy, but it was background. Worry was his primary emotion just then.

I looked at Asclepias again. "Is that why it hurts to use my powers?" Didn't want him to know this, in case he used it against me. But I had to know.

"Likely, yes. It, she, is punishing you, perhaps. You say it's worse when you're under stress?"

I nodded. "Can we do anything about it?"

"I have some ideas. But none of them are easy, I'm afraid."

"Nothing ever is," I said.

We sat back around the kitchen table, Asclepias and my mother preparing cups of tea as Nain poured fresh coffee for me, my father, and himself. Cozy.

Once we were all settled, I glanced toward Asclepias. Nain was sitting beside me, my parents across from us. Like one crazy little demonic family. And then Asclepias was seated at one of the ends of the rectangular table.

"So, you think I can keep this thing under control?" I asked the healer.

He took a sip of tea. "It won't be easy. Especially knowing what I know of you, my dear."

"Meaning?"

"You're not the calmest being I've ever met," he said, his voice very purposely mild.

I sensed humor from Nain beside me, kicked him in the ankle.

"What does that have to do with it?" I asked Asclepias.

"You say the Nether seems to get stronger when your emotions are stronger."

I nodded. "She gets more restless, for sure. It's harder to fight her down, keep her under control."

"Well, I'd begin there, then. You need to dampen your emotions. Is it all emotions she seems affected by?" he asked me.

I thought. I knew she was affected by my anger, stress, sadness. Happiness. I nodded, slowly. "Yeah. Pretty much any strong emotion."

"Well, that makes it even more difficult. I was hoping I could just recommend that you try not to get angry."

Nain and my father each started to talk and I glared at them. "Cram it."

They exchanged a look.

"Pardon?" Asclepias asked.

"They were about to tell you that it's not possible for me to avoid being angry."

Asclepias smiled. "Well, you'll have to learn to control yourself, my dear. Your emotions strengthen that thing inside of you. And you saw last night what can happen. May I ask if you were around your former, ah, mate, before it happened?" he asked, uncomfortable, trying to frame it delicately, with the obviously possessive demon sitting next to me.

"Yes, but it wasn't just that. Yesterday in general was pretty stressful, and then I fell asleep. I've noticed she manages to take control when I'm sleeping, so I've been doing without sleep. I failed in that last night," I finished, irritated with myself. Nain bumped my knee with his under the table, reassuring.

Asclepias nodded. "I can teach you some meditative exercises. I know, in your position, that it will be difficult. But you need to do this, Mollis. A lot of it is just focus. You will need to keep an iron-like hold on your emotions."

"For how long?"

He looked like he wanted to be just about anywhere but in my kitchen just then.

"Forever?" he said, looking like he wanted to run. Everyone around the table stared at him, and he raised his hands. "This being, Nether, is obviously angry. Unstable. Vicious? Yes?" he said, and I nodded. I had her inside of me, and there was no doubt about what she was. "All right. And the only thing keeping her under control right now, is you," he said, looking directly at me.

"So I just have to live with this thing?"

"Can't we get her out of Molly?" Nain asked.

Asclepias took a breath. "And release her to where, exactly? Set her free in your world?"

"Wouldn't she just go back to where she came from? Be the Nether again?" Nain asked, and I shook my head.

"She's had a taste of freedom now. There's not a chance in hell she's going back," I said, knowing it was true.

"And here's where it gets worse," Asclepias said, and my father glared at him. "You called me. Hades. Do you want to know everything or not?" Asclepias shot at my father, and Hades nodded, gestured his apology.

"How does it get worse?" I asked.

"That thing knows everything you know. It shares soul space with you, and a lot of it. Chances are, should it ever find itself free, it would be able to do what you do. Everything you can do," he said, emphasizing the "everything" part.

"Oh no," Tisiphone said.

"So it could destroy the immortals?" I asked quietly, and Asclepias nodded. "So I have to keep it in me. I'm stuck with this now?"

"What if Molly died?" Nain asked, and I knew from his emotions that he hated to even ask the question. "Would that destroy this thing, or send it back to where it's supposed to be, or what?"

Asclepias shook his head. "That would be the worst thing in the world."

I looked at my mother questioningly. "Remember how we said that the spirit daemons like Strife and Terror are basically avatars? That they don't die, really, that they'll just come back again?"

I nodded, dread knotting my stomach.

"I have the bad feeling he's saying Nether would be the same thing," she said, and I looked at Asclepias.

"Is that what you're saying?"

"My gut tells me, little Fury, that you are the only thing standing between that thing, that angry, malicious being inside you, and everything else. Should you die, she will be free. And she will know what you know, and she can do what you do. But she has none of your nobility, none of your humanity. If she gets free, you and everything you love will suffer."

I rested my head in my hands. "Who created the Nether? And don't tell me you don't fucking know. There has to be a story, a myth, something you can give me," I said, keeping my head in my hands.

"Emotions, Mollis," Asclepias said gently, and I took a deep breath, tried to make myself calm down. Nain put his hand on my back, rubbed up and down my spine. I didn't know if it was the comfort of his touch, or having another creature of the Nether touching me, but I was able to draw my stress and anger down, just enough to dampen its rage.

"From the myths we know, the Nether was created by Nyx, who created the Furies, the Fates, and several spirit daemons, including Strife."

"So, what? My grandma created the Nether? How?"

Discomfort from every immortal at the table.

"Spill it. Now," I growled. Nain kept his hand on my back.

"The story is that Nyx was born of chaos, that she is darkness. And she came into being, and created many of us. And there were two very powerful spirit daemons who became a danger to all that Nyx had created. So her final act, before falling into an everlasting sleep, was to create the Aether and the Nether, which were created with the power of the two powerful beings. Nether, she was punishing. Aether was Nyx's son, and Nether nearly killed him. Nyx turned him into the realm of the Aether as her last bid at keeping him alive. Their power powers the realms. And the realm Nether became was her prison."

"Except that now, I'm Nether's prison. That's what you're telling me."

Tisiphone nodded.

"And she probably kinda hates my grandma," I said, burying my face in my hands again.

"Damn you people are a mess," Nain said. "So she's supposed to just do this? Serve as a living prison for this thing inside her that's making her crazy and hurting her? And she's supposed to do this forever?"

"And if she fails, it will be so much worse, demon," Asclepias said.

"You said she's sleeping?" I asked, face still in my hands, trying to keep myself under control

"Yes. She sleeps."

"Where?"

"In the Nether, most likely," Hades said. "She can be whatever she wants, whenever she wants. No one has actually ever seen her. Including those she created."

I looked up, and Tisiphone nodded. "She created us. Molded us, and we have no memories before we were full-grown, powerful beings, undertaking our roles as Furies. We seemed to have come into the world just as we are now."

"She won't be any help to you, Molls," my father said, and I nodded.

I sat for a minute, trying to calm down, trying to wrap my mind around everything thy'd told me. "Okay. So I definitely can't die anymore. I have to keep a lid on my emotions so I don't give her any added strength to take over. What about when I'm asleep? Even I can't stay awake forever."

"You'll need to be guarded by someone powerful. Preferably someone from your own realm, since you seem soothed by them. Your parents would be the obvious choices here," Asclepias said, and both Hades and Tisiphone nodded. Asclepias glanced toward Nain. "He would probably do as well. You have an affinity to him because of the blood you've exchanged."

Right. I'd walk bare ass naked down Woodward before I'd ask Nain to babysit me while I slept.

"Okay. Well this has been completely and utterly depressing," I said. Asclepias and I walked out into my yard, and he gave me some advice for meditating, ways to keep my stress level down. I nodded. He recommended yoga, stretching, deep breathing. Counting when I felt myself starting to feel something. The thing was, I really didn't need much advice. I'd done all this, when my powers had first manifested when I was a kid. I'd learned to keep my emotions in check, trying to dampen both mine and everyone else's so it wouldn't drive me nuts, feeling what everyone else was feeling all the time. What it meant, though, was that I didn't let myself feel much of anything at all. That had ended with Nain entering my life. I'd have to go back to that place.

He finished talking, and I looked up at the healer god. "You know I'm not one to make idle threats," I said softly, hating myself a little.

He smiled. "No one will hear a word of this from me, Mollis. I swear it to you. It is in my best interest to keep you calm and safe as well, remember."

I nodded. "As long as we understand one another."

"Clearly, my dear."

"Thank you for your help," I said, holding my hand out. He shook it firmly.

"I'm sorry I couldn't give you better news."

I shrugged. "It's better to know than not. At least now I know what I need to watch out for."

He nodded, smiled, and then winked out of sight. I turned back toward the house. My mother was standing on the porch, watching me.

Great. Now I'd have a freaking babysitter watching me all the time.

Nain came out onto the porch, and my mother went back inside. He had his car keys in his hand.

"So how do you want to do this, Molls?"

"You are not watching me sleep," I said.

"Fine. But if you ever need to sleep and they're not around, come to me. I won't even act like a perv or anything."

I rolled my eyes. Then I glanced back toward the house. "I need you to do something for me," I said softly. I started walking toward his truck, and he followed. When he was behind me, I reached up my sleeve and pulled off the band I'd been wearing on my bicep, the one that held a stone that imprisoned the souls of Ares and Dionysus. He opened his car door, and I passed it to him, behind the door, so no one else could see it. He took it, stared down at it.

"What the fuck is this?" he asked, a look of disgust on his face.

"You can feel it?"

"Yeah. I don't even want to be touching this. You've been wearing it?"

"Nain," I said sharply, losing my patience.

"What?"

I need you to keep that for me. Hide it. Lock it away somewhere no one else knows about.

Why?

That adds to my power. If I lose control of her again, I don't want her having anything extra.

His eyes met mine, then he looked down at the armband. *I've got a couple places only I know about.*

If I come to you, asking for it… don't tell me. Don't give it to me. No matter what I say.

He hesitated, then nodded. *This is going to make you weaker when you're fighting though, right? You need to stay alive to keep her imprisoned.*

And I need to not give her extra power, in case she takes control again.

I fucking hate this.

Me too, I thought at him. *Please.*

I'll take care of it.

It needs to stay whole. If what's in there gets out—

It won't. I promise. I'll keep it safe.

I hate to have to ask this of you. Like you need one more thing.

He waved it off. *I'll do whatever it takes, Molls. You know that already.*

I nodded.

Call me if you need me. Or want me. I'm not picky. And then he got into his truck, and I watched him drive away.

The crazy thing was, I really, really didn't want him to go.

I turned back toward my house. My mom was on the porch, sitting on the top step, watching me. I went and sat beside her.

"Do you want to talk about Nether?" she asked as I sat down.

"No."

"Good. Neither do I. I want to talk about something else."

"What?"

"I have kept my opinions to myself on many things, including your choice in men."

"Oh, Christ," I groaned.

"And I'm going to tell you what I think. That shifter, though he's extremely pleasing to look at and probably not too shabby in bed, based on what I hear about shifters in general, is not strong enough to handle someone like you."

"We broke up."

"I know. I'm not sorry to hear it. I'm sorry it hurt you, but he was never right for you."

78

"He made me happy."

"For a time. Yes he did. A woman like you, an immortal, a powerful being of the Nether, has needs that can't be met by just anyone."

"I cannot believe we're discussing this," I muttered.

"Now, that demon. That huge, gorgeous, powerful, absolutely stunning specimen of a demon. That is a man worthy of my daughter."

I looked away, blushing. "Did you miss the part where he lied to me and destroyed me and practically made me lose my mind?"

"Did you miss the part where you rose from destruction stronger than ever? Or maybe you missed the part where the trauma his death caused you allowed you to come fully into your own powers. Or maybe you missed the emotions that roar through a room whenever the two of you are together. It's enough to make me require a cold shower after I've been around the two of you."

"You can't make a life together out of lust. I don't trust him anymore."

"That's a lie, and you know it."

"What? The lust thing?"

She rolled her eyes. "No. The trust thing. If I were a betting type of woman, I'd bet it all on the claim that you trust him more than you trust anyone else in your life. That he's quite possibly the only one you trust."

I didn't answer. Hadn't I just kind of proved that, by handing over something like my armband to Nain? And I'd done it without thinking twice, knowing that he'd take care of it, that I could trust him to do the right thing because I was the one asking.

I didn't want to think about it.

"It's not everyday you find a man who's willing to die for you," she said softly.

"No. But I am sick to death of people leaving me behind to save me," I said. "I need someone who wants to share my life, even if I'm not perfect."

I am sorry, Mollis. That started with me. I had no idea your life would be so lonely. I hoped it wouldn't be. Then, aloud, she said, "give him half a reason, and he will be. But stop lying to yourself about what you feel for him. I don't doubt that you loved the shifter. When you feel something, you feel it all the way, dear girl. But a blind woman could see that you and the demon are not finished. Not by a long shot."

I shook my head. "Never mind. Let's talk about Nether," I said, and my mom laughed.

"We do actually have to discuss that. I think Asclepias gave you some good advice, and do not hesitate to call on me or your father if you need to rest. We will come, if it's at all possible."

"What's that supposed to mean?" I asked.

She glanced at me, shook her head. "You don't need this right now."

"Spill it, mom."

She smiled, took my hand. "I love hearing you call me that."

I squeezed her hand. "Stop stalling," I said, smiling.

"Your father asked about the realm, the Nether, getting weaker as well," she said.

I nodded. "I remember. And you said it would be bad."

"Yes. It is beginning. We've been back there more often than either of us would like. We're seeing more escapes from Tartarus. Even the cells Megaera and I hold the damned in are weakening. We lost two souls recently. That has never, ever happened." Frustration rolled off of her, and I squeezed her hand again, trying to comfort her.

"Can I do anything?" I asked her.

She shook her head. "I think we both know that you setting foot in the Nether again would be a bad idea."

"I was wondering about that, if it would try to trap me again."

"I don't know. But I don't particularly want to risk it. And I know you don't either."

"Still, if you need me…" I said, trailing off.

She smiled. "You have enough to handle, my darling girl. If anything happens that will affect your realm, we will let you know. So far, the gateway has continued to be well-guarded."

I filled her in on what I'd learned about Strife, and she listened, not saying a word, just focusing on what I was saying.

"I think you're right. I think she is biding her time and building her power. The more chaos she causes, the stronger she will be."

"And when she's strong enough, that's when she'll come after me."

"Yes."

I took a deep breath. "How am I going to do this? How am I going to keep everyone safe from the mess I've made?"

She looked over at me and smiled. "The same way you do everything, Mollis. Through sheer rage and determination and sacrificing yourself for everyone else. I am so proud of the woman you've become."

I looked down at my feet, shook my head. "Mom. My world is in danger again because of my screw-ups," I said.

She patted my hand. "Nobody's perfect, my dear. But if your world knew what you've done for it, and knew the cost of having you, I still believe it would rather have you than not. These humans have no idea how lucky they are to have a champion in you."

I didn't answer. Maybe someday I'd feel like the woman my mother sees when she looks at me.

"I need to leave for patrol soon," I said. She stood up and folded me into her arms.

"You'll be fine. It isn't in you to be otherwise," she said, smiling. I shook my head and watched as she winked out of sight.

CHAPTER SEVEN

After two weeks of practicing what Asclepias had taught me, I was starting to feel a little better about my ability to keep Nether under control. It still freaked me out if I let myself think about it too much. The idea of an ancient, angry being who held a grudge toward not just me and my entire family, but also Brennan (who'd really only been brought to her attention because I'd been so stupidly goo-goo eyed over him) was nearly too insane to wrap my mind around. But she was there, and I was trying to get used to the idea of her being there. Sure, it was possible that Asclepias was wrong and everything would be fine if she became free. I wasn't willing to risk it, and the healer had never steered me wrong before.

It was after dark, and I had my team in my car. The radio was blaring "Back in Black" and we were each trying to get into our ass-kicking mindset in our own ways. I listened to music and tried to envision everything that could go wrong. I knew that Levitt was running through attack strategies in his mind. Heph was looking forward to cracking some skulls, and was enjoying this kind of work more and more as time went on. E was calm, as always. She was very good with a tiny knife she kept strapped to her waist. Shanti was deadly serious. These lost girl jobs always put her in this mood. She was going in looking to hurt somebody and make sure the girls got cut safe.

We'd gotten a lead from the imps about three young women who'd gone missing from different parts of the city. The authorities hadn't tied the three disappearances together, but we know better. There aren't many beings out there doing shit like kidnapping or killing. Even in a city that's considered "violent" as Detroit usually is, most incidents can be explained. A boyfriend, a stalker, someone you looked at the wrong way. It's when these mysterious, nonsensical incidents take place that we can safely bet a supernatural is involved.

The bad thing about when supernaturals do this shit is that if we're not fast enough, the women never make it home.

The good thing is that my team is goddamn relentless. And so is Nain's, and between our two teams and Queen Rayna (even if she wasn't technically cooperating with us) and Brennan's shifter coalition, we were saving almost everyone we got a lead on.

We drove through a quiet neighborhood near the Grosse Pointe border. Nice, big old houses. I leaned forward and snapped the stereo off.

"Okay. Let's go over it again. From what the imps say, the three of them are being held by a group of demons."

"Strife's work," Heph said, and I nodded.

"We think so. The imps are still frustrated, because they're not actually seeing Strife herself, but these demons are acting like the other groups we've come up against."

"Wrong area of the city though," Shanti said, shaking her head. "So this is either a copycat group or Strife's influence is expanding."

"Let's hope it's the first," Levitt said from his usual place beside Shanti. Everyone nodded at that.

"Let's hope. But we still go in assuming this is Strife's doing. Same as last time. Levitt and Shanti, secure the women. Heph, E, and I start hurting people."

"You three got to hurt people last time," Levitt grumbled, and Heph laughed. "No, seriously. Shanti and I like hurting assholes just as much as you three do."

"Which beings here are immortal, and which aren't?" Shanti asked him, taking the words right out of my mouth. "And which two, even if they aren't immortal, are still strong and fast enough to protect the women if one of the demons comes at them?" I glanced in the rearview, saw her giving Levitt an irritated, yet understanding look. I saw him glance up at her and give a small nod.

I took a small breath, let it go. The two of them seemed to be past most of their weirdness. Levitt still wanted Shanti. I could feel it from him every time they were together. But he seemed to be accepting that it was over, and they were sliding into a comfortable friendship.

It made me hope Brennan and I could do the same thing someday. Things were still weird between us, still tense. He was polite to me, and I'd stopped avoiding him (taking Nain and my father's advice, finally) but we were definitely not comfortable around each other. And that was fine. At least we didn't hate one another. I think maybe that's the best I can hope for as far as the two of us.

Nain was something else. As I drove to our location, my mind wandered. Brennan hadn't been wrong when he'd been pissed about me talking to Nain every day. We did. A day didn't go by without me talking to my ex and as much as it irritated me, I actually enjoyed talking to him. We'd be all business, filling each other in on what was going on, and eventually slip into talking about nothing, usually talking as one of us was driving to a call or home from dealing with some bullshit or another. It wasn't the Nain I knew. We'd never just talked about nothing. Not like that. We'd never had time, before. And we really didn't now either, but we were doing it anyway. It was almost like we were getting to know one another again, but really, it was like getting to know someone for the first time. He was the same, yet different, and I knew the same could be said for me.

I hated the way his deep voice soothed me as soon as I heard him on my phone.

I pushed thoughts of him out of my mind.

"So yeah. Grab the women. We'll bust heads, and then we'll look around for Strife's sign. I'm almost hoping it's not there."

The team nodded in agreement. If Strife was expanding her territory, that was bad for us, for so many reasons. We were already run ragged trying to keep up with the shit she was stirring in her current territory at Sever and Kelly.

We found the area we were looking for, and I pulled up to the curb a block or so down from where the imps said the women were being held. I tossed my keys to Levitt. There wouldn't be room in the car for all of us once we had the women, so Levitt, Heph, and Shanti would drive them home and E and I would fly off once they'd gone. As I got out of the car, I just felt more pissed off. All of this, the taking of women, holding them captive, was Strife taunting me. She knew it was my thing, to rescue women, so she'd started playing this game, taking women off the street, using demons and witches to hold them. And we'd get there and fight and save the women and find Strife's mark and be pissed off because we still didn't have her.

Really, it felt like she was just trying to keep us busy. I hadn't shared that concern with my team, because I was wondering how paranoid I was. That, and like she was trying to learn about us, the way we worked, and I feared that she was learning more with each rescue. I never felt her around, and we always destroyed all of her little minions, but that didn't mean she didn't have someone lurking in the shadows, watching us and reporting back.

Christ, am I paranoid.

The simple explanation would be that she's Strife, better known as Eris, the spirit of chaos and discord, and snatching innocent women off the street causes all kinds of chaos as everyone scrambles to try to figure out what's happening, as they become afraid, which only causes more chaos.

But nothing is ever simple, and Strife has a bone to pick with me over the death of her buddy Enyo and my imprisonment of Ares, her other best friend.

I don't like her much, either.

My team and I started walking down the street. There was no need to try to sneak or hide. They'd be able to feel us coming, especially Heph, E, and I.

"Destroy immediately," I muttered. "They won't answer questions, so don't bother. I'll grab whichever one seems like the leader and see what I can learn from him or her."

They nodded, and Heph led the charge, sprinting up the front steps and bashing the oak door in with one slam of his shoulder.

"After you, my Lady," he said to me, and I grinned. Shouts erupted within the house. My imps were already there with us, and they ran through the house, scoping it out, bringing info back for the rest of us.

"Demons in the kitchen and basement. Women tied up downstairs," Bash said. "One more demon upstairs with a Normal," he said, eyes blazing. Heph had heard.

"Okay. They're splitting us up. Stay with them. I'll go after the asshole upstairs."

"You know that's a trap, yeah?" Heph said. "For you or us."

I nodded. "I'm trusting you and E to keep them safe until I get back down here."

He nodded, then patted my shoulder and stalked toward the kitchen, where we could already hear the snarls and crashes that told us a fight had broken out.

I wanted to follow him. I wanted to make sure my team was okay, that the trap hadn't been laid for them instead of me. I shook it off. They were a bunch of badasses. I had my job to do, and so did they. I wasn't their mom.

As the fighting got louder on the first floor and in the basement, I sprinted up the stairs. All of the doors along the long hallway were closed, except for one at the very end. A lamp was lit inside it. I headed toward that, listening, opening my mind for the thoughts or emotions of anyone else nearby. I concentrated, and smiled a little when I picked it up.

Definitely a trap for me.

There was a Normal in the room at the end of the hall. I could hear her frenzied, terrified thoughts, feel her fear rolling through the house. She was tied to a bed, and the demons had threatened all kinds of sick things, but hadn't followed through on them yet.

I had to give Strife that. She did keep her demons on a tight leash. They'd kill if we didn't reach them fast enough, if we didn't play the game, but she didn't let them do the kinds of things I would have expected, the kinds of things demons want to do. Nain had said it before: before he'd changed his ways, he'd acted like a typical demon, causing pain, killing without remorse. Worse. He'd admitted that with absolute disgust. And I knew that was what most demons were like. They fed off of pain and fear, and were strong enough to do anything they wanted against even the strongest human. My own demons, Elsoloth and the gang, would be doing the same things if they hadn't sworn themselves to me, if I hadn't made it absolutely clear that they could hurt all the bad guys they wanted, but if they ever harmed an innocent I'd hunt them down. They were like Nain. They saw a better way and wanted it. They wanted to be better, to be noble. To use their strength for something good instead of destruction and pain. As I thought of them, I reminded myself that I really needed to check in with them. It had been weeks since I'd last touched base with Elsoloth. I had to be better about that.

I stood there and sensed. Seven demons in the closed rooms off to my left and right. One demon in the room with the woman.

Okay.

I pretended their little game had escaped my notice. I walked into the room at the end of the hall. There were no enchantments on me now, and I let my wings and eyes show. I'd found that it tended to terrify the enemy, and their fear fed me.

I am, after all, a child of the Nether. My parents, demons, the Guardians; they were all created by Nyx, darkness itself. She'd created terrifying creatures, but also managed to create the only beings in existence capable of punishing even immortals, of serving judgment after death.

So their fear fed me, and I headed into the room. The demon was wearing his true skin as well, deep reddish purple flesh, red glowing eyes. He wasn't as big as Nain, or even Levitt, in that form, and I felt a bit of scorn.

"What game are you playing, weakling?" I asked him, aware of the snarl in my voice that let me know my demon was being well fed, my lust for destruction increasing by the second.

"We don't play games, Fury," he said, and even his voice sounded weak. Too high for a demon.

"She certainly is scraping the bottom of the barrel, isn't she? I've killed all of her strong demons, apparently."

He snarled, and, just as I expected, leapt at me.

Stupid, undisciplined demons. This one was young. Not the leader.

The second he jumped at me, I heard the doors in the hallway crash open, and the woman on the bed screamed as demons flooded into the room. I could hear them easily enough. (Seriously? Did she even bother training her people to shield their thoughts?) They were supposed to capture me. One of them had a needle, and was supposed to inject me with some tranquilizers.

I laughed. Freaking pathetic.

I held my hand out, and my flamesword appeared. I didn't even need to use my powers for this.

"Is she getting desperate or what?" I asked, turning to the one who held the needle in his hand. "I'm a fucking immortal. You can take that needle and shove it up your ass," I said, and I felt surprise roll off of the other demons.

And then they were afraid, really.

Damn, it was good.

They were dead in a matter of seconds, my flamesword making easy work of seven of them. I kept one alive, and I held my sword at his throat. I glanced toward the bed. The woman there had passed out; the sight of me slaughtering the demons a little too much for her to handle.

I would have to take those memories away from her. That was too much to expect someone to live with. I turned back to my own captive.

"Okay. Did she really expect this to work?" I asked him.

He clamped his mouth shut. He was the smartest among them, and I'd seen clearly in the thoughts of several of the demons that he was the mastermind of this particular little plan.

"Answer," I snarled, forcing my will on him, enduring the pain that came with using my powers.

"She didn't know we were doing this."

"You're hers, though."

He nodded.

"I was trying to impress her," he said, and I felt it from him.

Oh, for crying out loud. He was in love with Strife.

"We were supposed to do what we always do. Take some women, wait for you to come."

"She wants to taunt me," I said.

He didn't answer. Then he leaned forward and impaled himself on the end of my sword, dying as the point pierced his spinal cord.

I pulled my sword back in disgust. Then I went over to the woman and quickly made my way into her mind, removed memories of me and the demons. She was still out. I untied her hands and slung her over my shoulder, carried her downstairs, where everything was already quiet. Shanti, Levitt, Heph, and E were standing in the living room with the other two women. I remembered to bring up my enchantment again before I headed down the stairs. My nose was gushing, my ears starting to bleed, and I swiped my sleeve across my nose to clear the blood away.

"That was too easy, boss," Levitt said when I reached the bottom step. I nodded in agreement.

"I don't like it," Heph said.

"Me neither. Did you see her sign anywhere?"

"It's scrawled on the walls in the basement, and Dahael said it's also carved into those two trees in the front yard," Shanti said.

I glanced toward Dahael and she nodded.

"These were weak fucking demons, boss," Levitt said.

"She definitely didn't throw her A-team at us," I agreed.

"Diversion?" Heph asked, and I shrugged.

"I have no idea. Let's get them out of here." We left the house, and I dialed Chief Jones and told him about the mess in the house. Nain or Jones always handled cleanup (removing bodies, getting rid of blood and other grossness. I had no idea what they did with the bodies and I didn't really want to know) and I'd tried to be better about calling them when I made a mess. This was closer to Jones' territory, so he'd deal with it.

I hung up and watched Shanti, Levitt, and Heph get the three women into my car and drive off. They turned a corner, and I reminded myself to remind Levitt to watch the hell out when he was driving my car. He'd nearly sideswiped a parked car.

I turned to E, and that was when I saw the mob coming toward us.

"Company, E," I muttered.

"Oh, good. I was just thinking I hadn't had quite enough stupidity for one night," she said, turning around and watching them come. "I call the vampires."

"You are so weird," I said, drawing my sword as the mob approached.

"This from you is laughable, my friend," she said, and I grinned as the mixed group of vampires, shifters, demons, and witches advanced on us. We watched as they surrounded us. We were outnumbered at least seven to one.

"No problem," I murmured to E, and I felt her humor in response.

"Angel," one of the vampires said. "How convenient. All we had to do was wait for those asinine demons to lure you here."

"You are a freaking genius," I said. "Congratulations."

I sensed irritation from him. I somehow always manage to forget that I'm supposed to be afraid at times like this.

"We are tired of you, Angel," he said.

I just watched him. I wanted to laugh at his bravado. The only concerning thing about his little display was that we were seeing, first hand, the way supernaturals were forming mobs to work against us. We'd only ever heard of stuff like this happening before. Now we had direct proof. And apparently, they were not pleased with me.

What a surprise.

"We tire of being under your thumb. You and the Nain Rouge. That bitch who calls herself our queen," he scoffed, anger snaking its way through his emotions.

"Aw. We're not letting you maim and kill whenever you want to. Poor babies," I said with a fake sob.

One of the vampires hissed, and I laughed. "So I guess the question is, which one of you wastes of space wants your ass kicked first?"

And that was when they started charging us. E and I stood back to back, fighting off the mob.

"You really have a way with people. You know that, yes?" E asked me, and I laughed.

This was a much stronger group than the demons we'd just faced. The vampires were old, much older than Shanti, and the demons among them were experienced fighters. The shifters were all wolves, and they snapped at E and I as we fought.

"Witch," I muttered to E as I felt the power around us spike. First signs of a spell.

"I see her," E said and I felt her arm pull back as she threw one of her knives. The power around us snapped out as the witch fell.

"Nice one," I said, slashing my sword out at the vampires who were currently trying to double-team me. They were all being very disciplined about this, attacking us in waves, watching how it went for the wave ahead of them. Once E and I messed up one group, another would take their place.

"Are we done here yet?" I asked E.

"Oh, we've already killed half of them. Let's just keep going, shall we?" she said. She was panting a tiny bit, but I could feel from her that she was enjoying herself. "Keep your mind open."

I did. The vampires were always a little tricky to pick up. The shifters, especially when they were in their animal forms, were mostly nonsensical, full of rage and bloodlust. We'd killed the two witches already, but the demons were only getting stronger in response to all of the pain and anger. I made my way into one of the demon's minds as I fought him back. I sifted through his thoughts as we fought. Memories of being given this assignment by another demon, a stronger demon. Part of a much bigger group.

Crap.

They were organized. More than we'd ever realized.

"Are you in my head?" the demon snarled, and I smiled at him.

"Empty place that it is, yes," I said, and it enraged him.

You can't use your powers now. What if there are more in waiting? E's voice in my head. She couldn't communicate telepathically, but she knew I'd be able to hear her if she focused her thoughts.

"I know. Sucks, huh?"

"What?" the demon I was fighting asked, and I used his moment of confusion to slice him across the stomach. He roared, and it died abruptly as his body failed him.

We were down to five opponents. E was minus both of her knives now.

"Fly," I said.

"Only if you do."

I growled and kept slashing with my sword. "Wish I could use them," I grunted, taking a stab to the arm and ducking away from one of the vampires who was looking crazed at the smell of all of the blood. Especially mine, apparently. The final demon and two of the vampires were facing off against me, while E faced the last two shifters. I heard one squeal, and then she was down to one. She could be damn vicious with nothing more than her bare hands when she wanted to.

Nether was getting excited by all of the chaos, too, and I felt her struggling against my control, even as I tried to focus on fighting off the trio facing me. I managed to remove one vampire's head from his body, and barely had a chance to watch him fall when I heard E grunt in pain. I looked over to see that the last shifter she was facing had clamped its jaw onto her arm. She was trying to kick it away, but it was huge and determined to hold on.

I spun away from the demon and final vampire, pivoted and brought my sword down on the back of the wolf's neck, and it fell over onto E.

"Thanks dear," she grunted.

"You owe me one," I said, bringing my sword up as the demon charged me. I got ready to swing out with the sword when I heard E shout my name, and I turned just in time to see the vampire leaping through the air. As soon as he had contact with me, he sank his fangs into my neck, and I felt him tremble, pleasure coursing through him.

Freaking gross, I thought to myself. The demon was still there, getting ready to charge me again, and I saw E take to the air and then land on his huge shoulders, and soon there was a knife sticking out of his neck where she'd plunged it, severing his artery. She shoved him and he fell over. In the meantime, I got my sword arm out from under the giant mosquito sucking my blood and sliced across his stomach. He was sprawled out on top of me, which meant that I ended up slicing my stomach too.

Only one of us would die, though.

He released me in shock, grabbing at his stomach, and I drew my sword across his throat, ending him.

I glanced around. E had several bites and cuts on her arms and face, her black pants shredded at the bottoms from the shifters' teeth. The ground around us was littered with bodies. E stumbled over to me and raised her fist, and I bumped mine to hers.

"Nice job, demon girl," she said.

"That would have ended in like two seconds if I'd been able to use my powers," I said, trying to catch my breath.

"Yes, but you can't. We did well enough without them. And now it's time to go in case another group is on its way. Can you fly now?"

I nodded. "You?"

"Of course. Let's go. I have wolf slobber all over me." I glanced down at the street again, then E and I rose into the air and headed toward my neighborhood.

When E and I arrived at my house, the lights were on inside and I could smell something cooking. Hamburgers, maybe. Levitt and Heph were always ravenous after a fight. Or any other time, really. E and I walked up the front steps, and the dogs greeted us, tails wagging. We each patted one of them on the head and went into the house.

My team was all in the kitchen, Heph and Levitt cooking, Shanti sitting at the Formica table leafing through a magazine. They'd all cleaned up and looked relaxed.

When E and I walked in they all stared at us.

"What the hell, Angel? You went and had fun without us?" Levitt asked, and I grinned at him. I explained how E and I had been ambushed, what I'd learned from the demon's mind.

"So we've had this rule all this time about not patrolling on your own. Even more so now. At least two of you go out, no matter what else is going on," I finished.

"And that applies to you as well, right?" Shanti asked, looking at me.

"No it does not. I can't die."

She sighed, seemed like she wanted to argue, then let it go.

"Can you fill Rayna in on this when you go back?" I asked her and she nodded. "Are you staying tonight?"

She looked a little embarrassed, glanced at Levitt's back. "I have somewhere I have to be," she said. And she thought the word "Zero," whatever the hell that meant.

"Okay. Be careful." I asked her, and she smiled.

"I always am." She stood up and gave me a hug, embraced E as well, and called a "see ya" to Levitt and Heph. I walked her to the door and watched her drive away.

I told my team goodnight, then headed up to my room. It was well after one in the morning, and I thought about Shanti. She must be meeting another vampire. Normal people are not just starting to move around at this time of night.

I stripped off my bloody clothing and threw them in the garbage. Disposable clothes. Someone needs to get on that, I thought to myself. I turned the shower on as hot as I could stand it and stood under the faucet, letting the water rinse the blood and gore from my body. As always, there was the desire to scrub my skin to the point of bloodiness, to try to wash away not just the new gore, but the memories of my time in the Nether. Months later, I still didn't feel clean. I could still feel the gritty soil of the Nether, my blood crusting over my body, the way it had flaked away when I'd finally been able to move again.

I fought the urge to scrub myself. It was something I was working on. I had enough to be freaked out about without my own mind playing traitor. And it never helped. I'd just start scrubbing, and scrub harder and harder as it became apparent that I'd never feel clean. If I was in the wrong mood, I'd break down crying.

I was tired of crying. I was tired of being afraid of myself, of fearing what would happen if I screwed up. I shook the thought away as soon as I had it, got out of the shower and pulled on some terry pajama pants and a sleep tank. I dried my hair with a towel, then went into my room and sat in the center of my bed. I grabbed my phone off of the nightstand and saw that there was a text from Nain.

Call me when you get a chance. N.

I hit his number and waited through two rings.

"Hey," he said, and the sound of his voice made my stomach flip, which was happening more often of late.

"Hey."

"Were you kicking ass or something? I called twice."

"I was in the shower."

Silence.

"But I was kicking ass before that. Listen." And I told him about the demons, about how weak and stupid they were. Then I told him about E and I getting ambushed.

"The ones who attacked us were one group out of a much bigger one. This was an assignment. I saw in his head that there was a strong demon who gave them the order."

"So they're organized, like we thought," he said.

"But more so than I realized. Bigger."

He didn't respond, and silence stretched between us for several seconds. "Well it sounds like you already know what I was calling to tell you. Brennan and I ran into a group tonight. Pretty much same as you, mixed demons, vamps, and shifters. There were only seven of them though."

"Where?"

"Seven and Kelly area. I kept one alive but he became useless after a while."

I didn't need to ask him what he meant. Nain was experienced in trying to force beings to talk. I'd listened as he'd tortured a vampire for information once, and I still couldn't quite get the screams out of my mind.

"This is a mess," I said. "I told my team to make sure they don't go out alone."

"You too," he said.

"No, not me. Them. The mortal ones," I said, irritated.

"You shouldn't go out alone either. I want to start patrolling together."

"Oh, hell no," I said, and I heard him huff in irritation.

"We'll hit the bad areas. You know how much damage the two of us can do together."

"Oh, we're not rehashing our marriage now, dear," I said.

"Ha ha," he grumbled. "I'm serious."

"I think that's a bad idea," I said.

"We're full of bad ideas. What else is new?"

I didn't answer. Maybe he'd forget about it eventually.

Right. As if that would ever happen.

"I was thinking about you earlier when we faced the house full of demons," I said.

"Was there a piano there?" he asked, and I blushed immediately. The first time we'd been together, he'd taken me against the side of a grand piano, and he knew as well as I did that I couldn't look at a piano without thinking of him.

"Oh, you're just hilarious. No," I said. "I was thinking about demon shit, and how you never see demon kids. Why not?"

He didn't answer right away.

"I mean, do demon women not get pregnant easily?" I asked, trying to urge him on.

"They don't. We're creatures of the Nether, just like the Furies and Guardians and all that. A little less so. We do reproduce, but it's rare, and that's probably a good thing. We live a really long time, and if we reproduced easily, we'd overrun everything."

"That makes sense. So there are demon kids out there somewhere?"

"Most of them are probably born in the Nether. That's where most demons live anyway. But even those that are born don't have much of a chance at survival."

"Why not?"

"Think about the demons you know, Molls. Me included," he said. "Do you think any of us would make great parents? Demon kids rarely make it out of toddlerhood."

My jaw dropped in disgust. "They kill their own kids?"

"Sometimes," he said. "Sometimes, they just don't care what happens and the kid wanders off. Sometimes they toss it out when they get tired of all the needy shit."

"That is… wow," I said. "What about your parents?" Then I thought. "Wait. Where are you? Can you even talk now?"

"I can talk. I'm driving home from Jones' house."

"Okay."

"I haven't seen my parents since I was maybe five or so. My father was a strong bastard. Violent as hell," he said. "He and my mother weren't bonded. They really didn't give a fuck about one another either way. And one day, she just got bored of playing mother and putting up with his fists, and she took off. And he never wanted a kid in the first place, so he gave me a choice: take off or let him finish me. I decided to leave."

"Where did you go?" I asked as I settled myself under the covers. I closed my eyes and let his voice wash over me, even if the story he was telling wasn't a soothing one.

"I just wandered. Stole food when I had to. Killed when I felt weak."

"Demons start killing that young?" I asked.

"I did. The ones that are alone do, or they end up dead at the hands of another demon."

"And then what?"

"When I was in my twenties, I ran into Astaroth. You know the rest."

I stayed silent. "Demons aren't good parents, yet you managed to raise several kids. Stone, Brennan, Veronica, George," I said.

"Yeah, but I was bad at it. They obeyed me, because they were afraid of me and they had nowhere else to go. I spent plenty of time wanting to kill them. And I never had a baby around, and I'll tell you that if I had the thing wouldn't have survived it. You have any idea how much babies fucking cry? That's all Sean does. Cry and shit."

I laughed. "You like Sean," I said, knowing it was true.

"I like him as long as he's not crying which is almost never," he grumbled. "Someday, he'll be strong and useful."

"He's cute," I said.

"Babies look like bald little aliens," he said. "They are not cute."

"Grumpy old man."

"Did that answer your question?" he asked.

"Yep. Demons are shitty parents and you've always been a badass. Got it," I said, and it ended on a yawn.

"Are you sleepy? Where's your mom and dad?"

"Mom's on her way," I said.

"Oh. Okay." Was that disappointment in his voice? "Well stay on the phone with me until she gets there."

"I don't need a babysitter, Nain," I said.

"You need something, woman," he muttered, and I didn't answer. Doing so would only send the conversation in a direction I wasn't ready for it to take.

"Tell me what else happened today," I said. So he did, telling me about Stone and Ada and how they were starting to talk about maybe getting married, and about how the assistant Ada had insisted he hire had ended up quitting after seeing one too many scary things in her time at the loft. I kept my opinion about that to myself. I was glad she was gone. She was too pretty. Long red hair, curvy. Big boobs.

And why the hell did I even care?

"She won't talk?"

"Ada used a spell to erase most of what she knew. She won't even remember she's ever been there."

"Good."

"You didn't like her," he said.

"I think you hired her maybe for the wrong reasons," I said.

"Yeah? What are those?"

"I can think of two," I said, and he laughed.

"You think I hired her for her tits?"

I didn't answer.

"Were you jealous?" he asked.

"I wasn't jealous. I just never understood why of anyone you could have hired, you hired a freaking Normal to help you out. Those were the only two assets I could imagine."

"I hired her because Ada is friends with her aunt and she likes her. I didn't especially want or need an assistant. As far as her assets, I prefer nice round, perky ones that fit in my palms. Yours come to mind."

My entire body flushed, and I took a deep breath, both to calm myself and in relief. "My mom is here," I said.

"Too bad. That was just starting to get interesting," he said. "Talk to you tomorrow." And then he hung up, and I sat staring at the phone. My mom knocked and I let her in, relieved to have something to think about other than my husband. Ex-husband.

Obviously.

CHAPTER EIGHT

I pulled up outside of the loft and idled, waiting for Nain. I was still irritated about this whole thing. I mean, I understood why we were doing this. As the two strongest people on our teams, we not only had the best chance of destroying Strife or Terror, but we'd also be likely to draw them out. It just pissed me off that I had to spend time with Nain today, of all days.

I looked toward the loft, waiting. There was no point in honking the horn or calling. He could feel me, the same way I could feel his presence, and that had nothing to do with bonds anymore. It had to do with the fact that we were both beings of the Nether, and we were both pretty powerful. When we'd first met, the amount of power swirling around the demon had nearly made me nauseous. And he'd said the same about me. And now he was even more powerful than he'd been before, thanks to my blood in his veins and the fact that the enchantment that had stolen some of his power from him had broken upon his death.

His death. Which had happened on a night almost exactly like this one, five years ago to the day. And him being alive, him walking toward me, the way he was at that moment, didn't do anything to erase the memories of that night.

I didn't even want to think about him, let alone sit in a car with him for four hours on patrol.

He climbed into the passenger seat, and as soon as his door was closed, I pulled away from the curb.

"Where are we going?" I asked him, keeping my eyes straight ahead.

"Downtown, see if we can dig up anything about the trouble there. If it seems quiet, then we'll head toward the riverfront."

I nodded and maneuvered the car through the mostly-empty streets. Weeknights downtown weren't exactly jumping. There were a few bars and restaurants open, but it was nothing like the way it was during the day when it was bustling with cars and pedestrians, people sitting on the benches and edges of the planters along the streets. As we drove, I clicked the radio on, making it loud enough that I wouldn't be expected to talk to him. And how he could sit there, acting like nothing was going on made me want to kick his ass.

He was watching me. I could feel his gaze on me, and I forced myself not to look at him. We should have taken his truck. My car felt way too goddamn small with him in it.

I ended up parking near Campus Martius (another stupid memory. We'd met in nearly that exact spot.) It was a convenient enough place and we could cover a lot of the surrounding area on foot and then circle back to the car when we were done.

We got out of the car and started walking down Woodward. The imps slipped through the shadows, scouting, watching out for us. It was hard for me, even after all the time I'd spent in the city, not to still be a little mesmerized by the skyscrapers downtown, by the way looking up made me feel dizzy and tiny. Insignificant. I liked it. I know some people feel uncomfortable when reminded how small they are. It was nice to feel small once in a while, and I could pretend that the weight of the world wasn't on my shoulders.

It would have been a more enjoyable stroll if I'd had different company.

We walked in silence. I had my shields down, trying to hear any threatening thoughts. I paid attention, trying to feel any demonic or immortal power signatures nearby.

After a while, we started snaking through other streets, the traffic thinner here, even more deserted. We walked for at least an hour, and I didn't pick up a single thing.

"This is a waste of time. If we want to catch Terror, if it's even her doing this, we're going to have to be here during the day. She's preying on people going about their business, and whoever she has working for her is depending on the chaos and noise down here during the day to shield what they're doing," I said.

"We can check out RiverWalk and Hart Plaza," he said.

"Fine."

We started walking back toward Campus Martius.

"What's your problem tonight?" he finally said.

I glared at him for a second, then looked straight ahead. "Nothing."

"You're supposed to be keeping yourself calm. You don't look calm. You look like you're going to rip someone's fucking head off. Probably mine."

"Mind your own business, Nain," I muttered.

"You are my business, Molls."

I didn't answer. I wanted to hit him so bad my body ached from holding myself back from it. We got back in my car and I drove toward the Renaissance Center, paid for parking on the street. The imps stayed with the car this time, and Nain and I walked toward the riverfront. We'd had a few reports of trouble here, mostly Normals acting up, which seemed a lot like it could have been Strife or Terror's influence. The RiverWalk was pretty well policed, especially near the Rennaissance Center. Nain and I seemed to be of one mind, walking automatically in the direction of Hart Plaza. That stretch of the RiverWalk tended to be more deserted, especially at night.

We were nearly at Hart Plaza when I felt it: a creeping, tickling sense of fear surrounding me, nearly suffocating me. I glanced at Nain, saw him looking around.

You feel this? he asked in my mind

Yeah. This must be Terror.

As if to punctuate my words, screams erupted from Hart Plaza, and Nain and I ran there. The Plaza wasn't crowded, but it was its usual mix of skaters and loiterers. There were maybe fifteen other people in the plaza, and they were herded into a small group, all of them looking around as if waiting for an attack.

That right there told you all you needed to know, made it clear that something was wrong. Sticking to your own and minding your own business were pretty much par for the course around here. If a bunch of strangers were herding together for safety, that was a pretty clear sign something was wrong.

And that was when I felt it. Strength. Immortal, ancient power. She materialized not a foot away from Nain and swung a huge, medieval-looking black ax at his head. I shoved him away just in time, and her blade just missed his throat.

Get them out of here. Their fear is feeding her, I told Nain, and he started running toward the Normals, shouting that they needed to leave. I knew him. He'd order, and then he'd threaten and anyone stupid enough to try to resist would see a little of his demon and they'd run. I couldn't focus on that, though, because right then Terror was swinging her ax at me. I ducked. I was trying not to use my powers, because I didn't know how long this would go on and weakening myself early, putting myself in pain, would only be trouble for me the longer it went on.

She was strong. She'd been feeding well in all of the fear she'd caused in this part of the city over the past several months.

As I spun around, I had a moment to look toward where the Normals had been. They were running, Nain shouting after them to go, fast.

Once I was sure no one was watching, I held my hand out, and my sword appeared, black flames leaping along its thin blade.

"Pretty toy, little Fury. A bit refined for my taste, though," Terror said. Her voice was soft, almost delicate. She didn't look the way you'd expect "Terror" to look. She looked like a Disney princess; big blue eyes, rosy skin. Long, wavy blond hair cascading down her back in waves. She wore jeans and a pale blue sweater. Really, the only thing that would mark her as anything other than a stupidly gorgeous human were the sharp, razor-like teeth she bared at me as I swung the sword at her. That, and the fingernails that looked more like claws than nails.

She darted away from my blade, practically pirouetting and reaching my left side. She wound up to swing again, and I remembered my lessons with Athena; as she opened herself up to swing, I sliced forward with my sword and ended up getting her across the ribcage, a slash of red appearing on her light blue top. She hissed, and it was more in anger than pain.

"I was playing nice, Fury," she said. "But fine. We'll do it your way." And then she rushed me, ax raised, and I readied myself for it. At the last second, the ax disappeared, and she held a knife, which she maneuvered with almost dizzying speed. I ducked away from her, but she still caught my shoulder, and I felt the tip of the knife hit bone as she stabbed downward.

I grunted in pain, trying to ignore it. At least it had been my left arm.

Nain was nearby, watching, looking for opportunities to jump in.

Stay back, I ordered him, and felt a torrent of rage and irritation come from him.

Fuck that Molly. You're already bleeding.

So is she. Stay back.

She was everywhere, using the knives, then a mace (seriously? A goddamned mace), swinging it above her head and then at me, nearly taking my head off as I tried to avoid her.

"Come on little Fury. Fear me. I can only imagine what your fear would do for me," she said, swinging at me again.

Shows how much she knows about me. The more she fought me, the angrier I got. There's no room for fear when I'm pissed off. It's a Nether thing, maybe. Or maybe it's just me. But my rage is all-consuming, and there is no room for anything else. She was doing a good job of helping me get my rage on.

I slashed out with the sword, catching her forearm, the flames of my blade sizzling as they met flesh. She shouted in pain.

I slashed out again, and she barely blocked me, making the ax appear again. I grunted as the contact reverberated, making my shoulders ache. She glanced toward Nain, and then she smiled. I panicked, tried to slash out at her again. And then she was gone and I looked around, seeing her rematerialize a few feet behind me. She had a gun in her hand, and she smiled as she let off a shot, just before I charged into her, knocking her down.

It didn't hit me.

I heard Nain grunt behind me, and I saw red. I could feel his anger. He was in pain. I grabbed the avatar of Terror around the throat, and she clawed my arms, bared her teeth at me.

"Better go, Fury. He's hurt bad," she said, grinning a feral smile. "I think I hit something important."

I heard myself roar. I lost all sense of myself. And I squeezed, as hard as my body would let me. I felt her struggle, and then I felt her go still, and still I squeezed, and I tore my way into her mind. I could see Strife there. Exactly as she had appeared to the Normals. They'd been working together. And I saw the source of her power.

Immortal power.

The power of the avatar of terror.

Ancient and terrifying.

Take it.

Take it.

Take it.

"Molly, don't," I heard Nain shout behind me.

Take it. You know you want it.

"Stop, Molly."

Imagine how strong we could be, a sinuous, sibilant voice in my mind.

"Molls!"

You have to fight me off, don't you? And then a throaty laugh, bordering on a cackle.

"Baby, come on," Nain, groaning now behind me.

Take it, you fool. Before it escapes this body.

I shook my head. Made myself let go of the avatar's body, made myself leave her mind. Once I stopped touching it, the body just disappeared, as if it had never been there at all, and I felt the spirit of Terror leave. It would inhabit another body at some point. But it would be new, and it wouldn't be after my blood.

I shook myself out of it, got up and ran toward Nain. His chest was a mess. She'd hit right near his heart. He was breathing heavily. Shaking. Blood was dripping from the corner of his mouth.

"No. No goddamn way," I said, falling to my knees next to him. I slashed my wrist, let the blood pour over his wound. "Why weren't you in your demon form?" I chided him. In his human skin, he was much more vulnerable. That, and the fact that I was almost sure the weapons used by the avatar of Terror were much more lethal than what we usually faced, had ensured that he wasn't going to be with me much longer.

"What the hell are you doing?" he grunted, trying to push my hand away.

"Healing you. Goddamn it," I shouted.

He groaned, tried to push me away. "You can't fix this."

"The hell I can't," I muttered. "Don't push me again."

I opened the vein again, let my blood pour into him. He stopped trembling.

"It burns," he groaned.

"That's how it feels when you heal. Now shut up," I said. I could feel myself weakening, my heart struggling against the massive blood lost while healing Nain. My nose was bleeding, my skin cracking, burning, from using my powers against Terror. Nether was raging in my mind, angry with me for not doing as she ordered.

I tried to ignore it all, and stared at Nain's chest. Watched bone reform itself, muscles and skin slowly but surely knitting back together.

One more time.

I slashed my wrist again, worked the blood into the last of the wound. My heart was thundering within me, sputtering as if it was ready to give up.

"No more, baby. I'm fine. Stop it," Nain said, sitting up and gripping my upper arms. I looked at his face. He was still deathly pale, but he was alert. No more trembling. No more blood from his mouth. I felt tears come to my eyes and my vision swam in front of me. One of the imps appeared at Nain's side, shoved a shirt toward him, still sporting its tags.

"Can't walk through the city like that demon," the imp, Falrog, said.

"Thank you," Nain said to it, and the imp thumped its fist to its chest, saluting him the same way they saluted me.

I sat and watched him strip off what was left of his destroyed, bloody shirt. He set it on the ground, and I threw flames at it. Leaving our blood sitting around was a bad idea.

"Thanks. Don't use your powers any more now."

"Fuck off," I said. I brought my knees up, rested my face against them, mostly so I wouldn't have to look at him. I didn't want to see his muscles bunching as he moved, or that trail of dark hair that led from his navel and into the waistband of his jeans. I sat, and refused to look at him, and forced my tears back, and felt myself burn as I healed. My heart rate settled back to normal, and I stopped trembling as my wounds, both those received at Terror's hands and those I'd caused to myself, healed. I sat there, and I felt Nain sit beside me. Close, but not touching. And I knew damn well what he was doing. I could feel my power building again, my body strengthening, healing faster, because of his demonic rage feeding my own demon.

After a while, I felt whole, full of power again. I stood up and walked away from him, back toward the RiverWalk. He followed me, and we didn't say anything for a long time. I tried to shut down all of the emotions I was feeling. I tried to focus on details: the sound of the river to our right, the lights twinkling downtown to our left. Anything but the man behind me and the feelings running through me.

Of course, he broke the silence.

"I didn't know you could do that. Thanks for saving me."

And something snapped. I growled, and I shoved him as hard as I could. He hit the wall of a building nearby. "Fuck you, Nain," I said.

He sprung up, eyes glowing red, an immediate demonic response to a threat of any kind.

"What the hell, Molly?"

"Just shut up," I growled, and I dropped my enchantment on myself, letting him see my eyes glowing, my wings. My own response.

"You've been ready to rip my head off all night. What's your problem?"

I rushed him, shoved him again, my rage overtaking me. "You are such an asshole," I shouted.

"Stop," he said, grabbing my arms when I tried to hit him. I fought against him. He groaned in response to my rage, my power swirling around us. And I couldn't get a lid on it, couldn't stop being angry, especially after what we'd just gone through, seeing him near death again.

"Do you even know what today is, you son of a bitch?" I asked him, still struggling, still trying to hit him.

He held me tight. "What the hell are you talking about?"

I growled again, determined to get loose so I could hurt him.

"I hate you," I said, feeling some of the fight go out of me, feeling stupid tears come to my eyes. I tried to push him away. "I hate you so much."

"Molls. What's going on?"

"It's the anniversary of the day I killed you."

"I'm alive."

"You are such a bastard. Is that supposed to make me forget the way it felt when I killed you? Am I supposed to forget the way my soul ripped when you died? Or the way I felt the pain I caused you? Or the emptiness I felt the instant you were gone?" By now I was crying, shouting, tears coursing down my face, still struggling against his iron grip, trying to get loose.

"Honey," he said and his voice was low. Guilt and sadness, regret coming from him.

"Get away from me," I said, trying to pull out of his grip.

"No."

I growled, and he pulled me into his arms, holding me against him. I tried to pull away from him, but I was exhausted and I felt the last of the fight go out of me. I felt my knees buckle, and then he was holding me up, supporting me as he held me against his body, huge strong arms encircling me as I cried. I fisted my hands in his shirt, gripping it.

"I hate you. You destroyed me. You lied to me. You made me hurt the one person in my life I ever loved."

He didn't say anything. He held me tight.

"Something in me died, too. And I don't know how to get it back," I said, and that seemed to do something to him. He raised his hands to my face, cupped my face between his hands. He leaned down and kissed first one eye, and the the other.

"I'm so sorry, Molly," he said, his voice hoarse, rough. He pressed his lips to the top of my head, stood like that. His hands were cool on my face, his body huge, hulking, protective over mine.

I'm sorry, baby. I didn't know it was today. I'm sorry.

Let go of me.

No.

I shoved him away, and this time, he let me go. I wiped at my eyes in irritation, drying the remaining tears with my sleeve. And then I glanced at him one more time. He looked stricken, haunted almost, standing where he'd held me. I turned away and headed toward where the car was parked, knew he was following me.

We climbed into the car in silence.

"Take me back to your house."

"Not a chance in hell, Nain."

"You're going to sleep tonight. You're exhausted. Your parents aren't around. I'll watch you."

"You are not fucking watching me while I sleep," I snarled.

"Yes I am. Or do you want Nether to make another appearance? You're upset, you're stressed out, you're tired.

You're hurting. I'll sit in that chair in your room. When's the last time you slept anyway?"

"The night with Nether," I said.

I felt his shock. "That was over a week ago."

I didn't answer.

"They told me you didn't sleep after I died. I thought they were exaggerating."

"I'm not talking about this," I said.

I felt his gaze on me. I just wanted him away from me. But I knew I couldn't get rid of him that night. He was right. I was ready to fall asleep driving. And I was a mess, and Nether was already pissed off at me. I drove toward my house, and thankfully, he didn't talk to me anymore.

I pulled up into the driveway, patted Kurt and Courtney as we walked toward the back door. Nain leaned down and scratched Kurt behind the ears. The dogs had lived with him at the loft after I'd died. He'd fenced off the empty lot next to the building, installed sod and everything. They even had custom-built doghouses.

We walked in the back door. Eunomia and Levitt were in the kitchen, washing dishes.

"Hey," Levitt said in greeting.

Eunomia looked me over, stopped still from drying the plate in her hand.

"Mollis? Are you all right?"

"I'm fine. We managed to destroy Terror," I said, and Levitt pumped his fist in the air, congratulated me.

"Well, that's a relief," E said, eyes still on me. "But are you all right?"

"I'm all right enough. He's here on babysitting duty tonight. I feel like I'm about to fall over."

She nodded. "Let me know if you need anything."

"Thanks."

I made my way up the stairs to my room, Nain right behind me.

I didn't want to be in my bedroom with him. In the room we'd bonded in, in the room we'd made love in. I gritted my teeth, refused to start crying again. I steeled myself and walked into my room.

He settled himself into the yellow chair in the corner of my room, the one I liked to curl up and read or doze in sometimes. I went to my dresser and dug out pajama pants and a t-shirt, then I went across the hall to the bathroom and took a quick shower. I pulled the clothes on and took a deep breath. Then I headed back into my room. He was still in the chair.

"There are books over there," I said.

"Lots of classics," he commented.

"I went through a phase where I was trying to read them. I thought at one point I'd try to go to college and figured it couldn't hurt," I answered, pulling the covers of my bed back.

"*Jane Eyre* looks pretty worn," he said, still looking through the stack of books.

"Yeah. That's one of my favorites." Nearly told him that I like *Wuthering Heights*, too, even though I hated it the fist time I'd read it. I kept my mouth shut, tried not to remember the way I'd come to my house to be alone a few months after he'd died, tired of everyone else hovering over me, trying to make me speak or eat. How I'd sat in that chair and flipped through my copy of *Wuthering Heights* until I found the part where Cathy says that "whatever souls are made of, his and mine are the same" and cried and screamed into the empty house, grieving, missing the other part of my soul. I'd written his name in the margins of that page, as if writing it would make him feel more real again. I shook my head, climbed between the covers. I turned away from him, faced the wall.

I heard him flipping pages. Felt the usual from him: demonic rage. Lots of guilt mixed up in that just then. Good.

"Do you really hate me, Molls?" he asked after a while, his voice low in the mostly dark room.

"Yes. I really do."

He was quiet for a long time, and I thought he wouldn't respond. Then he finally said "good."

"Yeah? What's so good about it?"

"It means you still care enough to hate me. And if you still care enough, then maybe someday you won't hate me anymore."

"Don't hold your breath," I said, closing my eyes.

CHAPTER NINE

When I woke up, I glanced toward the chair first. He was there, head resting back against the back of the chair, snoring quietly. He was too big for the dainty chair, and he looked like a giant. Even more than he usually did. I got up and shook him.

"What?" he asked, jumping awake.

"I'm up now. Take the bed for a while."

"Thanks." I watched as he climbed sleepily into my bed, rested his head on my pillow. Tried not to notice the way he pressed his face into my pillow, the same way I had so often with the pillow on his bed after he'd died. Within moments, he was asleep again. I looked toward the chair. *Wuthering Heights* was sitting on the little table beside it. I sat down in the chair and picked up the book. I leafed through it, noticed a piece of yellow paper from the legal pad I kept on the table sticking out of it. I opened it to the page he'd marked, which was the same page I'd been thinking about the night before, the one on which I'd written his name in the margins.

I looked at the paper. I'd thought it was a bookmark. It wasn't.

In his neat, exacting hand, he'd written to me.

You are my soul, Molly. Always will be.

My hands were shaking. I put the paper back in the book, set it down. Left the room before I did something stupid.

I went into my bathroom and locked the door behind me. I rested my hands on the edges of the sink, let my head fall forward. I tried to remember to breathe.

Focus, girl, I told myself. *That is a whole mess you can't even deal with right now.*

I tried to force myself to snap out of it. I brushed my teeth, washed my face. I brushed my hair and put it up, slipped into a pair of jeans and a black top.

I put on make up, which I'd been doing more often in the past couple of weeks, when I thought of it. It made me feel more human, I guess. Normal. As I did it, my mind kept going back to what he'd written.

I had two notes from Nain now. The one he'd left me after he'd died, and the one he'd left in my book. I had the first note memorized. It was in a metal box in my basement. It was creased from being folded over and over again, smudged.

I can't. I just can't even with this right now, I thought. I'm supposed to not be feeling anything, and when he's around, I feel every goddamn thing. Everything was bigger, stronger, when he was around. Especially the things that happened between us. Every word, every glance seemed weighted, tense. There was no way to be calm around Nain. Not really. I shook my head and took a deep breath, steeling myself to face him again.

I opened the bathroom door just as he was coming out of my room.

"You should sleep longer," I said.

"I can't sleep in there," he said.

"Why not?"

"I can smell you all around me. It doesn't make me feel sleepy."

I watched him. "It doesn't? How does it make you feel?"

His eyes met mine. "Is this really something you want to talk about right now?"

I blushed. "I guess not."

"Stone's on his way to pick me up."

"I could have driven you home."

He was watching me. "I think you've probably had enough of me for a while."

I glanced away. The hallway felt tiny with him in it. It felt as if all of the air was being sucked from my lungs. I rubbed my hands together, rubbed my arms. "Thanks for staying last night," I finally said.

"Anytime. Thanks for not fighting me on it."

I nodded.

We stood there a while longer, and I could tell he wanted to say something. He was tense, his emotions swirling around me. I tried to shut them out, remembering that I was supposed to not be feeling.

"Molly, I—"

At that moment, Stone walked through the front door, calling a raucous "good morning!" into the house.

I glanced up at Nain, met his eyes. We stood there like that, for just a second.

"I'll see you," he said, and I nodded. He headed down the stairs. I watched him go, and called a good morning to Stone. When they were gone, when I heard Stone's car going down the street, I headed back to my room, and I sat in the chair, and I held his note in my hand and tried not to feel anything.

I really didn't want to feel the things I was feeling anyway.

I made myself leave my room and try to stop thinking about things I had no business thinking about. For once, I was the first one up, and I let the dogs out and fed them, tossed the grungy tennis ball they loved so much a few times and watched them chase it down. It was early November, and the air had taken on its winter chill.

I was about to head inside when I felt a presence behind me, coming out of the gateway. When I saw who it was, I smothered a groan.

"Hello, abomination," Aphrodite said. How lovely that she'd adopted my stepmother's nickname for me.

"Good morning to you, bitch," I said in as pleasant a voice as I could muster.

Anger rolled off of her. "What did you call me?"

"Aren't we calling each other what we really are? I'm an abomination and you're a bitch."

She just glared at me. "You are vile."

I grinned. "Thank you. If you believe that, then I must be doing something right."

Okay. So I'm not a huge fan of the goddess of love. She's bitchy, walks around with her nose in the air, and she's spent eternity screwing around on Hephaestus. I don't have the world's highest opinion of her.

"Whatever. I am here to speak to my husband."

She hated me. I knew it. Part of it was that her husband had chosen to live with me instead of her. Never mind that the reason was that he'd felt spurned by the immortals over and over again, which made me want to kick every single one of their asses. He was a freaking genius. Loyal. Dependable. And I knew she wasn't the only one. There had been whispers, and flat-out accusations about why exactly Heph was so devoted to me. I tried to ignore it, but clearly Aphrodite hadn't.

"I think he's still asleep," I said.

"Well, I'll just go wake him up," she said.

"You are not stepping foot in my house," I snarled, and she glared at me.

"And who's going to stop me, abomination?"

I just crossed my arms and smiled. "Remember that you're calling me that for a reason."

I felt just a teensy bit of nervousness from her then.

"Yeah. That's what I thought," I said.

"Someday, you'll get your comeuppance, Fury. And I will be first in line to cheer whoever takes you down."

"I'm sure you will be. Probably on your knees if the person is the right gender."

Her mouth dropped open in shock, and I did my best to keep my bored face in place and not start laughing. I felt a good dose of humor from behind me and turned to see Heph walking down the back steps.

"Morning, queenie," he said, grinning. "And to you too, Aphrodite."

"Good you're here. You can go now, abomination."

At her words, Heph threw her a disgusted glare. "If you're going to talk that way, you can take your ass back to the Aether."

"Oh, right. Can't be insulting little miss perfect, can we?" Aphrodite sneered. "Speaking of knees, I wonder how often she's been on her knees for you. You do get around, don't you, Mollis? From your husband to his best friend, and now, what? Back to the husband?"

Rage rolled of of Heph, and I nudged his arm with mine. "I never two-time. That's more your thing, I think."

She smiled a vicious smile. "Ah, right. The shifter cheated on you, didn't he? How did that feel?"

I didn't answer.

"You can go now," Heph said to Aphrodite.

"Oh, right. Sure you want alone time with your little girlfriend. You know he wants you, don't you? Even if you haven't given him what he wants. The way he follows you around is embarrassing," she said, glaring at me.

"I think you need to leave now," I said, starting to get pissed. I turned to Heph. "Unless you want to talk to her?"

"Fuck no," he grumbled.

I produced my flamesword. "I'm in the mood to cause some pain. Are you volunteering?" I asked Aphrodite.

"You wouldn't," she said, though I felt a wave of fear roll off of her.

"Oh, I would. Definitely."

She snarled at me, and then she disappeared with a "crack." When she was gone, I let my sword disappear and turned to Heph. "Well that was a shitty way to start the day," I said to him, and he nodded.

Heph walked toward the back porch, and I followed. He settled onto one of the steps, grimacing a little. I couldn't imagine living with something that hurt you, for eternity, the way his leg did. I sat down next to him, sensing that he wanted to talk.

We sat in silence for several long minutes.

"You know nothing she said is right, yeah?" he finally asked. "That shit about me wanting you."

"You really know how to make a girl feel good about herself, Heph," I said, and he laughed. "Yes. I know that," I said. "But she's not the only one who thinks that."

"Artemis," he said, and I nodded.

"Aphrodite already hates me because of the Ares thing (Ares, her former lover who I'd imprisoned for all eternity) and then to have you living in my house it's just a little too much for her ego to handle."

"It is. I just feel like we need that spelled out between us, the way people's jaws flap. I don't feel that way about you. I mean, you're a good-looking woman and all that, and I like you a lot, but I'm not interested in you that way."

I smiled at how uncomfortable he seemed. "I know. I can sense emotions, Heph," I reminded him.

"I know. I just wanted to say it so there would be no doubt." He took a breath. "I like you. A lot. You're probably the best friend I've ever had. No one's ever showed me as much kindness as you have. You appreciate the shit I can do. I've never had anything like this before."

I looked over at him. "I'd be stupid not to appreciate all the help you give me. You're a fucking genius and an artist. Not shabby in a fight either. And you curse almost as much as I do."

He laughed. "I'll admit. The first time we met, I had a moment or two where I thought, what if? But the longer I know you, you're like a sister to me. I want to protect you. I want to kick the ass of anyone who hurts you. She said I'm loyal to you, and I am. Completely. But that's because you're the only one who's ever made me feel worthwhile."

"The immortals are a bunch of assholes," I muttered. "You've given them so much. Weapons. Hades' nifty little invisibility helmet."

"I'm imperfect," he said, shrugging.

I looked over at him and grinned. "All the best people are."

He smiled then. "That is why I like you so much, queenie."

"We're good, Heph. It's kind of nice having a brother-type person in my life. Never had one of those before."

"We tend to be overprotective," he said. "I still want to kick that fuckin' shifter's ass."

"I know. Shit happens," I said. "He said he needed someone who needs him. Someone who needs him to protect her and make her feel safe. I don't need anyone that way."

"What do you need, queenie?"

"I need someone who loves me for me. Not for what they think I should be. Someone who gets that I can't stop fighting, that whatever else I am, I'm Tisiphone's daughter. It's not in me to turn away from a fight."

"Can I say something?"

"Sure."

"You already have that. You know what I mean."

I glanced at him. "How much did Nain pay you to say that?" I knew the immortal and my ex-husband were becoming fast friends. It made sense. Similar personalities. Both of them badasses with chips on their shoulders.

He laughed then. "As an impartial observer, that's all I'm saying, queenie. A blind man could see how much he cares about you. And your mom likes him."

"I know she does," I said. "That's only because he's so much like my dad with the whole angry demon thing he has going."

He was quiet for a while. Then he laughed. "When word spread that your parents had done what they were definitely fuckin' not supposed to do, and that you existed, the Aether and the Nether were in an absolute uproar. There's never been a baby born that caused as much fear as you did. Of course, you were a grown woman by the time we all heard about it."

I smiled. "My mom probably did a good thing by hiding me the way she did."

"Oh, hell yeah," he said, nodding. "By the time everyone knew about you, they didn't have a chance in hell of destroying or using you."

"They tried, though."

"They tried. And I think you taught them how pointless that is," he said. "And despite the shit they put you through, you're still here, and you're still strong. I know you doubt yourself. Stop doing that shit. Trust yourself. I know I trust you, and I don't trust anybody."

He got up then, and I looked up at him. "Thanks Heph."

"Anytime, queenie," he said, going back into the house and leaving me alone to sort through my thoughts.

CHAPTER TEN

The rest of the day was mostly just me being frustrated over my inability to find Strife, me trying not to think about Nain, me thinking about Nain and then hating myself for it, and me listening to Heph and Levitt debate whether they were watching boxing or wrestling on their night off.

Honestly, I was ready to throw both of their asses out of my house if they didn't shut up.

A big part of it was that having everyone around me all the time, as much as I adored them, was starting to wear on my nerves. I was actually relieved when my mom arrived that night to sit with me so I could maybe, hopefully sleep.

I was restless, and my mom and I spent most of the night talking, mostly about nothing: stuff I'd done as a kid, places she'd been that she liked. She kept telling me to go to sleep, but I couldn't.

"Go to sleep, Mollis," she finally said, and then she opened a magazine and proceeded to ignore me.

She was sitting in the chair in my room and I was

looking at the shadows of the trees outside playing across my bedroom wall. The sky was already lightening in the east; it would be light out within an hour or so.

"I don't think I'm going to sleep tonight. I know you have stuff to do," I said.

"But you might. I have no other plans, love," she said as she leafed through one of the magazines she'd borrowed from Shanti.

"I'm really not tired."

"I know."

I sighed in irritation. I felt like I should try to go to sleep so she wasn't wasting her time, but I really wasn't tired. Not just then anyway.

"What's Aunt Meg been up to?" I asked.

Tisiphone laughed. "Are you trying to give me a taste of the things I missed when you were a toddler, avoiding your bedtime? Go to sleep."

I laughed a little, and listened to her turn pages for a few minutes. My mind kept straying to other things. Brennan. Nain. Nain again. I heard the dogs start barking from the fenced in area of the yard. Heph usually let them in for the night when he came home from patrol. I glanced at the clock. That should be just about any minute now.

Sure enough, within ten minutes, I heard the immortal and Levitt walk in, talking loudly. I smirked when I heard them rattling through the kitchen cabinets.

The dogs started barking again, and I was about to get out of bed and let them in myself. "Don't they hear them?" I asked my mother.

"What?"

I was about to answer when my bedroom window, the one right above my bed, crashed in, and a ball of fire landed on my bed. There was shouting throughout the house, more windows crashing. I jumped out of my burning bed, and my mother and I rushed to the other rooms. I could smell gas. Whatever it was, they'd used some kind of accelerant. My bed was up in flames. The room across from mine, where Heph and Levitt usually slept, was also engulfed in flames. I followed my mom downstairs.

"See if you can catch them. I have to get Shanti," I shouted at her over the roar of flames. My eyes were already stinging from the smoke. Part of my living room was burning as well.

Levitt and Heph came running in from the kitchen.

"I'm getting Shanti out. Go outside," I said, and Heph listened but Levitt ran for the basement. Groaning in irritation, I followed him.

"You have the key for this?" he asked me, pounding his fist on Shanti's door.

"It was in my nightstand, which is on fire right now," I said. We both bashed our bodies hard against the reinforced door. I was already pissed off at myself. We'd given her this door so she'd be safe while she slept. If she ended up dying because we couldn't get in to save her I'd never forgive myself.

Levitt and I both backed up and slammed against the door again, this time with me using a little extra power to back me up. It splintered more.

"One more time," I shouted at him. He nodded, and I listened in fear as the house groaned, creaked above us, flames crackling. The air was heavy with smoke, and Levitt was starting to cough. We both backed up and put our shoulders to the door, and I used as much of my power as I safely could without running the risk of hurting Levitt, who was standing inches from me. The door shattered into the room, and I grimaced as I became dizzy with the effects of smoke inhalation and using my powers. We leapt into the room and Levitt picked Shanti up off of the bed. Even trying to wake her at that point was useless. Vampires are like corpses when they're asleep; cold, still. They don't breathe, so they don't snore. It's eerie as hell, and the younger ones, especially, don't even start feeling like moving until well after the sun has set. Shanti had just gone to sleep a couple hours earlier, so she was in deep sleep.

Levitt slung Shanti over his shoulder and nodded at me, and we made our way back up the basement stairs. It was nearly impossible to see; the air was full of thick black smoke.

"Back door," I called to Levitt. I reached back and took his hand so we wouldn't get separated in the darkness. He didn't know my house as well as I did. I led him up into my kitchen. The wall near the living room was already engulfed in flames, and I had a moment of absolute rage, thinking of my house, my one solace for many years, being destroyed like this. I wanted to chase down whoever had done it. I wanted to destroy them, in every way I possibly could.

It wasn't even a "them." I was pretty sure I knew who'd ordered this particular attack. Strife was a dead woman when I found her.

Levitt and I managed to find the back door and made our way out into the pre-dawn darkness. Heph and E were there, and they helped us get farther away from the house. We were both coughing, and I felt like I'd never quite manage to get my breath again. My lungs and throat burned, my eyes stung. A glance at Levitt showed that his eyes were red and teary and I was sure mine looked the same. We both crouched on the grass, coughing up black phlegm, trying to catch our breath.

"Dogs," I said, jumping up. Heph grabbed me.

"They're okay, queenie, They're in the garage with your car."

I breathed a sigh of relief and glanced around. Strife or whoever she'd ordered to do this had been thorough. My house was a goner; flames leaping and roaring from every part of it. Levitt's car had been torched as well and burned in the driveway. So we were down to my car, for five of us and my two huge German shepherds.

"Where do we go now, demon girl?" E asked me,

coming over to me and rubbing my back in her soothing way.

I glanced at the sky, which was getting even lighter in the east, now. We had maybe a half hour until dawn.

"We need to get Shanti somewhere now. We're already cutting it close," I said, and E followed my gaze and nodded.

I took a deep breath. Knew where we had to go, even though it was the last thing I wanted. Spending time in the same house as both of my exes after I'd lost everything was probably bad for my mental well-being. I didn't have many options.

"Let's go to the loft," I said, heading toward the garage. I felt lucky that, unlike the keys to Shanti's room, I'd been smart enough to keep a second set of keys to my car elsewhere. I turned over one of the patio stones outside of the garage, where I'd buried the second set of car keys in a ziplock bag. I pulled them out.

"We probably need to put Shanti in the trunk," I said. "It's already getting light. I have a big blanket in there too. Cover her up with that," I told Levitt, and he nodded. I unlocked the trunk and let the demon go to work getting Shanti settled. Eunomia and Heph climbed into the front seat with me, and once he had Shanti tucked into the trunk, Levitt sat in the back seat with my dogs.

I pulled out of the garage and maneuvered around Levitt's burning car. One of the nice things about living in a deserted neighborhood is that there are no pesky things like fences or other houses in your way. I drove across the lawn, then back down my driveway and into the street. I glanced at my poor house one more time. "Did anyone call the fire department?" I asked, knowing it was already a lost cause.

"I called Jones," Heph said. "He said he'd deal with it and talk to you tomorrow."

"Thanks." I forced myself to look away from the flames, ignored the way every cell in my body wanted to be hunting down whoever had done it. I had responsibilities now, and my primary one was keeping my team safe and finding them a place to live.

Suppressing a groan, I turned onto Gratiot and started heading toward the loft.

The sky was already pinkish orange, the sun rising faster than I expected when I roared into the parking garage below Nain's loft. I reminded myself to thank him for buying a place with underground parking.

We climbed out of my car, all of us stinking of smoke, exhausted and tense. My main focus now was getting Shanti into her room before the sun came up. Too many damn windows in the loft. When we opened the trunk, she was laying there, awake.

"Did you hit every pothole on the way here, Angel?" she asked me when she looked up. "What happened?" She was sluggish; the ride must have been rough to have woken her, especially this close to dawn.

"Some jerk set my house on fire," I said, trying to stay calm, Nether raging inside me, wanting control. I'd been fighting her since I'd woken up, and now that I wasn't focused on getting everyone to safety, she was just getting stronger. I clenched my teeth and tried to stop feeling anything. Right. As if that was even possible.

"I am so sorry, Molly. What a bunch of assholes," Shanti said as I pulled her out of the trunk. I just nodded and we started heading toward the elevator. Levitt was supporting Shanti with an arm around her waist. She was barely awake now, and I tossed the heavy comforter Levitt had grabbed from her room over her head, leaving her face clear so she could see where she was going.

We took the elevator up in silence. I was dreading this. If there was another safe place we could go, I would have been there. But we needed darkness for Shanti, and Nain had a special room for any vamps on the team. Ada's shields and protective spells made the loft the safest place in the city. And I needed it. I just wasn't capable of trying to figure anything else out just then.

We straggled out of the elevator when it stopped, and I stepped forward and knocked on the door. Then I hit the buzzer, and a few seconds later, Nain answered the door. His hair was tousled and he was dressed in low-slung pajama pants and nothing else. Muscles rippling every damn where. Shanti gawked at him, and I threw her a withering glare. She ducked her head, grinning a little, mouthed a "daaaaaamn" at me before looking away. Goofy in her near-unconscious state.

"Molls? What's going on?" Nain said, looking me over, taking in the smudges, burnt clothing.

"Some asshole bombed my house," I said, then I bit the inside of my lip, hard, to keep from crying or otherwise making an idiot of myself. He reached out and pulled me into the loft, and my team followed. He kept hold of my hand, looked at me more closely. "You're okay?"

"We need a place to stay, just until I can figure something else out," I said softly, embarrassed to be asking anything of my ex.

"I have room," he said. "Shanti, your old room is still empty," he told the vampire, and Shanti nodded and Levitt helped her upstairs. Then he looked at Heph "You and the demon can share your old room. E, you can probably bunk with Shanti, right?" He rubbed his hands over his face. Clearly we'd woken him up. And it was when he raised his hands that I saw the hematite band on his finger, the one I'd placed there when we'd bonded. The one I'd found in a pile of dust after he'd died. The one I'd held, clutched in my hand, in the weeks that followed, wishing I could join him.

All I could do was stare at it and try not to feel anything as Nether raged, battling me for control. She could sense when I was weak, and she got stronger when I was emotional. Seeing that ring was almost enough to make me lose it, for so many reasons.

My team dispersed, each going to their rooms. Nain walked me over to the kitchen, sat me on one of the stools. "Wait there a minute," he said. Then he went to his room, came out with jeans, t-shirts, tossed them to Levitt, who was just coming out of Shanti's room. Levitt thanked him and went into the room he and Heph were bunking in. Then Nain came back to me.

"What can you tell me?"

I shrugged. "Not much. My mom was on duty, watching me. I was in bed, talking to my mom, and then all of a sudden we heard glass breaking throughout the house and a fireball landed on my bed. They tossed them into a few of the windows. The place went up so damn fast..." I trailed off, shaking my head. "We barely got Shanti out in time. Levitt's car was torched, so my whole team and the dogs drove over in mine." I knew I was babbling. Couldn't make myself stop.

"Where's your mom now?"

"Searching the area."

He nodded. "You want to get cleaned up?"

"Yeah."

"You can bunk with me."

I looked up at him, ready to argue.

"Just don't, Molls. You're ready to fall over and I bet Nether's just fucking loving this."

I nodded, let him steer me toward his room. He dug through his dresser drawers when we got there and handed me a t-shirt. I knew from experience that his shirts were huge enough on me to go down to my knees. I took it wordlessly and shut myself in his bathroom. I showered, scrubbed myself, hard, the stress of the fire just adding to the already insane state of my nerves. When I finally got out and pulled on Nain's t-shirt, I could see the sun was up, the sky bright in the east. I stepped out into the bedroom. Nain was sitting up, on his side of the bed. Reading. I knew, from the weeks I'd spent in his room after he died, that he liked science fiction, which had never really been my thing. And then I thought about how many changes he'd seen in his three hundred years, realized that compared to his reality science fiction was probably pretty tame.

I climbed into my side of the bed (just like old times, which I was trying not to think about. It was ridiculous how easy we seemed to slip into our old routines) and settled myself under the covers wordlessly. I took a deep breath, smelled the familiar warm, cinnamon and sunshine scent of my former husband surrounding me. Remembered how it comforted me, how it had broken my heart after I'd lost him.

I was not supposed to be feeling anything. Right.

I lay on my side, facing him. Glanced at his hand. The ring was still there. I reached out and touched it, gently, and he stilled.

"Why are you wearing that?" I asked him, pulling my hand back.

"Why were you still wearing yours the day you died?" he asked, his version of an answer.

I watched him. He wasn't looking at me. "You found it?"

He nodded. "I was the first one to reach what was left of you. It was there in the dust."

"Oh, shit," I said, realization striking me. He looked at me then.

"What?"

"You had to mourn me," I said. He looked away again.

"You went through it too. And it wasn't as bad as the first time. Brennan knew you were still alive."

"I'm glad. I was distracted this last time by all the getting murdered and stuff like that. And I was unconscious or dead a lot of the time."

He didn't answer.

"So why are you wearing it all of a sudden?"

"It's not all of a sudden. I've been wearing it since I found it after I got back. I take it off when I know I'm going to see you." He paused, glanced at me. "I'm surprised Brennan or Shanti didn't tell you that."

"Why did you hide it from me?" I was getting sleepy again, too much going on. My eyelids started to feel heavy.

"Because I know you. And I know that now that you've seen this," he said, holding up his hand, "you're going to be overthinking it and second-guessing things and focusing on shit you have no time to worry about. I'm wearing it because it still means something to me. And I'm wearing it to remind myself that there's something worthwhile in me, if I managed to bond with someone like you."

I didn't know what to say. Looked for something logical instead. "I wonder why they didn't get destroyed along with our bodies."

"Ada thinks it was because there was some kind of magic involved when we exchanged them. Like they became indestructible because we promised forever. Some shit like that."

I laid there watching him, smelling him. Feeling his emotions wash over me, and one, alongside his ever-present rage, was stronger than all the others. "How can you still love me?" I asked him quietly, the words coming out before I could second-guess saying them. He'd died for me, been imprisoned in the Nether because of who he was to me. He'd made it home to find that he'd been replaced, that I'd moved on and he hadn't.

He glanced at me, and his sapphire gaze met mine. "Because you're worth loving. Because you're the one person in my entire existence that I care about more than I care about myself. Because we're not done. Whatever is between us, it's forever. I said it before and I meant it." He paused, looked away from me. "Once upon a time I would have been pressuring you, ignoring every argument you threw at me. I would have goddamn *made* you see that you belong to me. But we've both been through shit and I hurt you and maybe I'm not the same either."

"We're a mess," I said, shaking my head.

"We always have been. Doesn't make it bad."

"I'm so tired of everything," I said, voicing the one thing I'd never been able to say to anyone. I both loved and hated the fact that I could say things like that to him, that I could let him see the weaknesses in me. When it came down to it, the demon beside me knew more about me than anyone in existence. He'd been in my mind, he'd shared my blood. He'd felt my emotions and heard my thoughts. He knew my past, my nightmares in a way no other being ever would. There was no hiding from him. "I can't do it anymore."

He put his book down and lay on his side, facing me. He put his hand on my waist, studied my face. "You can do it because you're fucking unbreakable. But you're tired and you're pissed off and everything's a mess. You're scared. There's nothing wrong with that, as long as you get your sexy little ass up tomorrow morning and go out and fight again. Giving up isn't an option."

"I know," I said.

"You're not alone," he said, voice rumbling, low. Comforting.

"Thanks."

He was silent a while. And I felt a different emotion taking over, helped along, no doubt, by the two of us being in bed together. "Well, if you feel the need to repay my kindness, I can think of a few things you could do for me." He opened his mind for just a second, sharing his idea with me.

I rolled my eyes, punched him in the stomach, not exactly holding back. He let out a grunt and ended up laughing.

"You know how much it turns me on when you hurt me, baby," he taunted.

I couldn't help it. I laughed. "Fuck off, Nain," I said, rolling over, facing away from him. He laughed behind me, gave my waist a squeeze before he pulled his hand away.

Damn distracting demon. I smiled as I closed my eyes and drifted off, finally giving in to the exhaustion that had set in once we'd reached the loft, knowing he'd make sure Nether didn't make an appearance.

CHAPTER ELEVEN

I was relieved when I woke up to find that just about everyone seemed to be out. I got up, dressed, and stepped out of Nain's room. The only presence I felt was Nain and he was locked away in his office.

I went into the kitchen and clicked on the radio on the counter. As always, it was set to the oldies station because Nain liked it. I started searching through the cabinets for the coffee; it wasn't where it always used to be and for some reason that annoyed the hell out of me. I finally found it and measured out the coffee as Elvis's "Suspicious Minds" started playing. I listened, humming along as I poured the water into the coffee maker. I turned it on, knowing it would feel like an eternity for it to brew. I started looking through the cabinets to see if my favorite mug was still there. It was, but it was pushed to the back of the shelf, forgotten.

I kept humming as I carried the cup to the counter. I leaned against the counter and waited, letting my mind wander. Elvis hit the bridge and I couldn't help singing along. It was my favorite part of the song.

I felt a healthy dose of humor behind me, turned to see Nain standing in his office door, which was just off of the kitchen. He was leaning against the door jamb, arms crossed over his chest, watching me. A rare hint of a smile was on his lips and it made my stomach twist, just a little.

"Shit," I muttered and he laughed. "How long were you standing there?"

"Long enough to hear your ad-lib on the bridge. I liked it."

I rolled my eyes, grabbed a cup out of the cabinet and poured a cup for him as I filled mine. He came up behind me, closer than he needed to be, and grabbed his cup off of the counter.

"Thanks," he said quietly as he reached past me. All I could do was nod. "Were you aware that you were swaying your hips side to side just a little while you sang that?"

"I was not," I said, my face burning.

"You were. Feel free to do that again for me anytime."

I could barely breathe. He was still behind me.

"Did you sleep okay?" he asked. I nodded.

"You?"

"I dozed off for a few minutes. It was crazy waking up next to you again." He stayed where he was, close behind me. He wanted to touch me. I could sense it from him. Desire, need. And it only grew the longer we stood there, until I felt like I'd be buried by it.

"Where is everyone?" I asked, mostly for something to say. He backed off a little then, leaning against the countertop behind him.

"Your team was going to meet with the Furies over in Hamtramck. They said they were supposed to be checking out for signs of Strife there."

I nodded.

"Ada and Stone went out to breakfast. Artemis is hunting. Brennan took off early this morning. Not sure where he went. Don't really care, either."

I looked up at him, my body still doing all kinds of crazy shit from having him that close to me, especially after the discussion we'd had the night before. "We'll be out of here as soon as I can figure something else out. I know it's crazy crowded now. And awkward."

"I don't give a shit if it's awkward. You don't have to go anywhere. This is your home too."

It was actually true. I hadn't known, but he'd put my name on the deed, signed everything he owned over to me shortly after we'd met. I didn't know that until after he'd died. Once I started working again, I'd taken his office as my base of operations. All of the paperwork was in a file in the top desk drawer. I just remembered spending that entire day in tears after finding it.

"We're not married anymore," I reminded him.

"So?" He stepped forward, leaned down closer to me, and I couldn't help looking at his mouth, remembering the way it felt to have his lips on mine. "All it takes is a word, one moment of your blood mixing with mine, and that whole 'not being married' thing could end."

"You said you weren't going to pressure me," I reminded him.

"No. I said I hadn't been pressuring you. But I woke up next to you this morning and I want to do it again. I want that, every morning for the rest of my life."

I looked away from him.

"And you want it too," he said quietly.

"Who says I want it?" I asked, looking up at him and raising my eyebrow.

"Please, woman. We didn't have long together, but I can read you like a book."

I just glared up at him.

"I'm not a patient man, Molly. Right now, I'm pretty much at my limit."

My heart was pounding. How could he still make me feel this way after everything we'd been through, after all that had happened since that night I'd destroyed him?

How could he make me feel something, anything, when I was sure it was impossible to open myself up that way again?

I put my hand on his chest, moved to push him away from me, when he covered my hand with his, held it there. I looked up, met his eyes, and he held my gaze for several long moments, need, hunger, anger washing over me in waves. Then he released me and stepped back and away without another word. He grabbed his car keys off of the entry table and walked out, closing the loft door behind him.

"Christ," I muttered, letting out a breath I hadn't realized I'd been holding.

I could have used another shower. A cold one. Instead, I downed another cup of coffee, grabbed the spare key off of the hook near the door, and headed out. My imps trailed me. I had a lead on a lost girl, and I needed to hit something.

When I got back, I was a mess again. I jumped into the shower and let the grime wash off of me. I'd crawled through a filthy crawlspace looking for a little girl. I found her, alive, and brought her home.

Worth every claustrophobic moment.

I was stepping out of my room when I heard the door open, felt Nain before I saw him. I watched as he hefted two large plastic storage bins, one stacked on top of the other, and carried them into the loft. He glanced at me, then set them down on the dining room floor.

"What's that?" I asked. I looked him over. He was filthy, clothing and hands smudged with something dark.

"Take a look."

I walked over and lifted the lid off of the top bin. My heart stopped.

Stuff from my house; dirty, smoke-smudged, but whole. I spotted a few of my McCoy planters from the bedroom, some of the jadeite dinnerware I'd collected. And that was just what I could see from the top.

I looked up at him, didn't know what to say.

"I know how you liked all of this shit," he said, shrugging. He looked away, almost seeming embarrassed. "This was all I could grab in one trip."

"Are you kidding? This is…." I shook my head, looked through the bin again. "I know it's stupid. It's just stuff, right?"

"It's stuff that's yours. Stuff you worked for and made into a place you loved. I'm sorry about your house, baby."

I was stepping toward him before I realized what I was doing, and when I reached him he pulled me into his arms as if it was the most natural thing in the world, held me tightly as I let myself cry over my house and all of the insanity of the night before. Over the craziness in my life and my fear of Nain and everything he meant. I put my arms around his waist, rested my forehead against his chest as I calmed down.

"You never used to cry," he said, running his hands through my hair.

"Sure I did. I just never let anyone see it."

He held me tighter, and we stood there, neither one of us moving. Neither one of us wanting to. And I knew it was wrong. I knew I should be running as far and as fast away from him as I possibly could. I knew he could destroy me in a way no one else ever could; that he'd done it before and if he thought it would save me, he'd do it again without a second thought. I knew he was brutal and ruthless and crude.

I knew he loved me, and that was the most frightening thing of all.

I made myself release him, pushed myself out of his arms, and he let me go. I glanced down at his hand, and he was still wearing the ring. No point in hiding it from me anymore, I guess.

"Is it true you and Eunomia messed around?" I asked him.

"I'm not Brennan, baby."

"Did you?"

"Yes. And we weren't together anymore."

"I know we weren't."

"It wasn't just her. For a year or so after I got back and learned all about you and him, I fucked just about anyone who wanted me, trying to get you out of my system. Didn't work."

"No?"

"No. You're so deep in me there's no chance of ever getting you out." He paused, stood there watching me, and the intensity in his gaze made my stomach twist. "Once I realized that, I gave up. I tried to make myself okay with the whole you and Brennan thing, because I know you. I knew you'd fight your way back here someday. And I thought I deserved to have to watch you with him. Especially after the way I made you hurt."

He shook his head. "I knew it would be bad, Molly. But knowing and experiencing it are two different things and I swear to you I didn't realize how bad it would be. How much it would hurt. I didn't believe it would destroy you the way it did. The second I woke up in the Nether and felt what it was like to have my soul and yours ripped apart, I knew that it was all so much worse than I imagined it would be. So I thought, if he can make you happy, if he can make you feel alive again, who the fuck am I to stand in the way of that?"

I looked away, unable to handle the way he was looking at me. "We argued about you."

"He mentioned that." We stood there for a few minutes, awkward. "Is it true you hunted down all of Astaroth's allies the night I died?"

I nodded. Still couldn't look at him.

"I saw those photo albums in your room," I said softly.

"Yeah?"

I nodded. "You've had a lot of girlfriends over the years."

"Only one wife, though," he said. "And you ruined me for anyone else. No one has ever made me feel the shit you do. No one's ever made me as pissed off and frustrated. No one's ever tied me in knots the way you can. I've never been the begging kind, but you're the one being in existence who's able to bring me to my knees."

I turned away, shaking my head. "I've heard this shit before."

"Yeah. But now you're hearing it from me."

I stood, facing away from him, looking toward the kitchen.

"Was there more stuff to bring back from my house?" I asked, desperate for a change of subject.

"Yeah."

"Is it bad?"

A pause. "Yeah. It's bad. I can dig out what's left, Molls."

I shook my head. "No. I should do it. It's my house."

"We can go back whenever you're ready."

"Now?"

"If you want."

I nodded. "There are boxes down in the garage."

He came over to me then and took my hand, led me toward the door. We rode down in the elevator together, and he was mercifully silent as we drove toward my neighborhood.

CHAPTER TWELVE

When Nain turned onto my street, I was tempted to close my eyes. I should have. I looked at my house as he drove up to it, the house I'd bought with money I'd squirreled away after two years of living in my car, the house I'd worked on and fixed up and turned into the first real home I'd ever had, and I couldn't help it. Tears sprang to my eyes, and I brushed them away. I was angry, and seeing my house like that was like an arrow to the heart.

Nain and I sat in the truck, him waiting while I got over the impact of seeing my house like that for the first time. I shook my head, opened my door. I grabbed a couple of boxes out of the back of the truck, and watched as Nain did the same. I walked toward the house, and when we met at the front of the truck, he took my hand in his, and we walked toward the house together.

"You can get in the back door still," he said, pulling me toward the back of the house. "The front is all caved in."

I nodded numbly, rage coursing through me. His rage, my rage.

"I am going to catch the bastards who did this," I muttered.

"Not if I catch them first," he said. "Probably part of Strife's group, right?"

"That's what I'm thinking. She's probably pretty pissed at me for taking out Terror. Did you see her mark anywhere?"

He shook his head. "I didn't look hard though. We'll check the area out before we leave."

He opened the back door, and the smell of smoke, soot was even stronger than it had been on the outside of my house.

"There might still be some kitchen stuff I didn't grab," he said. Then he took a box toward the living room. I could see that it was completely trashed, walls blackened, the ceiling and my bed and dresser from my bedroom upstairs now where the coffee table and sofa had been. Everything was charred, and I couldn't even recognize a few things, they were so melted.

We started rooting through the living room. My Moonbeam alarm clock that had been on my nightstand was there, but it was melted. I threw it aside in irritation. I glanced up. Not all of my bedroom floor had fallen in. Only where my bed had been, where the fire had started. Where the fireball had landed after it had sailed through the window. I was relieved now that the few things I didn't want to lose (Nain's notes to me among them) I'd kept in that metal box in the basement.

"How did you get the McCoy?"

"Those planter things?"

"Yeah."

"Went upstairs."

I turned and looked at him. "Are you kidding? You walked up those stairs and into what was left of my bedroom to get a few planters? You could have fallen through."

He shrugged, went back to sifting through the debris on the floor. "I liked a few of those, too."

"Yeah? Which one?"

"That blue one I brought you earlier."

I squatted down, found some of my jewelry, still intact, though its wooden box was destroyed. "What was so great about that one?"

"That was the one on my side of the bed."

I let that pass. Didn't want to think about how perfect it had been, for just a few hours. We'd made love, fallen asleep together. Woke up, and he'd made me breakfast. We'd performed the demon marriage bond again. We'd danced, sunlight streaming through the kitchen window.

He'd died hours later.

It was like watching someone else's life, remembering. And now we stood in the charred remains of what could have been our home, once upon a time, both of us having lived through death, a chasm now between us that felt wrong in every way. A chasm I was starting to despise, no matter how hard I fought against what I felt for him.

"You know what I thought last night, after I knew everyone was out and okay?" I asked as I moved aside some charred flooring from upstairs. Making conversation, rather than letting my thoughts continue on the path they were heading.

"What?"

"They were lucky they didn't hurt my dogs. I seriously would have gone all Ares on them if they had."

He grunted. "I was pissed when I realized you took them when you moved out. I was used to having them around."

"I think they missed the fancy doghouses you had built for them."

"Yeah? I think they're my dogs as much as yours at this point." He sifted through what was left of my living room bookshelf.

I shook my head, tossed a pair of silver candleholders that had managed to survive into one of the boxes. "Were you going to take me to divorce court over it?"

He looked at me. "We're not divorced."

"We're not married, either."

"Keep telling yourself that," he said. Then he stopped, looked around. "What are you going to do about this?"

I looked at what was left of my house too. "I think I'm going to have to let it go. I don't have insurance. Never needed it because I paid for it in cash. It would cost more to rebuild than the house would even be worth, in this neighborhood."

I glanced his way to see him watching me. "What do you *want* to do?"

I shook my head.

"You want to rebuild it?"

"It doesn't matter what I want. I can't."

"Why not?"

I stared at him. "It costs money, Nain. I don't have that much left in my account."

He looked up as if he was trying to keep his patience. I felt irritation rolling off of him.

"You own a fucking multi-million dollar loft. You have over three million dollars in your accounts. You can afford to rebuild if you want to."

"No. *You* have all of that."

"I gave it to you."

"Bullshit. It was mine upon your death. You're not dead anymore."

"It was yours the second you became mine," he said, walking toward the hallway. "And like I keep telling you, that hasn't changed."

I stared after him. After a few seconds, he started talking again. "You want to rebuild, do it."

"Like I have time to worry about that," I said, again, stupidly touched by the way he was looking at it.

"Nice thing about being rich: someone else takes care of all the details for you. We can have it rebuilt exactly the same if you want. I know you liked all that old-fashioned shit."

He came back into the living room holding a couple of small dishes, a vase. "Are these anything?"

I nodded, took them from him and set them into the box.

"One thing, though."

"What?" I asked, looking up at him.

"Keep the bedroom in the same spot. It was nice waking up with the sun coming in like that."

"You act as if you're going to wake up there again," I said, crossing my arms. "You sure you don't want a bigger room? Bigger bed?"

He stepped close to me. We were both filthy, grubby. We stunk of smoke. He leaned down, his face inches from mine. "That's because I will be waking up in your bed again. And no, I don't need a bigger one. We only ever used one body's width anyway. Me, on top of you."

And then he lowered his head the rest of the way, closing the distance between us, and his lips claimed mine. He held me tight to him, kissed me as if I was air and he'd been suffocating without me. I put my hands on his wide shoulders, trying to find something to hold on to, trying to get a grip because I was slowly but surely feeling myself falling all over again for this demon who wanted every part of me. Even my darkness. Even my screw-ups. He wanted me. All of me.

I kissed him back, bit his lower lip the way he'd always liked, and he rewarded me with a low growl, a deeper, harder kiss, his hands roaming, refamiliarizing themselves with what had once been his, squeezing my waist, my ass, as he ran his hands down my body.

Nether was silent. On top of everything else, he had the power to make her shut the hell up for even a little while. He brought his hands up to my hair, pulled my head back, forced me to look up at him. "I need you, Molly," he growled. "I'm out of my mind with it. Come back to me."

I met his eyes. My stomach twisted, and I found myself clenching my thighs together, my stupid body betraying me, just as it always had around him. He could have done it. He could have had me right then and there, and I would have given him whatever he wanted. We both knew it.

I let out a small laugh, still breathless, my body still trembling, still needy from being in his arms. "Haven't we had enough disasters in the past day or so?"

"We're creatures of the Nether. We thrive on disaster," he said. "Tell me you don't want us as much as I do."

I should have. Should have told him I didn't want him anymore, that I didn't still feel every cell in my body exalting when he was near, that I didn't dream about him at night. That the sight of my ring on his finger had satisfied a possessive streak I didn't know I had. So I said nothing.

"Yeah. That's what I thought," he said. He held my gaze for just a few seconds, but it felt like a lifetime. And then he lowered his lips to mine again and kissed me once, hard, before backing off and heading into the kitchen.

I took a deep breath, shook my head, trying to center myself. I grabbed my box and followed him. We went through the kitchen cabinets in silence, both of us adding items to our boxes. The plastic shit had all melted with the heat, but some of the older, sturdier stuff, the FireKing and jadeite, had held up all right. We finished grabbing what was salvageable, working mostly in silence, then we carried the boxes to his truck. We walked through my yard, up and down my block, looking for Strife's mark.

The area immediately around my house was a mess, trampled by the fire fighters who had apparently showed up not long after we'd left. I checked out the closest trees and my garage for Strife's mark. When I didn't find anything, I started looking for signs in the other adjoining lots, and Nain went off in the opposite direction.

In the end, I checked every tree between my house and the corner, as well as what was left of the burned out house on the corner, and didn't come up with anything. I took my time even though I was pretty sure I wouldn't find anything once I got away from the area immediately surrounding my house. Strife wasn't subtle. If her people had left a mark, it would have been near what was left of my house.

What the hell had I just done in there? I chided myself. This was Nain, for god's sake. The man who'd destroyed me. Lied to me. The man I'd sworn was wrong for me in every way once I had some time and distance from him. And now what were we doing? Starting down the same road again with one another. The problem was that I'd already seen the end of that road and I couldn't go there again.

Stupid. So stupid. He's bad for me. Not because he'd ever hurt me (unless he felt like it would save me somehow. Bastard.) but because when he's in my life, all I want is him. There is no halfway, nothing casual about Nain and I when we're together.

And on top of all of that, Nether was starting to push at my defenses again. "Calm down, bitch," I muttered, and it only made her start pushing harder, trying to find a weakness, trying to overpower me.

I took a deep breath, trying to ignore the insane immortal imprisoned inside me, and started walking back toward my house.

Nain was already waiting when I got there, leaning up against the side of his truck watching me.

He opened my door for me, and I climbed in. Then he climbed in his side and slammed the truck door closed behind him. "It had to be her. This shit isn't random."

I was grateful he was being professional again. Maybe he was realizing how stupid we'd just been, too.

"She would have left her mark. She likes that, especially here. Taunting me is her thing, right?"

He was silent. "Who else is pissed off at you?"

"Who isn't?"

I felt a little bit of humor from him. "Try to narrow it down a little."

"Strife, obviously. More than a few of the immortals. Probably a few I wouldn't think of."

"Because you forced them to listen to you," he said, and I nodded.

"Could just be any of the assholes we typically deal with, except that my mom would have caught up with one of them, I think."

He nodded. "Had to be an immortal, right? Able to do that thing where they disappear."

"I think that makes the most sense."

"Okay. So Strife. Zeus and Hera don't like you much, you said."

"Right. Apollo's not fond of me. Artemis likes me but I don't know how much Brennan and I breaking up affected her opinion of me."

"Aphrodite," he said.

"Right."

"That's mostly because of Heph, though." He was silent a minute "Did anything ever happen between the two of you? That's part of why she hates you."

"No. He's my friend, and he's not interested in me that way."

"You sure about that?"

"Yes. That's the last thing on his mind. He's been fucked over by Aphrodite so much he has zero interest in relationships or anything else. I can relate."

"Meaning?" he said, with a little growl in his voice.

"Meaning you can only take so much bullshit before you realize that none of it is worth it and you're better off on your own."

"You sure didn't feel like you didn't think it was worth it in your house just now."

"We're not talking about us."

"I agree." And then he reached over and pulled me close again, and his mouth was on mine, his arms like iron around my body. My hands were in his hair, and I was kissing him back as enthusiastically as he was kissing me.

I am so bad at listening to myself.

He bit at my lips, swept his tongue across my lips, demanding access, and I gave it to him, opening my mouth to him. His tongue invaded my mouth, and I moaned, knowing that he wanted more, so much more. His hands were roaming, and when he cupped one of my breasts in his huge, rough hand, I cried out at the sensation, pushing myself closer to him, needing his touch, and he gave it. He squeezed me, plucked roughly at my nipple, kissed his way down my throat, biting not exactly gently at the delicate skin at the side of my neck, right above my pulse point. Marking me, the way he had in so many of my memories and the dreams I'd had of him since. Claiming me.

He started kissing me again, and I started coming to my senses.

"Stop," I said, and he groaned, let go of me. He sat back against his seat, head back against the headrest, frustration flowing from him like lava.

"We're not doing this again," I said.

He didn't answer.

"Let's go."

"We're already doing it again," Nain said, looking over at me, meeting my eyes. "Why are you fighting so hard against what we both want?"

"You really need to ask that question? You don't think how it ended last time is reason enough? Or the fact that I ended up with Brennan, who is like your polar opposite in almost every way? Of the fact that we drive one another nuts?"

"I don't expect you to forgive me for the way it ended the first time. You know I did it to save you—"

"And to get back at Astaroth. Let's not pretend your motives were totally benevolent, demon."

"Fine. Yeah, I wanted Astaroth to meet his end. That was a bonus and I won't deny being happy he's gone. But I would have let him live if I thought you'd be okay. I fucking knew him, Molls. Hundreds of years fighting with or against him. Whether he wanted you for himself or someone else didn't even matter. He wouldn't have stopped. And no one knew you were immortal. All I kept envisioning was that day I'd come home and you wouldn't be there because he finally caught up with you."

He looked away from me, anger rolling off of him.

"I'm not going to apologize for doing what I thought I had to do to keep you safe. You can hate me forever for that if you want to. I'm sorry it hurt you. I'm sorry I lied. I wish I'd handled it a different way."

We sat in silence for a few minutes. It had started to rain, and the sky was dark gray. Fat raindrops splattered against the windshield.

"As for that Brennan shit," he started, and I looked back at him. "I'm not in competition with Brennan. I'm not some lovesick little boy who's gonna follow you around begging you to look at me. You have enough to deal with right now without that shit. You know I love you. You know I'd do anything for you. You want him? You know where to find him. But we both know you have no interest in going back to him. I don't need to try to convince you that we're right together, because you already know it. You want it just as much as I do."

I still didn't answer. Nothing he said was wrong. I'd felt his pull on me since the moment I'd broken him out of the cell at the Wayne County Jail that first night I was back from my time in the Nether. I'd done everything in my power to fight it, because there's just no way I could handle that particular brand of intense with everything else going on in my life. I looked over at him, and his eyes were on me. Being there with him, in the confines of his truck with the rain beating down after the kisses we'd just shared had my body on overdrive.

He leaned over again and lowered his lips to mine. This kiss was different; still demanding, still intense, but not as hard. This was more like him tasting me, loving me. This was the way he'd kissed me that morning in my kitchen, as if I was the best thing in the world and he'd never get tired of my lips on his.

He put his big hand on my waist, pulled me close to him, and deepened our kiss, and I was lost, kissing him back, my hands gripping his shoulders.

His mouth was on my throat, his hands roaming my body again, and I knew I would give him just about anything he wanted. I also knew I wasn't ready, I pushed him away again, gently, and I felt how much it frustrated him, but he pulled back, let me go.

I glanced over at him. His jaw and fists were clenched, every muscle in his body tense. His eyes were glowing. I glanced down at his lap, clenched my thighs together, his need and frustration very evident from that quick glance. I looked up at his face, and he was watching me.

"Yeah. That's nothing new. All you have to do is walk into a room and I'm ready to bend you over and make you forget about everything but me. And you know I can do it."

"Stop it."

"Make me."

My face was burning, my body aching. I looked out the window, tried to calm myself down. "Calm down. You're getting all demon on me."

"Only for you. You're the only one in my entire life I've ever let see all of me. And I know for damn sure I'm the only one who's ever seen all of you. All that darkness you try to keep bottled up, all that rage you try to pretend you don't feel. I know you inside and out. And I know there's not another being alive who can say the same thing."

"So, what? Do you want a gold star or something?" I huffed, still looking out the window.

"Nice that you didn't bother denying it."

I ignored him.

"What I really want to do is make you remember what it feels like. How fucking right it is when we're together.. You remember that night in your bed after we bonded for the first time? The way you came screaming for me? How hard we went at it until you were so exhausted that you couldn't even move?

His words, the memories he was evoking, had me on the verge of screaming with my own frustration. I looked back at him. His eyes were still glowing, his hunger rolling over me in waves.

"Nain."

"What?"

"Yes. I remember. I still dream about that night. I want that. I want all of it. I want your mouth on me. I want to taste you again. I want to hear you growl when I bite you and feel how much you like it when I rake my fingernails down your back. I want you inside me so much it's driving me insane. I want you holding me down, biting me, taking me so hard I feel it for days afterward even with my healing ability. But I need time, too," I said, shaking my head a little, trying to get my body under control. Nearly impossible considering the way his hunger had ratcheted up as I'd been talking. "It's so easy to lose myself in you. Just give me a little time to figure myself out so we don't mess this up again. Can you give me that?"

He reached over and took my hand. I felt him trying to settle himself down. I met his eyes. He brought my hand to his lips and pressed a kiss to my wrist, my palm. "Yes. I can give you that." Then his teeth scraped over the delicate skin of my wrist, and he nipped there, not exactly gently. "You are damn sexy when you do that."

"When I do what?" I asked.

"When you tell me what you want. When you stand up to me like that. You're a lot more confident than you used to be."

I watched him as he ran his thumb over my wrist where he'd just bitten me. Soothing and ridiculously sexy, reminding me again of the intense sensations I felt when we were together. I smiled. "You just like fighting with me."

"Only because when we start fighting, we usually end up fucking."

I pulled my hand out of his and crossed my arms over my chest. "Not today, demon."

He laughed and started the truck. "Not today, but soon. And I am going to enjoy making you beg, wife of mine."

"In your dreams."

He put his hand on my thigh, high, tips of his fingers very near where I was already aching for him. "You really don't want to talk about my dreams right now, Molly. Not if you want me to stay in control."

Nain and I drove through the city, back toward the loft. He kept his hand on my thigh, and I let him. We seemed to come to an understanding: I wanted and needed him, and he wanted and needed me, but we weren't moving forward until I was ready.

I put my hand on his, and he twined his fingers with mine. We drove in silence, and I would have been fairly content (even with all the insanity with my house) if it hadn't been for Nether fighting against me again. I closed my eyes and started focusing on calming my emotions. Too much. For someone who was supposed to not be feeling anything I was feeling way, way too much of late.

The anger and sadness over my house, the panic when I thought we wouldn't get Shanti to a safe place in time. Nain.

I took deep breaths and tried to settle down. When I'd first started trying to close myself off from my emotions, a few years after my powers manifested, I'd always pictured smooth white marble. I wanted to make myself like that: cold, hard, and pure. I found myself going back to that at times like this. The only problem was that back when I'd done that, I'd had nothing in my life that mattered. It was just me, living in my car and then my house. I had no friends. No family. No interaction with people in general, other than what my job required.

Life was way more complicated when it had other people in it.

My life before had been simpler, sure. The only life I really had to worry about was my own, and I honestly didn't care all that much. It had taken dying, over and over again, to realize that I'd spent the early part of my career with some kind of death wish.

And now, I couldn't die even if I wanted to. My life wasn't the important thing. But now, I had people in my life I cared about. People I loved like family, which is something I'd never thought I'd have. And I wanted to keep them safe. When you have stuff like that on your mind, it's hard to get to that cold, calm place.

Really, I needed some alone time. As much as I loved my friends and team mates, the fact that I was never alone was making me feel like I wanted to crawl out of my skin. I liked solitude. I could recharge when I was alone. It seemed like my life was one extreme or the other; I'd spent the first twenty-four years of my life totally alone, and now it seemed like there was no such thing as being alone.

I would make some time to be alone for a bit somehow, I promised myself as I continued to try to fight Nether back.

Why do you fight me so hard? The demon is right about that, Mollis Eth-Hades. You are a frustrating woman. Nether's sinuous voice in my mind. I was surprised. She hadn't talked to me since that night I'd killed Terror.

I didn't answer her.

Your line has always believed I'm a monster. That I'm something to fear. Do you even know why I was punished by Nyx?

I focused on staying calm.

"You okay, Molls?" Nain asked, and I nodded, kept my eyes closed.

I was punished because I made the mistake of falling in love. My duty, my life itself was owed to Nyx. But I fell in love with Aether, and he and I became consumed with one another.

I could barely breathe.

We were not supposed to love. We, the Creators, were born of chaos yet our duty was to bring order to the universe. We created everything. The immortals, the very land beneath your feet. There is no place in that for things like love. Devotion. Happiness or sadness.

Yet Aether and I felt it anyway. And we loved, and we kept it a secret.

We fought, as lovers do. Our fights were intense. At one point, Nyx decided we had gone too far. That we'd lost our focus. And she needed places to house her next creations. The immortals came only after Aether and I had been captured and transformed into the realms they call home.

Think about it, little Fury. I have spent millennia serving as a realm, as a prison. My prison all the worse because I watch beings live who are no better than I am. When you needed saving, remember who it was that saved you.

You keep hurting me. I couldn't even believes I was talking to the thing in my head. Time to be fitted for a straightjacket.

It hurts me when you use your powers You are only feeling what I am forced to feel.

Why?

You use a lot of power. It is agonizing, and you feel what I feel. I am not doing it on purpose, I swear to you.

157

I wanted to believe her. She was good. I felt sorry for her, and she already knew me well enough to know that I believed in second chances.

And the fact that she knew me made it harder for me to believe her, because I was almost sure she was playing me. I mean, everyone who'd talked about her had talked about how insane she was. And I'd seen it, the night she'd taken control of me. This wasn't some poor, helpless, innocent being. She'd purposely caused destruction and used my body to do it.

I can prove to you that I can be trusted. I can help you find the one you seek.

Strife?

I know her as Eris, but yes. I can lead you to her.

Now?

Silence for several moments. *No. Not now. We will need to rid ourselves of the demon first. He interferes with me.*

And that did it. She knew what Nain did for me, the way his presence strengthened me and made it easier for me to fight her.

Not a chance, Nether.

And that was when she started raging, calling me every foul name I'd ever heard and some I hadn't. Her anger, her frustration that she'd believed she'd been close to pulling one over on me and failed, was overwhelming.

I will destroy everything you hold dear.

I will take your life the way mine has been taken from me.

Believe it, little Fury. I will get my chance.

I focused harder, pictured that white slab of marble. Nain squeezed my hand, seeming to know that I needed a little extra something just then, and, eventually, her raging was nothing more than a dull roar at the back of my mind, muted but still very much there. I knew my breathing was elevated.

She was getting harder to fight.

I opened up my eyes and looked at Nain. We were in the parking garage. I had no idea how long we'd been there, but he was still holding my hand, watching me.

He reached into the glove box and pulled out a tissue. He brought it to my nose, and when he pulled it away, there was blood on it. I hadn't even realized it. He brought it back, held it there, and put his other hand on the back of my neck. His fingers rubbed along the back of my neck as he held the tissue to my nose, and his eyes stayed on mine.

Nether's pretty pissed at me.

You are white as a sheet right now, baby. I could feel how much power it was taking to control her. Nearly made me puke you were using so much of it.

I think she's getting stronger.

His eyes were still on mine. *I hate this. How the fuck am I supposed to destroy something that's living inside of you?*

You can't. No one can. I just have to be stronger.

He pulled the tissue away from my nose, and I took it and shoved it in my pocket. I'd throw it away later. He kept his other hand on the back of my neck, still soothing, still trying to calm me down and lend me his strength all at the same time.

"She tried to tell me she could help us find Strife. She tried to get me to trust her. She was pissed when I didn't bite."

"She knows how bad you want it."

"She told me why Nyx imprisoned her. I think she was trying to make me feel sorry for her," I said.

Nain was watching me. "Did it work?"

"Kind of. Doesn't mean I'm going to give in though."

"I love it when you're all badass like that," he said, and I rolled my eyes and opened my door.

We got into the loft and went our separate ways. I spent the rest of the day with E, scouring the city for Strife, and he went out on patrol with Stone. By the time E and I got home, it was very late but I was still full of energy. I took advantage of it and went up to the roof, pounded on the punching bag for a while. I sat and thought, and enjoyed being alone for a little while. I wasn't ready to climb into bed with Nain again just then, so it's a good thing I didn't need much sleep. Not because I didn't want to be near him, because I very much did. More because if I climbed into bed with him I'd probably end up doing a lot more and that wasn't a step I was ready to take.

A little after dawn, my phone went off and I glanced at it. Text from Nain.

"Good morning."

I texted him "good morning" back.

"Feel like going out for coffee w me?"

I smiled. "Are you asking me out on an actual date?"

"We never went on one of those before. Yeah."

"OK. Give me a few minutes."

"K."

I shook my head and smiled again and headed back into the loft. When I got down there, I could feel that he was in his office. I went to his/our room to shower and dress.

A date with my ex-husband. I must be insane.

CHAPTER THIRTEEN

I showered and dressed, tossing on my favorite pair of jeans and a red top I hadn't worn yet. Shanti and Ada were still trying to get me to dress like a girl and every once in a while a new shirt or something would show up in my laundry. Ada had already enjoyed replenishing my clothing stock after the fire. I put on make up and brushed my hair out, left it down. I made sure my enchantment was in place, my wings hidden, my eyes not glowing.

When I went out into the loft, Nain was standing at the kitchen counter. He was on the phone. He watched me hungrily as I headed across the loft and grabbed my shoes from the entry hall.

"Damn," he said after he hung up. He walked over to me, still staring at me. "The only thing that would be better was if you didn't have to hide your eyes and wings."

"They make me look freaky," I said, shaking my head.

"Not a chance." *You're goddamn beautiful, woman. You can feel what you do to me.*

I blushed.

"Are you ready to go?"

He nodded and pulled the door open, gestured for me to go through. We drove a few miles, ending up at the Fisher Building.

"There's a good place in here. Really I just like this building. The coffee could be shit and it wouldn't even matter," Nain said. "Is this okay?"

"Yes."

We parked and walked down the street. Walking into the Fisher Building always kind of took my breath away. Majestic was the only word for it. The tile mosaics, the gleaming floors, the soaring ceilings and amazing Art Deco chandeliers. It was almost impossible to believe that there could be that much beauty put into one building.

We walked through the lobby until we found the little cafe Nain was thinking of, which was the same one I'd come to with Ada once or twice. My hand was in his, and I was caught between wanting to stare at the magnificent surroundings or ogle him.

For the most part, I looked at the building. I'd have time to ogle Nain later.

We walked into the cafe and ordered coffees and croissants and found a table just outside of the cafe, in the lobby. We sat down and I sipped my coffee while I looked around. We chatted about the team, Shanti. How I was feeling regarding Nether. When I glanced back at Nain, he was watching me.

"Of all the things to be looking at in here, why do you keep looking at me?" I asked him.

"Because you're the best thing here," he said, and I shook my head.

"This building is amazing. Ada brought me here a few times for lunch. Every time I've been in here I find more to look at."

"I remember when they built this," he said. "I was on the construction crew."

I stared at him. "No way."

He nodded. "I worked on the exterior facade. I still remember the way the stonemasons obsessed over cutting every slab just right. They were like artists. I was just brute force, helping get the slabs up."

"Wow. So you worked construction and you worked in the factories, right?"

He nodded. "I did a certain job for as long as I could. Once it got to a point where I should have started looking like I aged, I'd move on. There was a lot to do. By the time it started getting hard to find jobs here, I'd already saved up and bought the buildings I wanted."

"What was your favorite time?" I asked him.

He looked like he was thinking. "I liked the early twentieth century a lot. The city was really starting to become something. And I liked it when I first spawned, when it was nothing more than a fort surrounded by wilderness. Watching all the people start flooding into the city over time was interesting." He shifted his glance to me. "But my favorite time is right now."

"What's so great about now? Things are falling apart. The city's in decline. We have raging immortals causing trouble."

"You're in my life now," he said, voice low.

I shook my head. "I never knew you were so smooth," I said, taking a sip of my coffee, trying to cover the fact that I was about to start freaking swooning over him. I am not a swooner.

Not usually, anyway.

He was watching me. "Well I'm hoping to get laid eventually," he said, and I laughed. He reached across the table and took my hand. "I wish we'd had the chance to do shit like this more often before."

I squeezed his hand. "Well, we're both here now," I said, meeting his eyes.

Satisfaction flowed from him. "We are." He pressed a kiss to my wrist. "And I'm supposed to be giving you time and space to figure shit out."

"You are. This is okay," I said. "Better than okay."

He kissed my wrist again, then released my hand. "Eventually we'll have to remind ourselves just how better than okay we are together."

"Horny demon," I muttered.

We stood up and he helped me into my coat, then wrapped his arms around me from behind. "Your fault," he murmured against my ear. He squeezed my waist firmly, then released me.

I took a deep breath and shook my head. He took my hand and we walked back out of the building. "I'm supposed to meet with some of the shifter leaders this morning to update them about your house and what we've learned about Strife," he said. "Which sucks because I really don't want this to end."

"Me neither. But I probably should go out looking for Strife anyway." My body was in complete disagreement with what I should do next, but I ignored it. Nain opened the passenger door of his truck for me and I climbed in. He got in and started the car, started driving back toward the loft. At some point, he rested his hand on my thigh, and in certain ways, in little things like that, it was as if we'd never been apart at all. And the fact that I could feel that way freaked me out a little. He'd lied to me. Destroyed me. I'd been messed around on, gone through hell. Was this just me wanting safety and comfort? Was it me rebounding from Brennan? And if I loved Brennan, how could Nain and I feel so right?

Was I the way Aphrodite had accused me of being? Was I just one of those women who now bounced from one lover to another? I sat in silence as Nain drove, and when he pulled into the garage at the loft, I still was wondering if maybe I wasn't losing my mind, starting up with him again. He turned the engine off and turned to me. "Where'd you go?"

"Hm?"

"I lost you a little on the drive back. Your whole posture changed. What's wrong?"

I shook my head. "Just wondering if this is a good idea," I said.

He was watching me. "You know what I think about that." He looked away. "Is it because of Brennan?"

"Meaning?"

"Do you want him back?" he asked, not looking at me.

"No. I don't. But I'm wondering if what is happening between us is just me rebounding from Brennan. That would really suck."

"I think what we have is bigger than that," he said, and I could feel the irritation coming off of him, the frustration. We got out of the truck and walked toward the elevator. He put his hand on my lower back as we stepped into the elevator, started absent-mindedly rubbing up and down my spine.

I sighed and rested my head against his chest.

"I hope it is," I said, and he squeezed me against his body.

He was about to say something when I felt someone freaking out in the loft. I pulled away from him. "Something's wrong with Ada," I said. The elevator stopped and we both charged off of it, heading into the loft.

When we stepped into the loft, we were met with chaos. Ada's terror. The reason behind it was evident almost immediately. Brennan and Stone were there, both of them bloody and bruised, sitting on stools in the kitchen as Ada tried bandaging them up.

Asclepias, come if you can, I thought as loudly as I could. I glanced at Bash and Dahael. "See if you can find the healer. I have no idea if he can even hear me or not."

They thumped their fists to their chests and took off. I headed toward the kitchen. Nain was already there. Ada was stitching up a huge cut across Stone's neck.

"Looks worse than it is," she said to me, though her voice shook and her hand was trembling so badly I was amazed she could even hold the needle.

Brennan was holding a towel to his side, and I tried to pull it aside so I could see. He held it tighter, and I looked up and met his eyes.

"Bren. Let me see it."

"It'll be fine."

"Let me see."

He still held it there.

"Or do you not trust me anymore?"

We watched each other. I could feel anger coming off of him. Pain. Sadness, and that was mostly because of me.

"Bren," I said softly, aware of Nain watching us as he helped Ada with Stone.

He took a deep breath, nodded. This time, when I tried to pull the blood-soaked towel away, he let me. I kind of wished he hadn't. The cut there was deep, ragged, the wound flayed wide open. No wonder he was so pale, trembling.

"You should by lying down," I said. "Let me help you."

"That's really not your problem anymore," he grunted.

"Brennan, don't be an asshole," I said, and he laughed, just a little, and it made him grimace. I helped him to the floor and pushed his shirt out of the way. I dug my knife out of my pocket.

"Don't freak out," I said, remembering the way Nain had reacted when I'd done this with him.

"I don't want your blood," he said, realizing what I was about to do. He pushed my hands away.

"It can heal you."

"I know. I don't want it."

"Why are you being so stupid about this? I've used my blood to heal you before."

"Without me knowing," he said with a grimace. "Don't."

166

"So what? You're just gonna bleed out and leave Sean an orphan? Don't be stupid."

He waved me away, turned and looked away from me. I was about to start telling his ass off when Asclepias popped into the loft.

He leaned down and started looking at Brennan, and I stood up and walked toward Nain, who was still standing near Ada and Stone. He reached over and gave my hand a gentle squeeze. I listened as Stone talked about what happened. They had been on patrol and come up against a group similar to the one E and I had run up against. This was apparently what they could do when they came up against a couple of non-immortals.

"They injured Bren so bad he couldn't shift back for a while, but I think that was for the best since he's a little stronger in that form," Stone said, and I nodded. "We did all right, kid. Six to two and we ended up kicking ass, huh?" he called over to Brennan, and Brennan gave him a weak thumbs-up from his spot on the floor. Asclepias was running his hands over Brennan's wounds, and I could feel the healer's power coursing through the loft. Artemis came rushing in just then and she was a mass of anger and worry. She crouched beside Brennan and started talking to him, then Sean started crying and she picked him up and took him to Brennan's room.

"This is insane. We can't patrol anymore without getting jumped? It's like they know where we're going to be," Ada said. "That night with you and E, they knew you'd be there. Today Bren and Stone were doing a patrol near Mack and they run into them? There's no way this is random." She tied off another stitch, her face close to Stone's. I watched the two of them as I thought about what Ada had said. Stone looked at Ada with complete adoration, and when she glanced up at his face, I could feel how much she loved him. She reached one hand up and ran it gently along first one side of his white mustache, then the other. It was beautiful, and the strength in that one glance between the two of them had me on the verge of tears.

My god I am getting sappy.

I focused my thoughts back to the immediate problem.

"Well we know Strife's organizing them. We know they have demons and just about everything else."

"Can Strife read minds?" Ada asked me.

"No."

"No. So how do they know where we're going to be?"

"You think we have a traitor?" Nain asked.

Ada glanced at me, and I sensed nervousness from her. Anger. "How do we know that thing inside Molly isn't communicating with her somehow?"

"I'd know," I said quietly.

"Would you? You didn't know she had control of you that night until you saw yourself on TV," she shot back. Then she took a breath, reached over and took my hand. "I'm sorry. I love you honey. I'm just saying... how do you know for sure?"

"This happened a little while ago. Molly hasn't seen the patrol schedule, and she's been with me since they showed up right before dawn. It's not her," Nain said.

"In your totally objective opinion, boss man," Ada said gently. "The alternative is that someone who lives here is selling us out. Who would it be? Me? Levitt? Artemis? Who?"

"Could be Artemis. I don't know her," Nain said. "I only let her live here because of Brennan and Sean."

"And I'm the one that got hurt today, and she's my grandmother. It wasn't her," Brennan said. Asclepias was still working on him.

"You sure? Maybe she wanted to raise that kid herself," Nain said.

"Fuck off Nain. It wasn't her," Brennan said.

"It wasn't," I said, agreeing with him.

"Heph knows our patrol schedule. So does Levitt. Shanti. E," Nain said. "And there's not a chance in hell it's Shanti."

"Or E," I said. "Or Levitt."

"You don't know that about Levitt. He's always been private."

"He's mine. He wouldn't do that," I said, glaring at him.

"Levitt's trustworthy," Brennan said. "It wasn't him."

"It wasn't Heph either," I said.

"He wouldn't mind hurting me," Brennan said.

"It wasn't him," I argued.

"The problem really is all the blasted immortals around here," Stone said. Then he glanced at me. "No offense, kiddo."

"None taken. I think," I said, and he grinned at me, threw a wink my way, Ada had finished stitching him up and was applying gauze to his wound.

"I'm saying, the way you all can do that thing where you just appear out of nowhere. And Ada's wards don't work against that, or Asclepias and your father never would have been able to get in here in the first place. Right?"

I stared at him. I'd never even thought of that. I'd just assumed Ada's wards kept us safe from everything, but he was right. My dad had just showed up without an invitation or anything else the first time I'd met him, when he'd appeared after I'd prayed to Asclepias.

"Thanks, man. You just gave me a whole new thing to stress out about," I told Stone, and he guffawed. "You're right."

"Shit," Nain groaned. "So it could be any of them, is that what you're saying?"

"Wouldn't we feel them, though?" Brennan asked. "Or wouldn't Artemis or Heph feel them at the very least?"

A thought struck me, and I felt my stomach turn. Please don't be true. Please don't be true.

"I'll be right back," I said. I knew it would hurt. Didn't matter. I knew where my dad was just then, and I needed to see him. I visualized the hotel room he'd been staying in, and materialized there.

Hades was snoring in the big bed, and I clapped my hands together.

"Wake up, dad," I said.

He jumped up and stared at me.

"What's going on?"

"Tell me you're not responsible for telling Strife's people where we're patrolling," I snarled.

"What? Why in the world would I do that. Why would I put you in danger?" he asked, getting out of bed.

Okay. I could have done without seeing my dad all au natural. Gross. I looked away as I waited for him to get dressed.

"Someone's responsible for spilling the beans about where we're patrolling. Bren and Stone got ambushed today, and it's not the first time."

"So what does that have to do with me?" I heard him moving around, zippers being zipped.

"Has to be an immortal who can rematerialize, because it's not anyone on our team," I said.

"Again, why would it be me?"

"And not be detected when they appeared. So someone who has something like, oh... I don't know. An invisibility helmet that hides not just his appearance but also his power signature." I chanced looking back at Hades then, wanting to see his expression.

He was staring at me, and anger rolled off of him.

"Well I'm so glad you assume your own father is the one selling you out," he snarled.

"Who else could it be?"

"Hephaestus made the damned thing. Did you ever think maybe he made another one? How do you know I'm the only one who has one?"

"Because Heph never makes the same thing twice," I said, recalling one of my many conversations with him. "He gets bored. Where is it?"

"I don't have it," he finally said, crossing his arms and watching me.

"Where. Is. It?"

"Don't threaten me, little girl," he growled, his power heightening, swirling around the room in response to the threat I posed, and I was reminded again of just how scary my father is.

But I'm just as scary.

"Didn't you learn anything the last time we went through this? You can trust me. Why won't you?"

"Oh, I don't know. Maybe because you were never there, my entire life, and then when you did meet me you fucking lied to me about who my father was."

"To keep you safe!"

I let out a shriek. "I am so tired of people lying to me to keep me safe."

He stared at me, held his hands out in a soothing gesture. "Okay. All right. Fair point. I'm sorry."

I just watched him, swiped at my bleeding nose. I was getting so tired of this.

"I haven't seen that damn thing in years," he said. "Last time I used it was shortly after you were born, and I came to see you before Tis put her enchantments on you. Then I put it in its safe in my bedchambers at my house. I don't need it very often."

"Persephone?" I asked quietly.

"You want it to be her," he said.

I sighed. "No. I don't. I don't want it to be anyone. Believe it or not, I don't just want to go around kicking people's asses all the time. I would rather not have to believe that the people in my life are selling me out. And to be honest, I actually kind of like Persephone. But she's your wife and it's entirely possible she has access to your safe. Yes?"

171

"It wasn't her."

I rolled my eyes, shook my head and looked up at the ceiling. Okay. Right that second I did kind of want to destroy something or someone. I wasn't picky.

"Who else?"

"The only other one who had access was our house demon, Elsoloth. But he serves you now."

"Can you go see if it's even still there, please?"

"Very well." Hades disappeared and I sat on the bed. It was obvious that my father thought I was barking up the wrong tree, but I had to know. Whether it was there or not really didn't solve anything. Whoever had used it could very well have just put it back when they were done with it.

And Heph could have made another one. Please, don't be that, I begged the universe or whoever the hell someone like me could ask for help at times like this.

A few minutes later, Hades rematerialized, and the first thing I felt was his rage.

"It's gone," he said, stalking back and forth across the room. "It wasn't me. I'm telling you that right now."

"Where's Persephone?"

"With her mother. I'm going to her next." I could feel his nervousness, his doubts. His guilt.

"What do you feel guilty about?" I asked him, and he glared at me.

"If she did this, it's still my fault. I trusted her. And I hurt her. I hurt her with Tisiphone, and I've hurt her many times since, every time she has to see me and Tis or me and you together."

"I'll check in with Elsoloth," I said gently. "It could have been him."

"Persephone has issues with you. Me. And we're not together anymore," he finished, and I stared at him in shock.

"Uh. You broke up?"

He nodded. "She made me break my bond to her. She said she couldn't take it anymore." He leaned on the windowsill, looked out over the city. "She caught me and Tisiphone. We were just holding hands, but it was enough. It was right after we realized Nether was in you and we were talking. She was upset and I took her hand to comfort her. You know how that works," he said, glancing back at me, and I nodded. It was the same way Nain was able to soothe me with his touch. Creatures of the Nether could do that for one another. "Anyway, she saw, and that did it. Tisiphone said the amount of pain coming off of Persephone when she saw us was almost too much to bear. I did that to her, after everything else I've put her through." Hurt, guilt, anger rolled off of him.

"Dad…" I said. "Maybe it wasn't her. I can talk to Elsoloth first, if you want."

He looked at me. "What reason would Elsoloth have to want to hurt you? Let's be logical here, daughter."

I shrugged. "Well. Let's find out. I'll talk to you later, okay?"

He nodded and turned back to the window, lost in thought, and I visualized the loft and rematerialized right where I'd been when I'd left.

Nain was sitting at the kitchen counter. Asclepias was gone. The rest of the main part of the loft was empty.

"So?" he asked.

"My dad's helmet is gone," I said, and he cursed.

"Okay. What do we do now?"

"Now, we go talk to my demons, because Elsoloth had access to it. That, and wait to find out what my father learns from his ex-wife."

Nain raised his eyebrow. "Ex?"

I nodded.

"Shit."

"Yeah."

He took my hand, and we headed out of the loft again. We walked the few blocks to the old house Nain had purchased for my demons. It was still dilapidated looking. The windows were still boarded over.

"I should have been watching them more carefully. I haven't checked in with them since right after I got back. Stupid to just leave a bunch of Nether demons on their own for so long," I muttered to Nain.

"Relax. We don't even know it's him yet," he said. I pulled my hand out of his, knowing he wouldn't take that personally. Holding hands when I needed to look like a badass in front of my demons would just ruin the whole effect.

I knocked on the sagging front door, listened. There wasn't a single sound from inside the house. "I don't feel any demons here, other than you," I said to Nain, and he nodded.

"Well, it's my house," he said. Then he backed up and put his shoulder into the front door, and it splintered in. Then he pushed it open and walked in, on alert, ready for an attack.

The house was filthy. Trash strewn around, a musty, urine smell permeating everything.

"It wasn't like this when I bought it for them. Fucking demons," Nain muttered.

We walked through the house. In the kitchen, food rotted in the refrigerator. The expiration date on the milk was two months ago.

"This doesn't make any sense," I said.

Nain looked around. "I don't think the stink is all coming from the refrigerator. Stay here."

He opened the kitchen door and headed down the basement stairs. As soon as the door opened, the stench hit me. Decay. Putrid. I covered my mouth and nose and within seconds, Nain was back in the kitchen. He closed the door behind him.

"Seven dead demons," he said.

"Elsoloth?" I asked, still hopeful that he hadn't betrayed me.

Nain shook his head. Then he took my hand. We looked through the house again, looking for any sign of what had happened, but the rooms all had that same dead, abandoned feel. We checked out the small backyard, then walked back around to the front. We'd just made our way to the front walk when my dad materialized in front of us.

"So?" he asked me.

"No sign of Elsoloth or the other demons. Other than the dead ones in the basement," I said. "You?"

"Demeter wouldn't tell me where Persephone is. And then she started throwing flower pots at me," he said. "Those hurt more than you'd expect them to."

I took a deep breath. "Okay. So it could be either of them. Or both of them. I really don't think it's Persephone, though." I remembered the night I'd realized Brennan's son had been cursed by his mother. Strife's witch. And how she'd removed the curse and reassured me. Told me that it was him, not me, and that it had made me feel better. I remembered the way she'd loved my father, despite her words to the contrary, and I felt bad for her. She'd taken a" chance on love and it had made her bitter and angry. That, I could relate to, remembering Brennan's betrayal, Nain's lies.

"Why not? She hates you, right?" Nain asked, dragging me back to the present.

"She isn't a fan of mine, but she's always been straightforward. She doesn't lie, she doesn't backstab."

"Maybe she didn't, but if she's upset you don't know how she's responding to it," Nain argued.

I shook my head. "She sees herself as above all that shit."

"Until someone gives her a reason to sink to that level," Nain pressed on.

"What? Do you want it to be her? Just because someone gets cheated on and screwed over, it's supposed to turn them evil? Is she less somehow because he broke her?" I asked, gesturing toward my father.

"We're not talking about you and me. Or you and Brennan," Nain said and I could feel the irritation from him.

I snarled, hating that he'd seen past my words. That he knew what was really bothering me. Angry at him, screwed up over the emotions running through me. "No? Maybe we should. Don't you wonder what it was like? What made me turn to him? What he did for me while you were gone?"

He glared at me. "I'm pretty sure I know the answers to all those questions. You're pissed off. Don't try to start a fight with me over it, Molls."

"You brought it up."

"I didn't fucking bring anything up," he growled. "It could be her, right?" he asked my father, who looked like he wanted to be just about anywhere else at the moment.

"It could have. I think it was," Hades said. "And it has nothing to do with hurting you and everything to do with getting back at me."

I rolled my eyes. "Full of yourself much, dad? Maybe her world doesn't revolve around you."

I glanced up at Nain and my father to see them exchanging a glance.

"If you're talking about me I'm gonna kick your asses," I said. Then I stalked away, back toward the loft. A couple of minutes later, Nain caught up to me, walked beside me in silence. We turned a corner where an abandoned factory stood on the corner, and he grabbed me and pressed me up against the wall, using his body to hold me there.

I shoved at him, and he lowered his lips to mine. I didn't kiss him back at first, still pissed at him and not even really knowing why. Eventually, I gave in and kissed him back. He kissed me hard. Angry. And it left me needy and breathless. I clung to him as he ravaged my mouth, crushed my body between himself and the rough side of the building. He pulled back and lowered his lips to my throat, nipped it with his teeth, and I gasped.

"Don't do that anymore. You can fight with me all you want, but don't throw Brennan in my face like that. I don't give a fuck what you had with him, or what you thought you had with him. All that matters is you and me."

I stared up at him. I'd hurt him. I'd been deliberately cruel. He was glaring down at me, his heart pounding, need and anger flowing from him.

"I get that you're pissed at me still. I get that you're scared about what's happening between us. It's going to take time for you not to be. And I have that coming to me. I'll take it. But we're not gonna fight dirty. And bringing him into it when you get pissed off at me, using that threat of hinting that maybe you want him more than me is beneath you. Like I said before: you want him, go to him."

"You don't have any room to make demands, demon," I said, shoving at him. He stayed put. His gaze was intense, and trying to push him away from me was like trying to shove at a mountain. Then he leaned down and kissed me again, gently this time. When he pulled away, it was only to press his cheek against mine. We stayed, and I let him hold me, needing it as much as he did.

"I'm sorry," I said softly, pressing a kiss to his jaw, then another one. "I was pissed and that was a shitty thing to do. This whole thing is just too much right now." I reached up and put my arms around his neck, and he picked me up, held me tight in his arms as I buried my face against his neck.

"Me too," he said, kissing the side of my neck. "And I'm doing a bad job of giving you time." Then he released me and backed away. I took a steadying breath, missing his touch the second he pulled away. "Tell me to get the hell away from you when you need me to. I won't like it, but I'll do it anyway."

I nodded. I pressed my fingers to my swollen lips, tried to ignore the way my body ached for him yet again. Then I tore my gaze away from him and started walking toward the loft again. When I got there, I got into my car instead of going up into the loft.

If nothing else, I could cover some ground and look for Elsoloth. Bash and Dahael climbed into the car with me, and we drove off. I felt okay. Nether wasn't raging too hard, even with all of the insanity of the day. I drove all over the city, going to places I knew Elsoloth had spent time. Restaurants and bars the team had said he'd liked. The house of the woman he'd been dating. The woman was there, but said she hadn't seen Elsoloth in over a month. And she was hurt by it. She'd been falling for him.

I hate feeling people's emotions sometimes.

It was pretty hopeless, and I knew it. If he was hiding, I wouldn't find him until I had a lead, and I'd already told my imps to start scouring the city for him. They were much better at that kind of thing than I am. Really, I needed a little more time alone. The fact that I'd done that to Nain, that I'd deliberately tried to hurt him... that bothered me. And I knew I could easily blame all of the stress in my life. I knew he'd forgiven me for it. I knew that it had been brought on by fear. I was in love with him again, and it scared the hell out of me. Well. I say again. I probably never was out of love with him in the first place. Angry at him, sure. Determined to never let him hurt me again? Hell, yes. I kind of wanted to smack myself for admitting to him that I wanted him, that I wanted us. If I could have kept acting like I didn't want him, maybe he would have backed off. And I would have been alone, but at least I wouldn't be risking losing my mind again when we end.

Brennan had made me believe in happily ever afters, and look how that ended.

I drove, and I thought. And every once in a while, Nether put her two cents in.

You are pathetic.
So afraid of everything.
If only everyone knew what a coward you really are.

The demon will die right after the shifter.

Love is a waste of time. Take it from someone who knows, Fury.

And every time she piped up, I'd push her back down.

When I ran out of places I felt like driving to, I headed toward home. I felt better after some time alone to think, even if I did feel guilty for not actually saving anyone while I was out. I pulled into the parking garage and took the elevator up to the loft. I was kind of relieved to find that Nain and Brennan were out on patrol together and I wouldn't have to deal with either of them just then.

Ada and Stone were watching TV, Stone cradling Sean in his arms. Levitt and Heph were eating. I glanced at the clock. Shanti was supposed to be coming over that night, and I'd be glad to see her. We hadn't managed to really talk since the night my house had been torched and I missed her. We were going to patrol together, which I was looking forward to. We always talked during our patrol time, and it gave us a few solid hours to reconnect without anyone else (other than those whose asses we were kicking) interfering.

I headed into Nain's room to change into my black cargo pants and black top. I braided my hair, and was just finishing up when my phone rang. I glanced at the clock. Shanti should have been there by then, but snow had been falling all day and the roads were a mess. Probably her, telling me she was running late.

I glanced at my phone, and it showed an unidentified number.

"Hello?"

"You really should take better care of your team members, Angel." A feminine yet powerful voice.

"Who is this?"

"Oh, I think you can guess. You're not as dumb as I once believed you to be."

"Strife."

"See there? Nice job, Fury."

"What did you do, Strife?"

"Me? Oh, nothing. But my men rid the world of one more vampire tonight. You took one of mine when you killed Terror. Now I took one of yours. I'm sure she won't be missed." And the line went dead.

I was shaking. Barely able to breathe. Telling myself she had to be messing with me.

But Shanti was never late. Ever.

I ran out of my room, dialing Nain's number. I told him what Strife had said, and that I was going out to look. Levitt and Heph overheard me and started moving too. They were going to check out Shanti's old neighborhood. I tried Shanti's number and got her voice mail, and I felt myself starting to lose it. I focused and rematerialized at Rayna's front door.

Ronan answered. "Angel!" he said, smiling.

"Please tell me Shanti is here," I said, hoping it had been a cruel joke.

His face sobered immediately. "She left right after sunset to see you."

I couldn't do it. Couldn't say what was happening. "Call Nain and he'll tell you what's going on," I said, and then I took to the air, kicking off from the ground and rising into the sky. I flew lower than I would have liked, tracing the route Shanti would have taken between Rayna's house and the loft.

She had to be out there. She had to be alive.

And even if she wasn't, I had to know for sure that Strife wasn't holding her somewhere.

CHAPTER FOURTEEN

I knew Shanti sometimes took a more leisurely route through the city on her way from Rayna's, so I looked along that route first. As I was flying, I felt my father's presence somewhere nearby, and glanced around. I saw him to my left, flying toward me.

"What are you doing here?" I asked, still flying, looking down at the streets and buildings below.

"The demon told me what was going on. We'll find her, Mollis." We split, me looking at the buildings and alleys on one side of the route, Hades doing the same on the other.

I couldn't answer him. I felt like I was going to puke. Felt like I wanted to scream.

This. Exactly this. This is why I shouldn't have people in my life. They get targeted because of me. The assholes who are my enemies know they can't actually hurt me physically, so they go after the people in my life. Every. Damn. Time.

I gritted my teeth and blinked the tears back from my eyes. My girl. The strong, gorgeous young woman who'd come to me because she'd feared herself and ended up being one of the most steadfast, disciplined supernaturals I'd ever known.

And I did scream then, unable to contain my fear and anger any longer. It echoed over the city, and I didn't even care.

Hades came to me and took my hand. Trying to calm me down.

"Mollis. This is not the time to lose it. Losing control now won't help you find her," he said softly. "Calm down."

I nodded, swiped my hands over my eyes. After a moment, we moved on, flying further along the route.

"Is that her car?" Hades asked after a couple of minutes. I flew toward him and looked in the direction he was.

And then I flew as fast as I could into the alley where the car was parked. A glance at the license plate told me it was definitely Shanti's little red convertible.

It was still running, the headlights illuminating the alley.

Hades landed beside me, and we started looking through the alley. There were several dumpsters. This strip had several small stores, a few restaurants.

"Please be here. Please be alive," I whispered as I opened the nearest dumpster. Hades was doing the same thing further down the alley. I swore I could feel her presence, or at least some vampire's presence nearby, but it was weak.

I checked another dumpster, then another. Hades started looking through the windows of the buildings, rose into the air to look at the area from up above.

I was losing hope. Her car was there, but they'd taken her. If they had, I had zero chance of finding her right away. The imps were looking already, but we were likely already too late, based on what Strife had said.

I was crying again, my fear overtaking me, the feeling of helplessness in this situation nearly overwhelming me. All I wanted to do was fall into a heap and wail.

I opened the last dumpster along that strip of alley, and the first thing I saw was a high-heeled black boot.

I rose into the air and opened the dumpster the rest of the way.

Jeans.

White top.

So much blood.

Shanti.

Still alive, I realized, but not for long.

"Dad," I called, and Hades came to me. I pulled Shanti into my arms and flew her out of the dumpster. I laid her on the ground as gently as I could.

She'd been stabbed several times, and the burnt look of the wounds made it clear they'd used a silver blade. She had to be in agony. Her eyes were closed. Unconscious.

"Will my blood work on her?" I asked Hades, getting ready to slice my wrist. Hades put a hand on mine, stopping me.

"It will. Mine will work even better. And you need to stay strong. Let me."

I nodded, prayed to I don't even know what as I watched Hades slice his wrist with my knife, letting his blood flow into first one of Shanti's wounds, then another.

They had definitely tried to make sure they killed her. They'd gone for the chest, the stomach. The throat. She was close. She'd likely lost consciousness from the torture the silver had caused to her system, and they'd left her for dead.

"They were careless. Thankfully," Hades murmured as he sliced his wrist again. "And she is strong."

"Stupid of them not to make sure," I said. "Not that I'm complaining."

"They were likely afraid of you appearing before they were finished," he said.

"I am going to find them. I am going to rip their guts out and make them watch. I am going to—"

"Mollis," my dad said.

"What?"

"Calm. Remember what you're supposed to be doing." His gaze met mine, and I took a deep breath. He was right. Me getting all berserker now would be a bad thing. I was tired. Stressed out. Pissed off. Perfect conditions for Nether, who was already fighting me again, sensing my weakness.

"You'll get your chance," Hades said.

I watched as he let more of his blood into Shanti's wounds, watched as they started closing up, as the burnt skin around the injuries started repairing itself.

"This will likely make her even stronger," he said. "Which is a good thing, considering."

"Does my blood make people stronger?" I asked, thinking of how I'd healed Nain.

"Probably. I know mine does. The same is true of the Furies, though theirs seems to have less of an effect than mine does."

"It makes like zero sense that the god of death has healing blood," I said, trying to stay calm, focus on anything other than my rage and the way my stomach still twisted, watching Shanti slowly but surely healing.

"All of the immortals have it in one way or another. That's why we can heal ourselves. Zeus, Poseidon, and I have the most potent blood, from what we know."

"I guess that makes sense," I said, and he nodded as he moved on to another of Shanti's wounds. He was starting to look pale. He'd sliced himself at least four times.

"Do you need a break?" I asked him, and he shook his head.

"I'll be fine. And I want you to stay strong."

Shanti's wounds had all closed. Hades sat down, and I settled next to him on the cold pavement.

"Now all we can do is wait. There was a lot of internal damage because of the effects of silver. As my blood works its way through her body, it will repair that. She'll likely be quite hungry when she revives."

"Thanks for doing that, dad," I said, bumping my shoulder against his.

"I know you love this one," he said, shrugging. "It's really the least I can do considering what a mess I've made of your life."

I looked over at him. "Well, considering I wouldn't even be here if it wasn't for you, I think that's being a bit harsh."

He smiled. "Are you truly happy to be alive?" he asked me.

I wrapped my arms around my knees, rested my chin on them. "I am. For a long time, I wasn't. But I'm needed and that's reason enough to be happy to be alive."

"I am sorry about the whole mess with my helmet. And several other things, obviously," he said, and I smiled at him.

"Any word from Persephone yet?"

He shook his head.

"Do you want her back?"

He didn't answer, and I was about to tell him it wasn't any of my business. Then, finally, he said "things are different now. I think our time was up a long time ago. I love her and she loves me. Or, at least she did." He paused, looked up into the sky. "I don't know how she feels now. But your being here and being the way you are proves that so many of the things we were told were wrong. Maybe I have a chance at something else."

I watched him. I wanted to press him, but I sensed that he really didn't feel like talking about it.

"And whether I want her back is irrelevant. If she is working against you, then we're so far beyond done there is no going back," he said.

"I still don't think it was her," I told him.

"I hope you're right," he said after a few moments. "Are things okay between you and the demon? You were less than pleased with one another when you left me the other day."

I shrugged. "They're fine. Just weird."

"If he hurts you again, I'll make him rue the day he was spawned," Hades said. And I totally believed him.

"Thanks dad." I smiled a little. I was feeling better. Shanti was healing up, and her power signature was getting stronger the longer we sat there. "I'm just trying not to rush into anything with him this time. Things are intense when we're together, and I'm just not sure I can deal with that right now."

He nodded. "Your mother says there is no doubt about how much he loves you. That she can feel it, and it's absolute."

"It is. I know it too. But there's a lot of shit in the past between us. He's mine, and I'm his. We both know it. I'm just not ready to move forward yet."

"You need to put that poor demon out of his misery. Give the man a break," Shanti said weakly, and I jumped up and knelt over her. I was crying again (damn it) but this time they were tears of relief. I bent down and hugged her. She hugged me back, wrapping her arms around me tightly.

"I'm sorry, Shanti. I am so sorry sweetie," I said, hugging her tighter.

"Don't you dare blame yourself for this," she said, pulling back and meeting my eyes. "Understand? They caught me by surprise. I thought I was saving someone and it was a trap. This is on me, and on them." She smiled. "This is the second time you've answered my prayers and saved me, Angel."

I shook my head. "I am so glad you're okay. If you'd died..."

She took my hand, held it tightly. "But I didn't. Which one of you healed me?"

I pointed at my dad, who was standing just behind me, and Shanti smiled up at him.

"Thank you," she said to him.

"You are very welcome. Though I have to admit I did it mostly for my daughter."

"Of course," she said, nodding. "But thanks anyway."

"Are you hungry?" I asked her, and she nodded, her fangs lengthening. I held my wrist up to her.

"Are you sure? I know this makes you kind of queasy."

"It's you. It's fine," I told her.

"I feel so special," she said, taking my wrist in her hands. I barely felt it when she bit into my wrist, looked away as she fed.

"She is going to be bouncing off the walls with all of this immortal blood flowing through her body," Hades said, and I nodded.

"Can you call Nain and tell him everything is okay?" I asked my father, handing him my phone. I sat and let Shanti feed, ran my hands through her hair. He took it, and I heard him talking to Nain, his voice low. Answering questions, assuring Nain we'd be back soon. Telling him he didn't need to come to us, that we had everything under control. Shanti and I looked at each other and rolled our eyes.

She finished feeding. "Thank you," she said. "Um. Your blood is really really good. That rumor is totally true."

"Great. I'll put that on my resume," I said, and she laughed.

"I need a shower so bad right now," Shanti said, and we stood up. Hades handed my phone back to me.

"You're driving home?" he asked me, and I nodded.

"I'll fly overhead and keep watch. Just to make sure," he said.

"Thanks," I said. Then I stood on tiptoe and kissed my dad on the cheek. I felt a jolt of surprise from him, and then he smiled a little.

"Thanks, Mr. Lord of the Dead, sir," Shanti said as she climbed into her car. Hades shook his head and rose into the air, and I climbed into the passenger seat of Shanti's car.

She started driving toward the loft.

"Are you sure you're okay?" I asked her.

"I'm fine. Your dad was right. I feel like I could do just about anything right now. I feel like I could fly. Like I could kick the ass of at least a dozen vampires without any effort at all."

I laughed. "Great. Except that the only thing you're doing now is coming home and relaxing for a while."

"Fine," she said, grinning.

"What was it?" I asked her, not really wanting to talk about her attack but needing to know. "Was it vampires?"

She shook her head. "Two witches and three demons. The witches were kind of the bait. I thought they were being attacked by two of the demons. And when I was focused on saving them, the third demon snuck up on me and stabbed me in the back. It was a stupid rookie mistake on my part. I should have been more careful, especially with all of the craziness going on now."

"You're like me in that way. You don't think of yourself until it's too late."

She glanced over at me. "That may be the nicest thing anyone's ever said about me."

"I didn't mean it in a good way," I said. "We're both reckless."

"You know what you are, Molly? You're a damn hero. What else do you call someone who rushes in without any regard for their own safety? So cram that whole idea that the way we are is a bad thing. If I'm anything at all like you, then I'm damn proud of it."

I stared at her. "You almost just died, Shanti. I can't die. There's no risk to me if I rush in to save someone."

"I'm pretty damn hard to kill too. And you can still be hurt and tortured and all that. So don't pretend there's no danger for you."

"It's not the same," I said, looking out the window at the passing landscape. Shanti had even more of a lead foot than I did.

"No. It's not. You have a hell of a lot more at stake than I do. If you get captured or whatever, look at how many people will suffer. Look at the way things fell apart when you died last time. And the only thing that's ever mattered to you is keeping everyone safe. We lose you, and none of us are safe."

"Thanks. I needed that additional pressure, kiddo," I said, and she laughed.

"You know what I'm saying. You blame yourself for every single person you can't save. That's worse than death, as far as you're concerned, and that's why you still risk everything when you go out and save someone, even if it means you'll live."

A thought kept coming through as she was talking, the same thing I'd heard from her before. Zero.

"Can I ask you something unrelated to this?" I asked her, and she glanced at me.

"Sure."

"Who's Zero? That name comes through fairly often when I'm talking to you."

She glanced at me again. Uncomfortable. Embarrassed. If she could have blushed, she would have been.

"Oh. He's this guy I know," she said, and the emotions coming from her let me know exactly how she felt about this guy.

I smiled. "Is he a vampire?"

"No. Normal. Which is why I haven't talked about him a lot. I kind of figure that the fewer people who know about him the better. And I don't want to get into it with Levitt and I'm kind of thinking you're about to tell me how stupid it is to put a Normal in danger by being involved with him."

I laughed. "I am not going to tell you that. You're a grown woman and you know the risks and I have no doubt you're doing what you can to keep him safe. I can put an imp or two on him if you want, just for an added bit of protection."

"Are they gonna report back to you with details about us?"

I shook my head. "No. I don't want to know."

"Good. Thank you then."

"Anytime."

We drove in silence for a few minutes. "How did you know something happened to me?" Shanti asked after a while.

"Strife called to taunt me about it," I said, just the memory of her smug voice enough to make me want to destroy something.

"Shit. So it was her people?"

I nodded. Clenched my hands in my lap.

"Calm down. Don't get all ragey now," Shanti said.

"I know. I need to find this bitch. She's spent too much time taunting me. And this was a sign that she's getting braver, coming at my own people. She's getting stronger, because all the chaos and fighting going on now is adding to her power."

"Well maybe she'll get cocky then. That's when people tend to make mistakes," Shanti said. She pulled into the parking garage under the loft and we got out of the car.

"Yeah, but who else is she going to hurt before I can get to her?" I asked. "This has to stop, and we still have no goddamn sign of her. How can she be hiding so well? The imps can't even get a read on her, and that's never happened."

We got into the elevator and Shanti reached over and took my hand. "We'll find her, Molly. And we'll all just have to be more careful in the meantime. Right?"

190

I nodded, took another deep breath. I took a moment to see who I could sense in the loft. It felt like our team was all there.

"You have a welcome wagon. I think I feel Rayna and Ronan up there," I said with some surprise.

"They are very protective of their people. She's probably not happy at all right now," Shanti said. The elevator stopped and we walked into the loft. The first few minutes of our arrival were taken up by just about everyone hugging Shanti and expressing varying degrees of "we're gonna kick their asses." Relief and love flowed through the loft, and I had to smile a little as I stood back and watched. Nain came over to me and wrapped me in his arms, and I rested my face against his chest, needing him. Needing the calm that only he could bring me. I put my arms around his waist and hid my face and just breathed.

"We can go somewhere else if you need to," he said quietly and I shook my head.

"I want to talk to Rayna first," I said, and he squeezed me to him for a moment, then let me go. I looked up at him, and our eyes met.

It amazed me how much this angry, powerful man could soothe me.

Thanks, I thought at him and then I started to walk away.

I'd give you a hell of a lot more if you needed it, he thought at me, and I shook my head. The bad thing (or was it maybe not such a bad thing?) was that all I really wanted to do was stay in his arms and let myself relax. But I had things to do. Rayna and Ronan were talking to Shanti in one corner of the loft, and the rest of the team had started to disperse once they'd seen her. Levitt, Heph, and E left for patrol. Brennan took Sean up to their rooms, and Ada and Stone headed to their room, tired after having been up early with Sean.

Rayna and Ronan both turned and looked at me.

"I'm going to go get cleaned up," Shanti said. "And then I think I'm going to sleep. The rush your blood gave me is starting to fade a little."

I nodded and hugged her. "I'm so glad you're okay," I said against her hair, and she squeezed me harder.

"Of course I am. Sometimes prayers get answered," she said, smiling. The four of us (Rayna, Ronan, Nain, and I) watched her climb the stairs to her room. Then I glanced at Rayna, who was watching me.

"That kind of attack cannot stand," Rayna snarled, and I felt the anger rolling off of her. One of her family had been attacked. And she genuinely liked Shanti.

"It won't," I said, turning and heading toward the couch. Nain sat beside me and Rayna and Ronan each took one of the chairs. "This was Strife. She called and taunted me with Shanti's death."

"How did you find her?" Ronan asked. "We started scouring the city the second I got off the phone with Nain."

"I know the route she takes from your place to the loft. I started with that, and my father joined me. We found her car in an alley and started looking around there." I filled them in on the details of the attack, of Hades healing her.

When I'd described Shanti's wounds, I felt rage rolling off of both of them. They both wanted a piece of Strife. I could feel that very clearly.

"We're in," Rayna said. "We'll work with you. We will avenge this attack on one of our own. This will be paid for in blood."

Ronan nodded, determined. I felt shock from Nain.

I nodded back at Rayna. "I agree. And it will be repaid. We're very pleased to join forces with you."

We spent about an hour filling Rayna in on what we knew about Strife and her team. Brought her up to date on the attacks, including the way we'd been ambushed. She and Ronan both listened intently, Ronan asking questions every once in a while. We discussed how we'd coordinate our teams. By the time they left, it was clear that our group of allies had grown in size and deadliness.

That could only be a good thing.

CHAPTER FIFTEEN

Once Rayna and Ronan were gone, I was about ready to fall over, but I also knew I was too wired to sleep. Nain went into his office to talk to Jones to fill him in on everything that had happened, and I went to our room and stepped into the shower.

I was alone, and I wanted to cry, wanted to let out all of the emotions the night had caused. But I knew I couldn't do that. I didn't have the luxury of letting myself feel everything, of letting myself rage against it. Nether had been fighting me all evening, and it had been a constant battle to keep control.

I stood under the searing hot water and scrubbed myself much harder than I needed to, my stress only feeding my already-insane habit of trying to get rid of filth that wasn't there. Nether raged, and soon the stress of trying to fight her back exhausted me, and I fell to my knees in the shower.

The water rained down over me and I pressed my face up against the tiles, gritted my teeth, fighting her for control.

194

So weak, little Fury. Just give in. You have no hope of controlling me forever, she hissed at me. I shook my head, focused harder. I was trembling.

I just grow stronger, Nether taunted. *Your time is limited, godling. And you will pay for every moment you've imprisoned me.*

I groaned at the effort of trying to keep her in control. My head was pounding, aching, and I whimpered and gripped my head with my hands.

I stayed that way, trying to fight her down, trying to keep in control. I felt myself starting to black out a time or two, and fought harder. The water went from searing to ice cold by the time I felt able to stand again. This had been her worst assault on me, her strongest attempt to take control, and she'd been so close.

This wasn't a battle I could keep winning.

When I was able to stand again, I stood up and turned the water off, and I tossed on some jeans and a top. Nain wasn't in the room, and there was no way in hell I was going to let myself fall asleep now without him nearby.

I went out into the living room, which was deserted. There was a lamp on in one corner, but other than that it was dark. I went into the kitchen and made myself eat a banana. It tasted like sawdust.

Nain wasn't in his office, and I wondered where he'd gone. I heard a door open upstairs, and glanced up. E was coming out of the room she was sharing with Shanti. She came down the stairs and smiled when she saw me.

"You should be resting, demon girl," she said, coming over to me and giving me a hug. I hugged her back, and we stood there. I felt tears come to my eyes, held back a sob, everything that had happened that night hitting me as I stood in my friend's arms.

She hugged me tighter, and I felt her cool hands smoothing my hair. "It's all right, my friend. It's okay."

I tried to stop my sobs.

"Let it out, Mollis. I'm here. The demon is here. You can't hold all of this inside."

I didn't think I could hold it in if I tried, so I didn't. I let it out, and E kept smoothing my hair, whispering that it was okay, that I'd saved Shanti, that everything would be all right.

When I was able to pull myself together, I pulled back from her. "Thank you. I don't know what I would do without you, you know that?"

She grinned. "Believe me, I know. I'm irreplaceable."

"You are."

"Come on. I am in need of hot chocolate and many marshmallows."

I laughed and followed her into the kitchen. She stood at the stove, mixing up some hot cocoa, and I sat on one of the stools, watching her.

E finished making the cocoa and poured it into two of the large mugs from the cabinet above the coffee maker. She held up the bag of marshmallows and I made a face, shook my head.

"You really are a barbarian. How can one drink hot cocoa without marshmallows?" she asked, setting my mug in front of me. I laughed. She took the stool next to mine, and we sat, waiting for the cocoa to cool.

"Other than death and chaos and all of that, how are things, Mollis?" she asked quietly.

I watched her. "Things are... weirdly good. I guess. Having Nain back in my life is confusing and awesome and maddening and just everything, all at once."

She sat in silence for a few minutes, seemed a little like she wanted to say something. She kept starting, then stopping.

"What's up, E?" I asked, and she gave a small smile.

"I am sorry for what happened between the demon and I. I didn't know him when you two were together, and the only one I ever knew you with was Brennan. I watched you mourn the demon, but I never got to see the other side."

"What side is that?"

196

She smiled again. "The way you work together like a matched pair, like two beings whose hearts beat in time to one another. The way you are both aware of one another without even knowing you are paying attention. The love in his eyes every single time he looks at you." She paused again. "If I'd known all of that, I never would have come on to him the way I did."

I hid a smile. "You came on to him? Really?"

She nodded. "We broke up a fight together, and you know how very attractive he is when he's all demon ragey."

I laughed. "Yeah. I do."

"And we got home, and I just sort of blurted out that I'd never been with a man and I wanted him to show me what I was missing. Except that I said it so fast I had to repeat it at least three more times before he understood what I was saying."

I laughed, and then I laughed harder, envisioning E asking Nain to take her.

"And you convinced him, I guess?" I asked.

"I made it clear I just wanted to see what sex was like. He was having sex with anyone who'd look at him at the time. I think he thought I'd be offended if he turned me down when he'd been with so many others." She paused, met my eyes. "And I think, maybe, I reminded him of you. Creature of the Nether, glowing eyes, short and thin. All of that. When it was over, he thanked me, and he was sweet, but he looked like he was a million miles away. Likely, wherever you were." She paused. "He stopped sleeping with other women after that night."

I put my hand over hers. "You don't have anything to apologize for."

"If I'd known the depth of feeling that was still there, I never would have. I swear it. And I am so happy that the two of you found one another again. I know you're afraid. And I understand. But I also know that you're a brave woman. Be brave now, my friend."

I leaned over and hugged her, and she hugged me back. "Can I adopt you as my sister?" I asked her, and she laughed.

She got up, taking her mug with her. "Demon girl, you already did." And then she smiled again and carried her hot cocoa upstairs. I shook my head, then I got up and washed my mug. With nothing else to do, I wandered back into the living room.

I paced the loft, restless now with nothing to do, no disasters I needed to avert that moment.

I felt like I was going to go nuts just hanging around, unable to sleep. There was one place in the loft I'd always been able to relax. Well, not technically in the loft, I guess. I took the stairs up to the roof, opened the door. It wasn't until I stepped out onto the gravel surface of the roof that I felt Nain's presence, realized he'd beaten me to it. I looked around and there he was, sitting on the old metal glider, the one snow-free spot on the roof. The same place I sat whenever I came up here.

The one I'd always thought of as "our glider." The place we'd sat so often early on. The spot we were sitting the first time he told me he wanted me. He knew I was there, and for once, I had no desire to run from him.

I walked across the roof and sat beside him, leaving a little space between the two of us. He corrected that immediately, silently reaching over and pulling me closer, sliding me effortlessly across the smooth seat of the glider. He kept his arm over the back of the seat, and within moments, he was twisting a lock of my hair between his fingers, absentmindedly, just as he always had. His thigh was pressed up against mine, and, as always, I felt tiny beside him.

"We're probably the only two idiots in the entire city sitting outside right now," I said, at a loss for anything else to say.

He grunted. "It's quiet. One advantage to not being bothered by the cold." We sat in awkward silence for a little while, my stomach in knots, just being near him. I was surrounded by him; his arm draped behind me, his thigh pressed up against mine, his power and emotions roaring over me, making it feel like I was at the mercy of a hurricane. And I craved it, more than I'd ever craved anything in my life. It was comfort in the way nothing else ever had been, and I knew he felt the same around me.

"I used to come and sit here, after you died," I finally said. He stayed silent, listening. "I wasn't sleeping. At first, I wasn't eating. Wasn't talking. I couldn't make myself do it. I just didn't care. But I'd come here, and I'd sit in this spot and stare up at the sky and I'd feel closer to you even as it made me miss you more."

"I didn't know that," he said after a while. "They told me you didn't talk, refused to eat for a while. You want to hear something crazy?"

I nodded, and his fingers kept twisting my hair.

"I did the same thing after I got back. Came up here, sat in this spot, and thought about you. I thought about how bad I fucked up, lying to you at the end. I thought about how in my entire existence, no one has ever made me feel the way you do, and I destroyed that. Typical demon, right? Destroying anything good in life."

We sat in silence for a while, and the longer we did, the harder it became to breathe, the more my stomach twisted. I felt it from him, too: desire, pure, raw hunger. To his credit, he was being remarkably well behaved. Doing what I'd asked of him, giving me time.

I was starting to think I'd had enough time.

"I know why you did it," I said. "And when I'm not pissed off at you over it, I recognize it for what it was. You did whatever it took to keep me safe, and you did it because you loved me."

"Love. Not loved. There's nothing past tense about what I feel for you," he said, voice low.

I met his eyes for just a second, glanced away. The words, the serious way in which he'd said them, were exactly what I wanted. He wasn't flirting. He wasn't trying to hide his feelings behind his bad attitude or dirty jokes the way he usually did. I felt my last bit of resistance start to give way.

"I spent so much time angry at you after you died. My anger was easier to deal with than my grief, and I held on to that. Without that, I wouldn't have gotten out of bed most days. And I would have been fine with that. But I knew assholes would still be out there, causing pain, that the world wouldn't stop just because my soul was bleeding. So I started to focus on the anger instead, and I worked, and I buried my grief under everything else."

"I'm glad you did. I know how I felt when I woke up in the Nether and felt our connection ripped away. I wanted to die again, rather than keep feeling that. But I knew that I couldn't make my way back to you if I just crawled into a corner and waited to die," he said. I put my hand on his thigh, rested my head against his chest, and he stopped toying with my hair, lowered his arm and wrapped it around me.

"I'm even glad you had Brennan, as much as I want to kill him every time I think about you in his arms," Nain said after a while.

"I learned a lot about myself when I was with him. I don't regret any of it, really, even with the way it all ended. I was kind of stupid. I wanted to believe everything was perfect, when I knew better. I mean, the Puppeteer had said it all, everything I already knew--"

"What?" he asked.

"That night with the Puppeteer," I said, glancing over at him.

"You told me the two of you killed the Puppeteer together. You never told me anything else, and I always had a feeling there was something you were hiding from me that night."

Oh. Right. I'd kept the whole Puppeteer incident a secret from Nain. "She got into his head. Used him against me. I ended up having to fight Brennan off, under her control, before I killed her."

"And what did she say about what was in his head?"

"That he wanted me. Which I knew. That he was really angry with me for choosing you instead. That like many shifters, he was prideful and the way I'd turned him down over and over again made him feel anger and contempt for me, even as he wanted me."

His anger washed over me. "You knew that was in him, and you ended up with him anyway?"

I glared at him. "Don't even, demon. We worked our way through it. He was there for me during the worst time of my life. He was the only comfort I had. And he loved me and he wanted me. And maybe I'm fucking weak, but I needed it." I paused, took a steadying breath. "But it never was as perfect as I tried to believe it was. Right? I mean, if it had been, he wouldn't have been tempted away. He wouldn't have gotten pissed off at me when I tried to tell him what I needed. When things were good, we were amazing. When things got a little out of the range of normal…" I shrugged.

"Speaking of which, I think we need to get something straight."

I smiled. "Yeah? What is that?"

"Did you really mean it when you said you believed we would have broken up eventually? That we would have hated each other?"

I remembered. We'd talked about it, after I'd gotten home from the Nether. Made jokes about how we were a terrible match. I snuggled closer to him. "Mostly, I was still pissed off at you. And for a little while, anyway, I was determined to make it work with Brennan, and telling myself that we were never meant to be was part of that." I paused. "And you're not the same, and neither am I."

We sat in silence for a few moments. I took a deep breath. There was something I needed to say, something I knew he needed to hear. And I was finally ready to say it.

"Like you said. I was still wearing your ring when I died. I never took it off. Brennan and I were on borrowed time the second we realized you were alive. And if you hadn't died... if I'd had any idea at all that you were alive somewhere out there, Brennan and I never would have happened."

He held me tighter, and I pressed my face against his chest, soothed by his presence, his touch.

"You're very different in some ways," Nain finally said, running his hand up and down my waist as he held me. "You're more confident. Tougher, which I wouldn't have thought possible. Calmer. Less trusting, though, too."

"More afraid than I used to be," I said softly.

"And what scares you, baby?"

"You do," I whispered.

"Yeah?"

I nodded.

"Why?"

"Because you're making me feel things I really didn't want to feel again. And when we're together, it feels right and that scares the shit out of me. I'm going to end up hurting you again. And we're going to lose each other, and I don't think I can take another heartbreak," I finished in a whisper.

He reached up, tilted my chin up toward him, forcing me to meet his eyes. "You think I scare you? I'm fucking terrified of what you do to me. You make me need, and that's something I've never done, not this way."

I reached up and pulled him down for a kiss. The need coming off of him was only making me want him more than I already did, and I couldn't get close enough to him. He held me pressed tight to his body, then he buried his hands in my hair, holding me close to him as he devoured my mouth. My hands gripped his biceps.

His hands had just started making their way beneath my top when someone cleared their throat behind us. Nain pulled away from me, irritation, hunger rolling off of him. We both turned around. Stone was standing near the door.

"Uh. Sorry," he said, genuinely embarrassed. "There's a call for you, boss. Jones."

"Oh. Right," Nain said. He stood up, pulled me up with him. Stone turned and went back inside, and Nain bent down, kissed me again. "I have to take this."

"Okay." I kissed him again, nibbled his lower lip before I broke away. "Do you need me for anything?"

He smirked down at me. "I need you for plenty of things."

I rolled my eyes. "One track mind."

"Like that's news." I pulled away, held his hand as we walked into the loft. He put his hand behind my neck, pulled me in for one more kiss before heading into his office. I watched him walk away from me, appreciating his broad shoulders, the way his ass filled out his jeans. I took a deep breath, shaking my head in admiration.

I sat down in his chair in the living room, intending to wait for him. First, my mind was on him, on the feel of his lips on mine. And, more, the way he'd been there for me, supported me through all the crazy shit that had happened in the past few weeks. And that made my thoughts turn to Shanti, to the way she'd looked when we'd first found her, and I tried to shut the vision away. My mind wandered again, to the increasing amount of fighting between supernaturals, but I really didn't want to think too much about that either.

I was exhausted, but I didn't want to sleep. My mental state was just right for Nether to force her way through. My eyelids started getting heavy, and I forced them open, stared at the television. For the most part, there was nothing on but late night infomercials.

Nain's office door opened a while later, and he came over to me.

He knelt down in front of me.

"You're exhausted," he said quietly, and I nodded. He stood up and pulled me up with him. "Come on. Get some sleep."

"You're just as tired as I am," I started to argue.

"Well. I'll just have to hold on to you while we sleep then, so I know if anything's happening," he said as he steered me into his room. I didn't bother arguing with him. Since our talk in his truck after my house had been bombed, he'd been attentive without being overly demanding (I mean, he was still a little demanding. This was Nain we were talking about) and when I'd needed to sleep, he'd stayed awake, sitting up on his side of the bed, reading. He'd planned for those nights, making sure he'd slept late or napped so that I'd have plenty of time to sleep. We had a kind of rhythm worked out, but the whole Shanti situation had taken its toll, and I could feel that he was just as tired as I was.

"Any excuse, huh demon?" I asked as I started pushing my jeans down.

"Pretty much."

I glanced up and he was watching me as I lifted the sweater I was wearing over my head, down to panties and a tank top now.

"We really need a vacation," he growled, hunger coursing through him as he looked at me. "It is a fucking crime that I have you in my bed all the time and all we do is sleep there."

I blushed, shook my head. "You're giving me time, remember?"

He pulled off his shirt, which did nothing to calm the way my body was responding to the situation. Nain in nothing but boxers is one of those images that pops into my head at very inconvenient times. Seeing him standing across the room like that was enough to start making me reconsider how tired I actually was.

"I'm giving you time," he said. "And you are going to reward me for my exemplary behavior someday."

"Exemplary?" I asked, crawling into bed. "I think that's stretching it a bit, don't you?"

He turned off the lamp, and as soon as we were both in bed, he pulled me close to him, his hand on my hip, his body just a fraction of an inch from touching mine.

"Considering what I want to be doing to you right now, I'm being a fucking saint," he said, giving my hip a rough squeeze.

We lay there in silence for a while, his hand heavy on my hip, his breath warming the back of my neck.

"Nain," I said softly, knowing he was still awake.

"Hm?"

"There's nothing past tense about what I feel for you, either."

He rubbed my hip, dipped his head and pressed a warm kiss to my bare shoulder. I shivered, and he kissed the side of my neck.

"It always did amaze me, how sweet you are when it's just the two of us," he said against my neck. "You are so warm. So giving. I never expected that. When I fell for you, I fell for the hard, cold, strong woman I knew."

"And then?"

"And then I started seeing more. I started seeing how kind you are. How good you are. How you would do anything for the people you love, and just as much for those you don't even know. And that was when I was lost. That was when you took a part of me, and I'll never get it back," he said.

It was hard to breathe. I knew Nain had this ability to be sweet. The letters he'd written me had showed another side of him, one I hadn't seen much of in the short time we'd been together. Now, with time and a lot of insanity behind us, he was letting me see him. And he was freaking irresistible. "You're going to ruin my rep as a badass, saying shit like that," I finally said. He squeezed my hip again, pressed his lips to my shoulder.

"Your secret's safe with me. *You* are safe with me," he said.

"We'll see," I said, wanting to believe him. Wanting to take that final step, back where I knew I belonged.

"Take your time, then. I'm not going anywhere."

I put my hand over his on my hip, and we twined our fingers together. I fell asleep, and when I dreamed, I dreamed of the demon beside me.

"Molls, wake up." Nain's voice, his hand shaking my hip. I rolled over and looked at him. He was standing beside the bed, pulling on a shirt.

"What's going on?" I asked, pushing the covers off of me.

"Shit just went crazy out there. There are fights breaking out all over the city. Strife's people are attacking in broad daylight."

I stared at him, and he pointed toward the television. It was showing a live news report of fighting in a neighborhood I knew well, East English Village. I could see shifters, demons, in their true forms, just destroying shit. It looked like there were other shifters fighting against them, and I glanced toward Nain.

"Brennan got the shifter coalition moving on it as soon as we started hearing about any weirdness."

I got out of bed and grabbed a pair of jeans and a black top out of my dresser, went into the bathroom and got dressed. I came out, braiding my hair, to find Nain on the phone. I pulled my shoes on and we left the loft, heading down the elevator toward his truck.

He hung up. "Jones. Shit is crazy in East English Village, Hamtramck, Mexicantown, and Delray. He says Delray is the worst of it right now."

"So that's where we're going,"I said, and he nodded. "I could just rematerialize us there."

He shook his head. "Save it. We might need all your scary powers later. And I don't want you in pain."

"I wonder if this is organized or just the effect of her prolonged influence here," I said. "I mean, I know the thing with Shanti last night was her. She planned that and taunted me with it. That's what she does here. That's her whole thing, trying to get back at me for Ares and Enyo."

"Yeah, but didn't you say that chaos adds to her power, the same way fear added to Terror's power?" he asked as he maneuvered the truck through the streets. It was eerily empty; smart people had decided to stay off the streets today. Good thinking.

"Yes." I glanced over at him. "So you don't think this is random."

He took a deep breath. "I know I'm a suspicious, crusty old man, but this feels like a set up. Maybe she's trying to get herself all powered up to come at you."

I remembered Tisiphone predicting that it would probably happen that way. "So she's probably going to make her move against me soon."

"I'd bet money on it. Plus word probably got back to her that she didn't succeed in killing Shanti. That probably pissed her off."

I nodded.

He pulled up to a red light and looked over at me. His eyes met mine. "This is going to be bad. They're putting us out in the open. They're attacking whoever the hell they want."

"We'll just have to be badder than them," I said, and he reached over and took my hand.

"We're pretty good at that," he said as he started driving again.

When we reached Delray, it was obvious that there was a whole lot wrong. The Delray neighborhood was one of those places that had once been a bustling neighborhood, and then had been slowly but surely destroyed by the mess and stink that comes with manufacturing plants. It was destroyed even more over the possibility of a second bridge to Canada that would have seen most of the buildings bought up and demolished. The bridge issue just kind of lingered for a long time, and in the meantime, no one wanted to risk buying a home or business in a place where the neighborhood would cease to exist if the bridge happened. It was usually like a ghost town.

We parked the truck on Fort Street and got out. We could hear screams. Buildings were on fire. About a block down, we saw a group of demons facing off against some of our shifters. We stalked toward the group. Nain reached over and pulled me close, kissed me hard on the lips.

"Be careful," he murmured.

"Always," I said, and I felt a little humor from him mixed in with all the anger and excitement.

Yes, excitement. We enjoy battle. As much as we hate it, as much as we hate that it causes pain to people and makes a mess… battle is one of those things that gets our hearts pumping. Nain and I had always been the same in that way.

We dove into the fight and I lost all track of time as Strife's people just kept coming at us. We got it mostly under control, and Stone and a few shifters showed up to take our place and tell us we were needed in Hamtramck, which had gotten progressively worse as the day had gone on.

"My way," I said to Nain, taking his hand. I focused on a street I knew well in Hamtramck, and a few seconds later, we rematerialized there.

Right in the middle of a huge freaking fight between the vampires who'd joined the fight as night fell and our own people. E was there, using her daggers against as many vampires as she could.

The neighborhood burned. DFD couldn't even get in to put the fires out if they'd wanted to.

"E," I shouted.

"Yes, demon girl," she answered, stabbing a vampire in the throat.

"Can you go tell my parents their baby girl would really appreciate their fucking help right now?"

She laughed, stabbed the vampire again.

"Should I use those words exactly?"

"Yes." I kept fighting, noting that she'd disappeared. I hoped they'd come. This was beyond out of control. We'd been fighting since a little after eight o'clock that morning, and it seemed like the supernaturals who were hell-bent on starting trouble just kept coming. Their numbers seemed almost limitless.

I fought, my arms starting to ache with the constant swinging of my sword. I wanted to use my powers, but I knew that the way they weakened me would only make trouble for me in these conditions. Nether was raging, excited by all of the violence, and there was not a chance in hell I was giving her a chance to take control.

So I'd just have to kick ass the old-fashioned way, and be extremely annoyed by just how many enemies we had.

I mean, it was clear we had them. We all knew that. We knew that those of us who tried to keep things in control were in the minority in the supernatural community. Most supernaturals didn't care one way or another how things fell. And those who wanted to take whatever they wanted, whenever they wanted, had always outnumbered us. It was just kind of shocking to see them all at once, working together instead of alone or in small groups. They generally didn't trust one another, constantly fighting for dominance.

Fucking Strife.

That was my most common thought as I cut my way through the group that was attacking this particular neighborhood of bungalows and mature oak trees. I could see Nain a few houses down, fighting his own group of vampires.

I felt E return, and she started fighting back to back with me.

"Do you want the good news first or the bad news?"

"Good news," I muttered, slicing out at a werewolf.

"Your parents are fine. They are keeping busy."

"Okay. Bad news?"

"They're busy fighting to keep the Titans in Tartarus. They can't come."

I cursed.

"But they send their regards and say they'll see you as soon as they possibly can."

I grunted, swung the sword again. My arms felt like jelly. "Why does everything have to go insane at once?" I complained. "The universe couldn't have scheduled this shit out better? 'Okay, Detroit becomes a war zone on the twenty-fifth of November. The Titans try to escape on December eleventh.' See? How hard is it really?" I muttered.

E laughed as she kicked out at a vampire. "You'll have to fill out one of those suggestion forms I keep hearing about."

I shook my head and kept fighting. It was all I could do. We were outnumbered and very much on our own.

CHAPTER SIXTEEN

I was taking a breather, hunkered down in one of the houses we were using as a base of operations. It had been abandoned long ago, and you could see daylight through the roof, but there was food and water stored inside, and several witches were administering first aid. I was holding a compress against a nasty wound a shifter had taken, waiting for the witch to help him, when I saw Jones come into the house. He looked around, then walked toward me.

"How are you holding up?" he asked me.

"I'm okay. This is insane."

He nodded. The witch came over and thanked me for my help. Then she went to work cleaning and stitching him up, and Jones and I wandered away. I slugged back most of a bottle of water, and Jones grabbed a small bag of pretzels.

"I need to talk to you for a minute," he said, and I nodded. He gestured toward the back porch, and I followed him. You could still hear sirens. The occasional booms and crashes. Screams and shouts. I glanced at Jones, and he was watching me.

"Things are a mess, Angel," he said. He rested his hands on the rickety railing and stared out at nothing. "Times are changing."

"We're not hidden anymore," I said. "There is no pretending we don't exist."

"Exactly," he said, nodding. "The thing is, we weren't all that secret to begin with. The government has apparently known we exist for a long time now."

I watched him. "Seriously?"

He nodded, and I felt nervousness from him. This entire thing had freaked all of us out. We'd been used to a certain way of life, to living in the shadows. And because of Strife and the chaos she'd stirred up, we were out in the open. It was terrifying for us, and I could only imagine that it was even more upsetting for the Normals, who now had to face the fact that there were powerful beings out there. And that some of those powerful beings were just fine with hurting them.

"I was approached this morning by an agent. Department of Homeland Security," he said, meeting my eyes.

"What did he want?"

He took a breath. "He wanted me to talk to you. He knows we know one another. Knows we work together."

"How do they know that?"

"That's what I asked him. He got all shifty on me. All he said is they know about Nain's team. Your team. The shifter coalition. All of it. And they're particularly interested in you."

"Why?"

"Probably for the same reason just about everyone is. You've got a certain amount of fame here in the city. People believe in you. Pray to you."

"Which is nuts," I muttered.

"I don't think it's a bad way to go, for what it's worth. You might not consider yourself a god, but I'd bet everything I have on you saving the day. And there are a whole lot of people in this city, supernatural or not, who feel the same way."

"I was getting the feeling I made you nervous," I said.

"You do. But that doesn't mean I don't believe in you."

"So what did they want you to talk to me about?"

He was silent a minute. "They want you to be the face of supernaturals here in the city. They want you to do a presser, talk to the people. Reassure them to try to contain the chaos."

"They want me to give a speech?" I asked in disbelief.

He laughed a little. "Yeah. I think they want it to be a regular thing, at least until things calm down."

"Hell, no," I said, crossing my arms. "Not a chance in hell."

"I think it would help, Angel," he said, meeting my eyes again. "I think you could do some good here."

"Did they tell you to say that?"

"They wanted me to ask you. And I did what they wanted. I'm telling you now what I feel, and think you're exactly what this city needs right now. You always have been."

"Oh, please," I said.

"You gave people something to believe in. Do you have any idea how it feels to feel powerless, and then to find out there's someone out there who will stop at nothing to kick ass on your behalf? Those who believe in you, those who are alive today because you saved them… they feel that way about you. My daughter feels that way about you. And for what it's worth, I do, too."

I didn't know what to say. "I'm not a hero. I'm just a nutcase who runs into trouble instead of running away from it. And I don't think weird, awkward me would reassure anyone."

He shook his head. "We need something here, Angel. It can't keep on this way. There are people getting hurt."

"And I'll do what I do best. I'll go out there and try to protect them. From the shadows, the way I always have. This isn't a comic book, chief."

"No. This is real, and so are you. You say you love this city? Prove it."

I glared at him. "I do. Every single day of my life. I want to know how they know so much about us. Can you try to find out?"

He nodded. "At least consider it, Molly."

"Maybe when hell freezes over," I said. Then I turned and went back into the house, prepared myself to enter the fray again.

It seemed like for every fight I put an end to, two more started in its place. And it wasn't just supernaturals anymore. Our insanity had stirred the Normals, and now there were non-superpowered idiots out in the streets fighting and looting and adding to the chaos.

Strife must have been freaking nauseous with power. This is what feeds her. And the stronger she gets, the more chaos she causes, and that sure the hell was what was happening.

The teams were spread out in a few key areas. Nain and I were near Hamtramck, where the fighting had started in the first place and which was still freaking insane. Brennan and a team of shifters were near the Grosse Pointe border. Rayna's people, including Shanti, were near Mexicantown. Stone, Heph, and Levitt were trying to get the Delray neighborhood under control.

I fought.

I lost track of time. All I knew was that morning gave way to the brightness of afternoon, and eventually that waned to darkness again. It got to the point where the supernaturals who were causing trouble in Hamtramck started running from me and Nain.

We didn't let them get far.

After the fighting, things in the area Nain and I were focusing on were eerily calm. We started checking the fallen to see if they could be saved. Too many Normals had been caught in the crossfire, had been targeted by Strife's people in the hopes of drawing me out. And it had worked, but each and every injury they'd sustained added to my guilt, to my determination to find her. I had every single imp in my command looking for her non-stop. I called in favors from witches who were adept at performing location spells, though with only a description of her to guide them, there wasn't much hope there. I had to try.

As Nain and I checked the injured, people started coming out of their houses. At first, I was worried they would attack us next, angry with us for what had happened.

An older lady in a colorful hijab came out of one of the nearby houses bearing a first aid kit and water. Down the street, a young couple came out with blankets. Within five minutes, several people had opened locked doors and come out bearing supplies, or simply offering assistance.

"Where do you need us, Angel?" the older woman asked.

I started directing them to the survivors. One of the men started boarding up windows that had been broken in the skirmish.

"Two days. I thought it would never end," one of the young women said to an older neighbor.

"Would have been so much worse without these two protecting us," the man said, gesturing toward Nain and I. Nain was carrying an elderly man back into his house, and I was holding the door open for them.

There were still three bodies lying in the street. Three people who had lost their lives because of Strife.

"What were their names?" I asked the elderly woman as she bandaged up one of her neighbors.

"That young man there is Jason. He just moved here a while ago. The older white man over there? That's Arnold Sawicki. He has been my neighbor for over twenty years. And the woman next to him is his wife, Maggie."

I memorized the names. I wouldn't forget.

I heard a distinctive "crack" nearby; an immortal appearing. I was on guard immediately, and then I realized it was Heph. He walked out from between two houses, and I had to respect the man's smarts. Appearing in the middle of the street would have only freaked these people out more.

"Queenie," he said in greeting, and the Normals helping us stared at the huge man.

"Heph. How are you holding up?"

"I'm okay. Got a status report for you."

"All right," I said, bracing myself.

"We got all areas under control. Fights are still springing up here and there, but it feels like the worst of it is behind us. Delray, East English Village, and Mexicantown are all secured. The team is still canvassing the city, going wherever Jones is getting reports of trouble starting up."

I nodded. "Losses?"

He shook his head. "We're all alive and accounted for. A few human losses, and Jones is handling those."

"I have three here as well," I said.

"I'll call it in. I think he was on his way back here anyway."

I nodded.

"The good thing though, Queenie," he began, and I looked up at him.

"Yeah?"

He grinned. "We took out a whole lot of assholes today who won't be causing anymore trouble around here. It's something."

The group of Normals around us started clapping, and I smiled up at Heph.

"We've all had rest breaks here and there. You and the d—, Nain," he amended, aware of our audience, "haven't had a break since it all started. We got this. Go home and get some rest."

"We can still help," I said and Nain came up behind me and put a hand on my waist.

"I'm about to fall over, and you are too. We can rest for a little while." Then he looked up at Heph. "You'll call us if anything comes up."

"Of course. She'd kick my ass if I didn't."

I smiled and shook my head. "Fine." Nether had been raging, and it had only gotten worse the more tired I got. Sleep probably wouldn't be a bad idea, especially if I had Nain by my side. I hugged Heph, and Nain shook his hand, and then the Normals started coming up to us, thanking us and shaking our hands. I promised I'd be back if there was trouble, and then I took Nain's hand and led him down an alley, and I focused and seconds later, we were back in the loft while our team worked to keep the city under control.

Nain led me into his room, and he closed and locked the door behind us. I flipped on the TV.

"I don't want to watch that shit, baby. We've been living it," he said as he pulled his t-shirt off.

"I want to know right away if anything changes," I said, watching the screen. "You can shower first and then I want to look at those bites."

He came up behind me and rested his hands on my shoulders as I watched the screen. He pressed his lips to the side of my neck and I took one of his hands in mine and kissed his knuckles. He gave me one more squeeze, then turned and went into the bathroom. I sat on the edge of the bed and watched the news. Most of it at this point was the newspeople bringing in "experts" to talk about what was happening. Jones had been on earlier, and now they were showing the clip of him again, saying the DPD was working on it, and that the Angel was also working to contain the chaos.

I could have killed him for dragging my name into it. There wasn't anything I could do about it now.

A few minutes later, I heard the shower turn off, and Nain moving around in the bathroom. He opened the door, and when he did, I went in to look at his injuries. He was standing at the sink, where he'd just finished brushing his teeth. I looked at him and tried to settle myself down. How could I be this horny when we'd been fighting for the last forty-eight hours straight? He looked mouthwatering. Pajama pants sitting low on his hips, bare chest, still slightly damp from his shower. His shoulders alone were enough to make me need a cold shower.

I forced my mind out of the gutter and walked up behind him, looking at the injuries he'd gotten in our most recent fight.

"These bites look bad," I said, dabbing some antiseptic ointment on a gauze pad. Anyone else would have flinched when I started rubbing it on, but he stayed completely still. I looked up and he was watching me in the mirror, sapphire gaze tracking my every move.

"Afraid I'm gonna get rabies?" he asked, and I laughed a little. I kept working, knowing he was watching me. The feel of his cool skin under my fingertips, his broad back and shoulders inches from my lips made it nearly impossible to concentrate.

I worked on him carefully, not wanting to hurt him. I glanced up again and he was still watching me.

I focused on him. On being gentle. I let my fingers wander over the many pale scars across his shoulders and sides, the results of past battles. That was only three years' worth, since he'd been back from the Nether.

I ran my hands down his back and his muscles jumped beneath my touch. The raw need coming from him was making it hard to breathe, hard not to beg him to do what we both wanted. The only thing holding me back at the moment was the knowledge that he'd been fighting for nearly two days straight, and I could feel how tired he was.

Though I had a feeling he would have been up for a little more action.

I pressed my cheek to his bare back, stood there pressed against him. It was soothing, and I needed it after the insanity of the last two days. And the two of us were both safe and alive for the time being, and he loved me and I'd made my way back to him.

I pulled back from him and looked at him again in the mirror. His hands were gripping the sides of the sink so hard I thought he'd crack it. Being touched by me, cared for by me was just as intense for him as it had been for me. He'd been touched by my tenderness as I cared for him. It wasn't something he was used to. Wasn't something he expected, and he would have hated for anyone else to take care of him in any way. But tenderness from me was something that made him feel good. I pressed a gentle kiss to the center of his back, and I felt a tremor go through him when I did it.

The idea that I could affect this powerful, dangerous man as much as I did still amazed me.

And he was keeping himself under control. Not touching me, not even moving. Giving me time, because I'd asked him to.

I pressed another kiss to his back. "Go to sleep before you fall over," I said, and he turned around and pressed a quick, hard kiss to my lips. I closed the door behind him and shook my head.

As I showered, I ran through everything that had happened the past two days. The insanity of the fighting, the fact that my parents weren't around to help. The way they just kept coming as soon as we fought one group back. It was insane.

And yet. I was happier than I'd been in a very long time.

I've never said I was a normal person.

I finished up and pulled on panties and a sleep tank and dried my hair. When I went back into the bedroom, Nain was sprawled out on his side of the bed, snoring quietly. I smiled to myself and shook my head, then I turned the television and lamp off and climbed into bed next to him. I turned on to my side, watching him. The rise and fall of his chest, the way he looked like he wanted to kick ass, even as he slept. He had one arm thrown up over his head, another resting on his stomach. I curled into his side and let myself drift off to sleep.

At some point during the night, my usual Nether nightmares woke me up, and I jumped, sat up in a panic. Then I remembered where I was. I was safe. I was alive. Not trapped. I couldn't suffocate and die again.

Nain reached over and took my hand. He was used to these nightmares already, just in the short time we'd been sharing a bed again. I settled back into bed, facing him.

"Sorry," I said softly.

"Don't be," he answered. Love, worry from him. Anger, that it still haunted me. A whole lot of raw need, picking up right where we'd left off before he'd fallen asleep.

That, I could do something about.

I reached out and trailed my fingertips down his chest, down his stomach. Felt his muscles jump beneath my touch, his need only heightening when I touched him. I kept my eyes on his, and he was watching me so intently I couldn't have looked away if I'd wanted to.

I lowered my hand, sweeping my palm over the front of his pajama pants, where he was already hard, straining against the fabric. He fisted the sheets in his hands as I touched him. I felt the raw desire flowing from him, the hunger. The desire to hold me down and take what he wanted.

Instead, he was doing what he'd promised me. Giving me time. Waiting until I said I was ready.

And I so definitely was.

How tired are you now? I asked him.

He grinned. *Not too tired for what you're thinking about.*

Prove it.

He stood up and pulled his pajama pants off, and the sight of my husband's body illuminated by nothing but the pale moonlight outside nearly had me crying with need.

Holy shit. It was better than I remembered. Huge, everywhere. Muscles to spare. A light bit of dark hair across his chest, leading down to his navel, down further. I was kneeling on the bed, and he was standing in front of me. He leaned down, kissed me.

"We've got a whole lot of time to make up for," he murmured against my lips.

I nodded, and he lowered himself to the bed, kissed me, our tongues tasting one another's mouths, my hands running along his huge shoulders as he pushed me back onto the pillows, crawled into bed after me. Soon, he was kissing, licking, biting, touching me everywhere, ravishing me in a way only he could. The tank and panties I was wearing didn't last long, ripped from my body as if they'd been made of tissue paper. I whimpered and moaned as he reminded me how it felt to be with him, when he was barely in control, when his demon was unleashed. The mixture of pleasure and exquisite pain he caused me, the way I begged him to do more. And I was no different. My fingernails scratched his back, and I bit his neck, his shoulders. The first time I did it, he let out a wild, animalistic growl.

"Do that again," he said in a rough voice, and I did, and that was when he spread my thighs open and entered me in one long, hard thrust. The second he entered me, we both groaned in pleasure. Relief. It felt like coming home again, like being exactly where you know you belong.

He pressed himself deep inside me, and I cried out, the sensation of being filled by him almost too much to handle. Everything after that was kissing and low, rough

221

curses, biting and sucking, and my body moving helplessly beneath his as he took what he wanted from me. Soon, he was thrusting into me so hard my hips were coming off of the mattress, his hands clasped with mine, pinning me down. He was terrifying when he was like that, totally in control of me, hulking, eyes gleaming, mad with lust, and it turned me on more, feeding my own demon.

"Who do you belong to?" he growled.

"You," I panted. Aching. Aching in places I'd forgotten I could ache, and wanting more. He thrust into me, hard.

"Say it again."

"I'm yours," I whimpered.

Another deep, hard thrust. "For how long?"

"Forever," I said, looking into his eyes.

"And who do I belong to?" he asked.

"You're mine," I said, meeting his eyes.

"Glad we finally understand one another," he said as he started moving again, harder, faster, his hands now gripping my hips. I whimpered, moaned, cried his name over and over again as I lost control, lost any semblance of sanity, his demon feeding mine as he reminded me how good it was, how frightening and dirty and addictive he could be. When I felt him explode inside me, I went right over the edge with him.

When he was finally spent, he stayed on top of me, our bodies still joined. We were both breathing hard, sweating. I trembled beneath him, exhausted in every way by the experience. I reveled in the sensation of being crushed by three hundred pounds of cool, muscled demon, of the feel of his hands in my hair, his lips on mine. Of the delicious way my body ached from the things he'd done to me. He kissed his way down my jaw, my throat, and ended up nuzzling my neck. We stayed like that a long time, and I never wanted to be anywhere else, ever again.

He rested his forehead against mine. "I love you, Molly," he said in a hoarse voice. "I swear to whatever god you want me to that I am gonna spend the rest of my life showing you how much. Remember that when I inevitably fuck up."

I smiled and rubbed his back, feeling the long scratches I'd left with my fingernails. "I will. Remember the same thing with me." Then I wrapped my arms around him. He stayed on top of me, our bodies joined, and I whispered how much I loved him.

"I know you wanted to take this slow," he murmured against my throat.

"We both know where this is going. I'm tired of being without my husband," I said softly. "I just want you."

He stilled, and I felt happiness, possessiveness flowing from him. "It feels like I've waited an eternity to hear you say that."

"I love you, Bael," I said, reaching up and bringing his face back down to mine, kissing him, nibbling his lips and feeling desire roar through him again.

"I love you too." And then he released me, rolled off of me, and I missed the sensation of being filled by him. He was rooting around in the nightstand drawer on his side, and I turned over and watched him.

He found what he was looking for, and he settled back into the bed, facing me. He opened his hand, and in his palm was the wedding band that matched his, the smaller of the set. Mine.

"We can do the bonding ritual another time. When we can enjoy it and everything isn't chaos around us. But this is a pretty good start, right?"

I was on the verge of crying. "Yes," I whispered, and I felt so much happiness from him it nearly broke me. How in the hell could someone like me make anyone this happy?

He took my hand, and placed the ring slowly on my finger, back where it belonged. I looked at our hands, then I smiled up into his face. He was watching me, staring at me as if I was the most fascinating thing he'd ever seen.

I started kissing his jaw, letting the coarse stubble there abrade my lips.

"I love you, my husband," I whispered to him. "You are my soul. You are the other half of me. If you ever fucking hide anything like your Astaroth plan again I will kick your demonic ass and you will never, ever get laid again."

He laughed, squeezed me tighter against him. "I love you too, wife." He was smiling, a rare, pure, open smile on his face. "But we both know you won't keep to that threat of never sleeping with me again. You like it too much."

I kissed him, nibbled his lower lip, sucked it between my teeth, and he groaned. "I wasn't kidding, Nain," I said when I finally released his lip.

"I know you weren't. Point taken. As long as you understand the same thing."

"Fine."

He kissed me again, and I turned over so we could fall asleep the way we liked best, his chest pressed to my back.

"Better now?" he asked, his breath tickling my ear.

"Yes," I whispered, smiling as my eyelids started to droop.

"Good. Rest now, baby."

I didn't think I'd fall asleep, not with his thigh pressed between mine, not with his hands each cupping a breast, not with my very naked husband pressed up against me. But I did, and I slept more soundly than I had in years.

CHAPTER SEVENTEEN

When I woke up, it was the way it was in so many of my dreams, so many of my memories of him. We were in his bed, bare skin to bare skin, his front to my back, my wings stretched forward. His leg was between my thighs, tangling with my legs beneath the cool white sheets. I laid there, reveling in the feel of waking up next to him, marveling over the way my body still ached, hours after he'd finished with me. I smiled, shook my head, remembering the things the man snoring beside me had done to me the night before. The things he'd said to me. The way he'd woken up again a while later and we'd driven each other insane all over again, his eyes glowing red in the darkness as we loved each other. I'd done things for him, let him do things to me I never would have even imagined. And I hadn't given them a second thought, fulfilling my need to please my husband, just as I knew he needed to please me to feel whole.

Demons: taking possessiveness to new levels. And I was no less possessive than he was. I understood that about myself now, better than I ever had

I closed my eyes and just tried to enjoy these moments of peace, knowing that, living the life we lived, they were few and precious. I turned over in his arms, trying not to wake him. I settled in again, looked him over as he slept. Strong, bare chest, shoulders, complete with scratches from my fingernails, bite marks I'd left the night before, because he liked it. The large black tattoos he'd had when we'd first met were gone; when he'd been reborn in the Nether, his body was remade, unmarked, the same way mine had. Dark hair, dark stubble on his cheeks and chin.

Damn. What was he doing to me? How could I even be thinking of going down this road again?

I knew him. There was no turning back now. There wasn't a chance in hell he'd let me walk away from him. There never had been. Not really. And I didn't want to. By his side was where I wanted to be, but I was afraid. We were like two fireflies in the night, always aware of one another, always circling each other, somehow coming back, meeting again, no matter what else was happening around us. The ache in my body, the ring on my finger, both signs that we were back, and I was afraid of it ending too soon, the way it had the first time. If I lost him again, there would be no coming back.

"Stop thinking," he murmured, running his hand lazily over my hip. His eyes were still closed.

"Could you hear me?" I asked, running my hand over his shoulder, down his arm.

"No. But I know you. Fifty bucks says it was something like 'I can't believe we did that, this is gonna turn out bad I just know it but goddamn that was the best fuck of my life,'" he said in a slightly higher-pitched voice, a very bad imitation of me.

"Not that you're too cocky or anything like that."

He opened his eyes, raised his eyebrow as he looked at me. "I seem to remember you begging for my--"

"Shut up, Nain," I said, grinning. I ran my fingernails down his stomach, earning a groan, a rough squeeze of my waist.

"You trying to start something?"

"Maybe," I said, leaning forward and kissing his chest.

He was watching me, and he ran his fingers through my hair. He was content. As relaxed as I'd ever seen him. And he seemed to be happy doing nothing more than just looking at me, as if the sight of me in his arms was the best thing on Earth.

Maybe it was. I knew I couldn't get enough of the sight of him, the smell of him. Running my hands over his broad shoulders, his arms, his back was something I'd never get tired of. I loved the trail of dark hair down his stomach, the muscled "v" of his abdomen. His strong jaw, those sapphire eyes with their long black lashes. I felt like I could spend eternity just staring at him, and it still wouldn't be enough.

"I think I love you even more now than I did before," I said softly as he pressed a row of kisses along my shoulder.

"I didn't think it was possible, but I know I love you more," he said, kissing my collarbone. "There's less bullshit between us now."

"We had to fight hard to get here," I said.

"We did." He kissed his way up my throat. "Every second of the fight was worth it. Every moment in hell, every second I had to miss you. Every bit of it was worth it for this moment."

I was on the verge of tears, and he just kept kissing me, loving me. "It hurt when you died," I said.

"Still worth it," he murmured against my neck. "I'd die a hundred times if it meant I'd have you with me again. There is nothing in this world that could keep me away from you now."

"I can't lose you again," I whispered.

He cupped my face in his hands, met my eyes, and the intensity in his gaze took my breath away. "You are never,

ever getting rid of me, Molly. I'll destroy the whole fucking world before I'd let anything come between us again. I am not going anywhere."

"I'd chase you through hell if I had to. I'd use every scary power I have to keep you safe and with me," I told him, and the pride that roared over me, from him, was overwhelming. "You're mine, Bael."

"From the moment I laid eyes on you, woman," he said, kissing my temple, then my cheek, my earlobe. "I knew I'd never want anyone else. It took you longer to want me."

"It did."

"And once you finally did, I knew I'd do anything to keep you safe. Even if it meant losing you."

"And now we know I'm unkillable."

"And nothing is coming between us again. I promise, Mollis Eth-Hades," he said, his voice low, intimate.

We stayed like that a while longer, in each other's arms, both of us knowing the moment had to end because we were still needed, both of us grateful that neither of our phones had rung yet. We showered and got dressed, and, cheesy as it was, getting ready with him again in the morning made me happy.

"What are you smiling about now?" he asked when he caught sight of me in the mirror over the dresser.

"What do you think?" I finished pulling on my jeans and grabbed my brush, started working it through the tangles.

He smiled and leaned down and kissed me on his way back into the bathroom to shave. I turned the television back on. Not much had changed from the night before. There were still random battles raging, and people were starting to ask stupid questions like "why doesn't the SWAT team just shoot them" and "why not just use tear gas?"

Simple answer: because you can't look at us and tell who the good guys are and who the bad guys are. The good guys aren't wearing uniforms.

Hm. Maybe we should be, I thought to myself. Not for ourselves, but so people know we're trustworthy. Something to think about later.

As I was finishing braiding my hair, I felt my mother's power signature nearby. Nain felt it too, and he glanced toward me.

"Your mom will be happy. She likes me, you know," he said.

"I know she does. Believe me, I heard all about it."

He shook his head and went back to shaving. I headed out into the loft just as E was letting my mother in. She was better than most immortals that way; she at least tried to adhere to mortal protocols about stuff like not just appearing in someone's living room.

As soon as she noticed me, she walked over and folded me in a hug, and I hugged her back. She stepped back and looked me over.

"You look surprisingly relaxed, daughter," she said. "And is that a... smile?" she asked, a look of disbelief on her face.

I grinned, shook my head. I knew I was blushing. "Maybe." I brought my hand up, so only my mother could see it. Her eyes lit on the hematite band on my finger, and I felt a barrage of happiness from her. She hugged me again.

"I am so happy for you," she whispered as she hugged me. "You deserve to be happy, my girl. And as often as you fight, I know the demon is your heart."

"He is," I said, and she gave me another squeeze. We went to the living room and sat down. I glanced around. E and Ada were in the kitchen. Brennan was in the dining room, feeding Sean, who was in his high chair. He was watching me, and I was dreading some kind of anger or something there after he'd seen me come out of Nain's room. Our room. Instead, he gave me a small smile and looked away again.

"I wanted to check in with you," Tisiphone said as she settled into one of the chairs by the windows.

"I'm glad. I was hoping to talk to you. Things are bad here. We could use you and Aunt Meg and dad. A lot," I said.

She shook her head. "As bad as things are here, they are worse in the Nether. That's what I was coming to tell you. And I wanted to check on you as well."

I took her hand, felt the worry rolling off of her. "I'm fine. She's still fighting me, but I'm managing," I said. "What about you guys?"

"Things in the Nether are an absolute disaster," she said, and Nether (the being) was starting to get all hyper, faced with one of the beings she hated. "Is she getting stronger?"

I nodded.

And that seemed to be Nether's cue to add her two cents. *Damn right I am, you worthless piece of—*

I held a finger up, signaling for my mom to give me a second, and I focused on shutting Nether out again. After a few moments, her raging was just background noise again, and I opened my eyes and looked at my mother. I shook my head. "Yes. She is."

Tisiphone reached out and took my hand again. "I wish there was another way. This is asking too much."

"It's not. I'll deal with it," I said, shrugging. "Stop stalling and tell me about the Nether."

She rolled her eyes, exasperated with me. "Fine." She took a breath. "It's bad, Mollis. Tartarus is weakening. You know that Tartarus is a living thing too, yes?"

I nodded. "And its strength is dependent on the strength of the Nether, so weak Nether equals weak Tartarus."

"Right."

"That was kind of poorly planned. Why are they tied together that way?"

"I think the plan was that the power of two powerful beings keeping the souls of the damned and other monsters imprisoned was that it would never fail. Apparently, Tartarus and Nether became more entwined as time went on. I don't think anyone foresaw either of them ever weakening, though. I know I didn't. We just assumed they'd remain the same forever."

"So, escapes then?"

She nodded. "There have been all manner of nasty things getting out. And because Hades and Meg and I are the ones who imprisoned them, they're not too happy with us."

"Are you getting much help from the Aether gods?"

"Some. Artemis and Apollo. Asclepias. Mostly it's your father and aunt and I."

"Are they complete morons? Why aren't they helping you?"

She gave me a look. "Do you really need me to answer that? You know how they are."

"Do you want Heph and E to come and help?"

"You just said you need more help," Tisiphone said. "I can't take two of the most powerful beings on your team."

"Well if you guys aren't able to fight back the things escaping from Tartarus, this will look like fun in comparison."

"If it gets to that point, I'll tell you. Right now I would feel better with both of them here. Hopefully the mess you're currently dealing with will get sorted out soon." We both glanced at the television at that moment, as one of channel seven's field reporters cut in with an update.

"While fights continue to pop up around the city, we've seen an increase in violence in downtown Detroit in the past five minutes or so. We're seeing large mobs of supernaturals now, and they're very clearly fighting against one another. I also want to take a moment to say that, watching this, it's very clear that some of these beings are more bent on destruction, and others are focused on protecting innocents and getting people out of the crossfire. I would suggest that any children leave the room before we go to video that we shot just a few minutes ago."

The video started, and Tisiphone and I stood up. Downtown looked like a war zone. Buildings were on fire, windows smashed. Shifters, demons, and immortals fought. I could clearly hear the sounds of screaming, booming in the distance.

Nain came out of his room, jaw set. He bowed his head to my mom. Both of our phones rang.

"Ready?" he asked me, and I nodded. I hugged my mom, and she held me tightly.

"Be safe, my love," she murmured against my ear.

"You too, mom."

At that moment, Hades showed up.

"What the hell are you doing here?" my mom asked. "The Nether—"

"Threw all of us out and we can't get back in. I don't know what the hell is going on," he said, worry rolling off of him. "Meg and I are here now."

"Good. We need you," I said, pointing to the television. He nodded, and he and my mother winked out of sight.

I took Nain's hand.

"You shouldn't," he said, realizing what I was going to do.

"We need to get there fast. I'll be fine."

He planted a hard kiss on my lips, met my eyes. I squeezed his hand, and focused on the streets downtown where the news had showed most of the fighting. We went through the familiar, painful experience of being pulled apart and rematerializing, and the second we did, we were greeted by screams, shouting. Flames everywhere.

I love you. Be careful, I thought at Nain.

I love you too. Let's hurt some fuckers.

Now that Nain and I had appeared, we were both immediately surrounded by a mixed group of demons and shifters. I recognized one of them.

"Elsoloth. You bastard," I growled.

"I am sorry, my lady," he sneered. "She promised me more than you could ever give me."

I snarled and struck out, and Nain and I made our way through most of our attackers, but Elsoloth managed to slip away. Brennan had arrived in the meantime, and fought nearby. I could feel Levitt nearby, as well as Heph and E. My mom and my aunt Meg fought, back to back, about halfway down the block. I was at the corner of Griswold and Congress. The skyscrapers around us just made every scream, every roar echo louder. Cars were stopped at the intersection, their owners having abandoned them once fighting broke out. The windows of the sandwich shop were all blown out already, and the awning of the Ford Building was crashed in, as if something or someone heavy had been thrown into it.

Over there, Nain thought at me, and I looked toward the Guardian Building. A group of demons was stalking toward me, Elsoloth at their lead.

I held out my hand, and my flamesword appeared. I had brought up the enchantment to hide my wings, knowing Normals would be seeing us and not wanting them to connect me to Nether's little exploit on Hayes. I let my eyes glow, though, because it freaked my opponents out. I started stalking toward the demons, letting myself fall into my rage, letting myself embrace destruction.

Letting myself be what everyone's afraid I'll become.

Within moments I was surrounded by demons. I was punched, kicked.

They were eviscerated by my sword. They donated limbs to my cause, and I watched them fall. I cut another one down and glanced to my left, where Nain was.

He was now in full demon form, as the other demons we'd faced had been.

This was only the second time I'd seen him in this form, and he was completely terrifying. Reddish black skin, glowing red eyes. Bunching muscles. He stood around seven feet tall in this form. Claws on his hands, two vicious-looking horns on his head.

He was looking at me.

This is a good look on you.

You're ready to jump me, aren't you? He thought back at me.

I rolled my eyes, didn't have time to answer before another group of assholes surrounded us. Fighting had shifted, just about everyone fighting near the Guardian Building now. It was clear who the assholes wanted, and now that I was there, they had gravitated to me. I cut my way through a few shifters, heard Nain roaring as he ripped the head off of a demon's body. (Not a pretty sight, that). Levitt and Heph were fighting some warlocks a few feet away, and I could see E finishing off a witch. My parents were making short work of the mixed group of shifters and demons they were fighting, and here and there I'd catch sight of one of my imps (who I'd summoned back once it was clear how bad this was) stabbing or cutting our enemies.

Vicious little bastards. I loved them.

The only real problem was that we were majorly outnumbered. There were around twenty of us, between our combined teams, my family, and Jones and the shifters he'd brought with him. Strife's people? They just kept goddamned coming. Mostly demons. The bitch had taken all of my demons, plus done additional recruiting, it seemed. She also had plenty of shifters, along with witches and warlocks. Sprites, who seemed intent on facing off against my imps. Plenty of beings with powers. Normals with just a touch of something else. She had a couple of pyros, and I wondered which of them had set my house on fire. She had a chick who could melt your skin with a touch. A couple of telepaths.

"Mental shields up," I roared, and I heard my team echoing the call. Fighting raged on. I watched the sun setting and knew it was only about to get worse. Yeah, we were outnumbered now. But the vampires had fallen pretty solidly on Strife's side. We'd have maybe another dozen or so coming from Rayna's family, but that was nothing compared to the number of vampires who hated me and her and everything we stood for. Vampires who chafed under our rules and control.

I didn't have time to dwell on it. Another demon rushed me, holding a huge axe similar to what Terror had used, and I fought him off. He was strong Old, and my bones rattled every time I blocked his ax with my sword.

I wanted to use my powers. Wanted to destroy as many of these beings as I could and keep my friends and teammates safe before something went wrong. But I knew I'd need them more later, when the vampires arrived and joined the fight. They wouldn't stay away. This was their chance to be out in the open and show what they really were.

So I fought, and I seethed, and I tried to keep an eye out for my teammates. I was proud of them. They were more than holding their own, and our enemies' bodies littered the street and sidewalk.

And then darkness fell, and within minutes, the street swarmed with vampires.

And immortals, who arrived by their side.

Aphrodite. Zeus. Hera.

"Oh, fuck," I heard Levitt mutter behind me.

I felt Athena's presence nearby. Artemis and Apollo. Athena put a hand on my shoulder.

"I hope you remember what I taught you, Fury," she said. "We're going to need it."

"Thank you for coming."

She nodded. "Once the Nether and Aether kicked us out, it was clear that a few of them were planning to join your opponents. They blame you. Idiots."

And then I felt Persephone. So did Hades, who was standing near me. She walked toward us, and a demon charged her.

A tiny dagger appeared almost out of nowhere, and was soon sticking out of the demon's throat. She snatched her dagger out back from its body and kept walking toward us, leaving him gurgling on the ground.

I stared at my stepmother. Former stepmother. Whatever.

She was watching me. "I'm not here for him," she said, gesturing toward my father. "I'm here because this is the right side of things."

"Thank you," I said, and she nodded. Asclepias was behind her.

"I will do my best to heal. You know I'm not a warrior," he said apologetically.

"Healing will be needed, my friend," I said. "Thank you."

Fighting had resumed again after the pause that the arrival of the immortals had caused. I said a silent prayer to whatever there is left to pray to, and charged back into the fight.

Shanti, Rayna, and Ronan found me.

"Where do you want us, Angel?" Ronan called in greeting.

"Wherever there's a piece of shit who needs his or her ass kicked," I called back. "Try to make sure none of our people are isolated."

He nodded and stormed off with Rayna. Shanti stayed and fought beside me. She had her favorite weapon with her tonight, the katana, which she'd taken up after joining Rayna's team. It suited her.

"Okay?" I asked her.

"This is freaking terrifying. What the hell?" she said, and then grunted as her sword made contact with a demon's torso.

It was worse than I'd imagined. Nain was fighting off to my left, and blood streamed down his chest, his arms. Too much of it was his own.

It was time.

I waded into a group of our enemies and released flames, setting them all ablaze. Around a dozen demons and vampires fell, the stench of burning flesh surrounding me.

I walked out of the flames and was charged by another group of vampires. I could feel panic setting in. They'd become complacent, sure I wouldn't use my powers. And I'd pay the price. I was already in agony, just from that one attack. Nether was raging, massively excited by the fight, battling me for control. I released mental knives at the vampires, and another ten or so fell, screaming. That wouldn't kill them, though, and I was proud of Shanti for knowing what needed to happen. She followed me and beheaded each of them as they lay writhing on the ground.

My team felt better, seeing me use my powers. They needed it. It energized them, and they fought harder. Heph charged into a group of vampires, swinging the light silver sword he'd fashioned for himself. He cut them down like a lawnmower, and released an exuberant battle shout, which was echoed by the rest of our team amid the chaos and screams of battle.

I torched another group of vampires and watched them fall. My nose and ears were gushing blood now, my flesh splitting along my hands and neck. I gritted my teeth against it, determined to stay strong. The only good thing was that all the pain and fear I was causing was feeding me. I could keep going as long as I needed to. I could ignore the pain.

I could almost even ignore Nether raging within me, her screams, her curses. Her constant attempts to gain control of me.

The tides seemed to be turning. We were still badly outnumbered, but our enemies were afraid. My immortals made it their job to keep the other immortals busy, which seemed to cancel out the effect of having them there at all. I could have kissed each and every one of them. Even Persephone.

Athena was enjoying herself as she fought against Zeus. He constantly tried to throw lightning bolts, and she struck out at him before he was ever able to get an attack off. Which affirmed my impression of Zeus in general: privileged asshole who never actually had to fight for a damn thing. Against a seasoned warrior, he was nothing. A one trick pony who'd had his trick taken away from him.

Persephone was fighting beside Artemis and Apollo against Hera and Aphrodite. Heph and E were still fighting demons, and my parents were fighting against several spirit daemons. I didn't know their names or what they were the spirit of, but they were clearly on Strife's side. Apparently, a few had joined my side as well. I saw them standing back to back with Rayna's vampires, Jones' shifters. Brennan and Jones fought against more shifters. We seemed to have it under control.

I should really, really know better than to ever think that.

CHAPTER EIGHTEEN

I was watching Levitt when it happened. I was telling myself to congratulate him on being one of the fiercest damn fighters I'd ever seen as he cut down three vampires, then fought a demon who tried to sneak up on him. I cut down the last of my current wave of attackers.

And that was when Aphrodite appeared behind him. I screamed my warning, but I was too late. Her sword appeared, stuck through his chest, blade sticking out of the front of his body. I screeched, charged her, but she disappeared, leaving her sword in Levitt's body. Levitt fell, and I crouched beside him.

"Levitt. Come on, man. Wait for Asclepias," I urged, putting my hand on his head. He was already pale, his yes unfocused.

"I'm done, my Lady. Thank you for helping me live a life of purpose," he said, his voice weak already.

"Hold on, damn it," I ordered. Shanti had made her way over to us, and she was sobbing as she bent over him.

He looked at me one more time. "I'm going to die protecting innocents and fighting by your side. I'll take it."

And then his gaze shifted to Shanti, who was holding his face between her palms.

"Thank you," he whispered to her, and she started sobbing harder.

And then he stilled. Gone. I screeched in rage and rematerialized in a group of vampires, just wanting to hurt something, just wanting to destroy. I was crying, snarling, and the vampires didn't stand a chance against my rage. I was lost in my anger and grief, cutting down or setting any enemy I could reach on fire. I was so lost I barely heard Jamie's scream from a few feet away.

I looked that way and watched Jones fall, his head taken from his body, still in wolf form. Jamie herself was caught between shift states, more human than wolf, but with an elongated snout, ears. Her scream was something between a scream and a howl.

Aphrodite again. And she was studying her work with pride as Jamie continued to howl.

She wouldn't get another chance.

I took a play from her own book of dirty tricks, rematerialized behind her and grabbed her by the hair. Jamie charged her and tore into her throat, ripped with such viciousness it nearly made me sick. But she needed it. Her father, her pack's alpha, had just fallen. Vengeance was hers, and I was glad I could give it to her.

Aphrodite fell, gurgling, missing most of her throat, eyes glazed over.

I tore into her mind, destroyed whatever was left as she lay bleeding on the ground.

So ended the goddess of love.

She was shitty at her job anyway.

When it was done, I fell to the ground. Exhausted. Sad, Angry. Full of rage and loss and guilt. Bleeding.

And I saw Brennan a few feet away. Watched him cut down an enemy.

I felt rage rise within me. Excitement. I fought it down.

I tried to, anyway.

Nether's excitement only heightened as she freed more and more of herself from my control. I fought, begged. Did everything I could to keep her in control.

Watch this, Fury, she said in my mind.

And then I heard myself/her cackle and now our situations were reversed. She was the one in control, and I was the one forced to watch, forced to fight for control. I raged against her, fought harder than I'd ever fought anything in my life.

She zeroed in on Brennan, and I heard her laugh again. I heard Nain shout, heard my father say Nether's name. Chaos.

And then she released a barrage of pure power, something I'd never seen before. In her insanity, still focusing on Brennan, still determined to destroy him. She didn't even know why anymore. And I raged against her as I watched her release the power straight at him. And just when it was about to hit, my mother jumped in front of it, took the attack.

Saved his life, and fell, still, to the ground.

I screamed from my place inside Nether, fought her harder, raged against her. In her confusion over what had happened, I had a chance to fight through, and I did. Barely. I wrestled control back from her, pushed her down again as she raged against me.

My father was roaring as he crouched over Tisiphone's still body. The battlefield had gone silent. Some of Strife's people started running, coming to the conclusion that maybe this wasn't a fight they wanted. Not today anyway. I crawled toward my mother. Hades snarled at me.

"It's me, dad," I said. "Oh my god." Tisiphone's body was a mess. A gaping, smoking wound in her stomach, where she'd taken the attack meant for Brennan.

"Save her," Hades shouted, and I looked up to see him staring at me. "Save her, Mollis."

"I.."

"Use your blood, damn it. Now!" Hades shouted. He looked insane. Desperate. Afraid. He sliced his veins open with one of Persephone's daggers and let his blood pour into my mother. I dug my knife out of my pocket and did the same.

"Come on, mom," I murmured. She was still there. Just barely. Nether, using my powers... shit. She could die. She was close to it, and there would be no coming back because of the nature of what I could do. I felt panic rise within me as my father and I tried to save her. Hades and I let our blood, our life forces, pour into her. I lost track of how many times I sliced my body.

I could feel myself weakening. I could feel my heart start struggling against the demands set on it by the constant loss of blood, I could feel my mind clouding, my body tiring.

I couldn't lose her. Not this way. I couldn't live, knowing she'd died by my hands. My mother, who'd done what she thought best to keep me safe. Who'd wanted nothing more than my happiness, my safety. My mother, who taught me what it meant to be a Fury.

I started crying as my body started giving out. She didn't look a whole lot better. I couldn't feel any improvement in her. I let out a gasp, struggled for breath as my body started failing me.

"Enough, Molls," Nain called. His voice sounded all weird and echoey.

A being appeared out of nowhere in front of me, and I looked up.

Right into Strife's glowing purple eyes.

"Remember who freed you, My Lady. Find me when you are able."

And I felt her blade slice across my throat. I heard Nain roar.

And the world went black.

CHAPTER NINTEEN

I rose from the darkness slowly. Black faded to gray. I felt air fill my lungs. I felt the moment my heart started beating, wildly at first, then slowing to a normal tempo.

I was in a soft place. The first thing I felt was him. His energy, his rage, feeding me. His love for me surrounding me, so real it was nearly as physical as his arms wrapped around my body, the beat of his heart against my arm. I slipped in and out of the darkness, and the only constant thing was him.

I opened my eyes, glanced around, remembering. I remembered my name. I remembered what I was. Bit by bit, I remembered everything.

Everything.

I started shaking, my breath coming raggedly, and Nain shot awake from his spot beside me.

"Molly," he said. His voice was hoarse, and his arms went tighter around me, trying to calm me. I was practically hyperventilating, and he held me, whispered to me, tried to calm me down. His touch did more than anything else could have, and I started to pull myself together. "Molly," he whispered against my hair, and I could feel the gratitude coming from him, the remnants of his fear. "Do you remember?"

"I remember that I failed," I said, and it felt strange to use my voice.

He sat up and took my face in his hands. "You failed? How can you say that?"

"I was supposed to keep Nether imprisoned. She got out, and I didn't even save..." I trailed off, bit my lip against the pain. Wished I could blot out the memory of seeing my power destroy my mother. My father's anguished roar, the way he'd pleaded with me to save her.

"Molly, you saved her," he said, still holding my face between his hands.

"I... I did? Really?"

"Really," he said softly. "Really. She's okay, Molls. She's weak still, but she's alive. She and your dad have been staying here."

I breathed, and ended up crying. Relieved, overwhelmed. Nain held me as I fell apart, and kept holding me as I tried to pull myself back together.

"How long have I been out?"

Nain's eyes met mine. "Eight days."

I tried to jump up, and he held me still. "Eight days? Oh my god. I have to get Nether. I have to find fucking Strife. I have to—"

"Molly, stop," he said. "You'll handle all of that shit later. And you know you're not at full strength yet."

I growled, frustrated.

He laughed a little, and I glared up at him. "It's good to see you back to your normal, calm self."

I shook my head. "Eight days? Really? Why did it take so long?"

He had been looking at me. Now he looked away. "You were really weak, baby. You'd used all of your power to save your mom. So much blood," he said, shaking his head. "We carried a husk here. A husk without a head, so pale you looked like you'd disappear at any second. You were on the brink of falling to dust. This body nearly failed you, and your dad was freaking out because the Nether would have been a really bad place for you if you ended up resurrecting beyond the gateway. I guess things are bad there." He stopped talking, overwhelmed by the things I was making him remember.

"We weren't sure even you could fight back." He curled himself around me, holding me, shielding me as if he was trying to protect me from any threat that appeared. "For the first three days, nothing happened. They started telling me it was time to let you go," he said, and he clamped his lips together, and I could see he was fighting back a wave of anger and fear. I raised my hand to his face, gently stroked his jawline. "I told them I'd destroy every fucking one of them if they tried to take you. I told them I could still feel you." He bent his head, rested it against my chest, and I knew he was listening to my heart beating. "And then on the fourth day, we started seeing your body healing. Your heart didn't start beating until the fifth day."

"Nain," I whispered, his anguish, his fear washing over me. "It's okay. I'm here." He wrapped his arms tighter around me, and I held him, too. "I'm here," I murmured again, and he just held me. I'd never seen him look the way he did then. Pale. Tired. Drawn, like someone who's been sick for a long time.

He sat up, got out of bed. "You should drink something," he said, and he grabbed a bottle of water off of the dresser. I glanced down at myself. I was dressed in clean pajama bottoms and a tank top. My body was clean. I knew it had been covered in blood. Mine. The blood of too many others.

"Did you clean me up?" I asked him. He nodded, and handed me a bottle of water. I was sitting up now. I took a few sips of water, and the liquid going down my throat made me want to throw up. I set the bottle aside and pulled his hand, made him sit next to me. "What's wrong, honey?" I asked him, and he pulled me into his arms again, buried his face against my neck, and I knew he was breathing me in. The scent of me, my touch, calmed him just as much as his calmed me.

He shook his head. He couldn't stop touching me, holding me, running his hands over my body, as if trying to reassure himself I was real. "That was... don't ever make me live through something like that again," he said. "I am never going to get the way you looked out of my head. I'm never gonna forget the way it felt to be next to you and not feel your power roaring around me." He kissed my neck again, nuzzled it as he held me tight to him.

"We have a long time, Nain. I'll do my best to make you forget," I said softly. I ran my hands up and down his back, trying to relax the tension there.

"I had a moment there where I thought, 'if I lose her, the whole world is going to pay.' I remembered how angry I was early on, before I tried to be somewhat decent. I wanted someone, anyone, to hurt. I was there again, waiting for you to come back. I wanted someone to pay for what happened to you, and I didn't even give a fuck who as long as I had someone to hurt."

I rubbed his back some more. I knew how he fought for control, much the same way I did. It's in his nature, as a demon, to cause pain. He'd made a life of causing it to people who deserved it. I understood what he was saying. People who turn to booze when things get bad don't really care what they're drinking as long as it'll make them forget. Pain is the demon's booze. I thanked whatever it is out there that you thank for things like this that I'd held on, as much for his sake as mine. "And I would have been eternally pissed at you if you'd acted like a typical demon over me," I told him, knowing he needed that. "I can't die. You goddamn know that."

"I wasn't the only one. Asclepias and your dad were freaking the fuck out too. Your body was there with us, and nobody could feel you, at all. I wasn't even sure I could feel you, but I kept telling myself there was something there. Asclepias said it was like you were stuck somewhere between death and resurrection."

"Limbo?"

He shrugged. "Something like that. He didn't really understand it either. He said you guys live or you die. And that *you* just live. If there's a body, we should feel you coming back right away. That's how it works. There is no in between. Except with you, there was."

"Well. I'm grateful for it, then," I said.

"Me too. Do you remember anything?"

I shook my head. We sat in silence, holding each other, the only sound in the room the clock on the nightstand ticking the seconds.

"I'm surprised Bash and Dahael aren't in here," I said after a while. I was feeling sleepy again, my head resting on his shoulder, my body close to his.

"It's weird. They haven't been around. None of them have. Maybe they're hunting Strife for you," Nain said.

"Maybe." I ran my hands over his shoulders. "You look exhausted. Sleep with me." We settled back into the bed, and he pulled the blankets up over us.

He kissed me. "I love you, Molly."

"I love you more."

"Not even possible, woman," he said, kissing me again, groaning when I sucked and nibbled his lips.

He held me, and I felt myself start dozing off again. "I gotta get up soon. Nether—"

"Isn't going anywhere. She doesn't even have a body yet. Asclepias figures we've got a couple months."

"And Strife is fucking dead," I muttered as my eyelids got heavier.

"Rest, Molly. You have the rest of eternity to kick ass," he said, and I started to fall asleep again, comforted by his arms, his breath on my neck.

We stayed in bed, both of us slipping in and out of sleep, for at least another day. And eventually, I felt like myself.

Actually. I felt better than myself. I felt new. Whole. A lot of it had to do with Nain, who still looked drawn and pale after spending so much time worrying, so much of his power, his essence, feeding me as I'd healed. I'd never taken enough from him to affect him in any way, so I felt guilty about it and when I'd tried to tell him that, he'd given me one of his Nain glares and kissed me hard and told me he was mine.

So, I'd shut up and told him to go back to sleep. And then I got up and took a shower, got dressed. My wings were all screwed up from being in bed so long, the feathers skewed and kind of flattened. In general, my wings don't require a whole lot of care. I'm not a bird. I don't have to preen (thank god. I am not the preening type.) But this did require some fluffing with my fingers, straightening errant feathers with my fingertips.

I went back into the bedroom, where Nain was snoring in our bed. I leaned down and kissed his bare shoulder, and he tried to pull me back into bed with him.

"Sleep," I told him. "I'm going to go talk to my mom. Where's my armband, babe?"

"Don't go kicking any ass yet," he said.

"I have to. I got this."

He sighed. "There's a loose floorboard in the closet of my office. There's a safe under that." He told me the combination.

"Thanks. Go back to sleep," I said, leaning down and kissing his cheek.

He brought my hand to his lips, kissed my wrist. "You are in so much trouble when I get my energy back," he murmured sleepily.

"I am looking forward to it, husband."

He smiled a little, then closed his eyes and drifted back to sleep. I watched him for a few minutes. I wanted to claim him, as I'd done with Brennan. That would have helped him get his strength back faster. But I didn't want to do it without telling him first. I didn't want to do it behind his back, the way I'd done it with Brennan.

This was my husband. My heart. My partner in life, death, and everything else. There would be no more lies between us. No more secrets. I watched him for a few moments longer, then I left the room, closing the door behind me.

The loft was more crowded than I'd ever seen it. Nain's team, my team, several of the immortals who were on our side. Jamie and a few of the shifters from the chief's pack. Ronan and a few vampires. They all stared at me when I walked out of our bedroom.

"Hey," I said, and was immediately surrounded by people. My teammates were hugging me. The only one I didn't see was Brennan, and I figured he was out on patrol. Ada kissed me on the cheek, and Stone pulled me into a one-armed bear hug, his other arm in a cast and sling. I answered questions, accepted hugs and kisses and congratulations on not dying. I looked around for Shanti, who was sitting in the corner of the living room with a man I didn't recognize.

He was holding her hand. Watching the room as if he was ready to hurt anyone who bothered Shanti.

I liked him. I could feel his adoration for the vampire, his protectiveness of her.

I walked toward Shanti, and she watched me. She was sad. She felt guilty. Confused.

I knelt down in front of her and took her hands.

"Are you all right?" I asked her. And she nodded, even as blood-tinged tears came to her eyes. Her eyes met mine, and I could see the pain there. The guilt. Levitt.

Tears came to my eyes, too, remembering the loyal demon. The way he'd never, ever let me down. The way he'd been grateful every day that I'd spared his life and given him another chance.

"We lost a good man," I said, and she nodded, crying harder now. "And you knew him better than anyone. He never let any of us get close to him. Except for you."

She nodded again, lips trembling. "And I turned him away. I hurt him."

I squeezed her hands. I was impressed by the man beside her, who listened to her words and didn't become angry or jealous. He rubbed her back, and I felt her calm a little at his touch.

"Sometimes, things just don't work out. It doesn't mean you didn't care for him. It doesn't mean the things you shared together are any less meaningful. You showed him something he's probably never had. You cared about him, and you stayed friends through it all. He appreciated that. I know he did," I said softly. "Don't feel guilty for living the life you want, Shanti. He's worth remembering fondly, and, as much of a demon as he was, he still wouldn't want you to hurt every time you remembered him."

"I know," she said, taking a deep breath to steady herself. "We did a little ceremony thing while you were recovering. We were going to wait, but..."

"But you needed it, and so did everyone else who knew him. I'm glad you had it. I will say goodbye in my own way."

Shanti leaned forward and hugged me. "I am so glad you're back. Stop doing shit like that."

I hugged her back. "I'll try."

"Liar," she said, smiling as she released me. "This is Zero, by the way."

I chatted with Shanti and Zero for a few moments, and then asked where my parents were. Shanti pointed to the room that had always been considered "the vampire room." I hugged her again and then headed up the stairs, listening to the din of conversation in the loft. All of the various teams, our allies, had bonded over our grief, over the experience of going into battle together. And based on the news reports, we weren't done. Supernaturals still fought in the streets, though it was much more random now. Even as I'd talked to Shanti, about half of the team, including Jamie and Ronan, had left to patrol and try to fight back the chaos.

So much to do, I thought to myself as I walked up the stairs.

I reached the room and knocked. "Come in," my father said, and I opened the door, ducked into the room.

The scene in here was similar to the way it was in the room I shared with Nain. My mom laid in the bed, dozing. My father was in the twin bed beside her, arm around her body, lending her his strength. I sat on the small chair, looked at my mom for a few moments. She looked healthy, but I could feel that she was still weak.

"How is she?" I asked Hades.

"She is alive. Thanks to you."

"She was nearly dead because of me."

"Because of Nether. Do not even start this nonsense, daughter," Hades said sternly.

"I should have controlled her better," I said, shaking my head.

"You did everything you could. Tis and I talked about all of it a lot after Asclepias saw you that day. We both had a feeling it was only a matter of time. You have too many powerful enemies, and hiding and playing it safe just isn't in you."

I tried to sense for him, to see if he harbored some anger toward me. I didn't feel anything other than typical demonic/Nether rage.

"We're proud of you, Mollis," he said. "And you saved your mother's life and I should be sorry for asking so much of you. When I saw what it did to you…" he trailed off, shook his head, guilt rolling off of him. "I can't choose you or her. I want you both in my life. And I was willing to risk you, to risk Nether's prison, to save her. I knew you'd come back, though you did give us all a fright there for a while. I'm only sorry it hurt you so much."

"She'll be okay, right?" I asked, looking at my mom again.

"She will be fine. I think we started giving her our blood just in time. There was only the tiniest speck of life left in her when we started."

I sensed for my father. My mother.

"What about Tartarus?" I asked him, remembering the insanity with the realms of the immortals.

He watched me. "Something is happening. None of us can get back into the Nether since it kicked us out that day."

"Maybe the Nether doesn't exist, because Nether is free now?" I asked, and he shook his head.

"No. The gateway is there. It's just not letting anyone through. I have never seen anything like it."

"Weird," I said, thinking.

"Yes. But I'll take it. I am not leaving her side until she's back to normal."

I watched my father for a few seconds. "You love her."

He didn't answer.

"You loved Persephone too."

He looked at me from his place beside my mother. "If it hadn't been for that stupid, nonsensical prophecy, Tis and I would have been together immediately. There has always been something between us. Always. And we did our best to avoid it, to avoid one another as much as our roles would allow, because for our entire existence, the Fates and everyone else were warning us that we would destroy everything. We reached a point where we could barely be in the same room together, the tension between us was so high. And then one day, I was out in the woods in the Nether, and she was there, and no one was around. I don't think either of us had a second thought. Being with her was like coming home. Everything was right. And we parted ways after we'd exhausted one another, and swore we'd try to forget."

His eyes had a faraway look, as if he was remembering.

"But I've never forgotten. You can't forget the feel of the body of someone who was absolutely made to be yours. You can't forget the way it feels when two souls fit together so perfectly you can't sense where one begins and the other ends. Can you?" he asked me, meeting my eyes.

I shook my head, thinking of my husband, who had given me his energy the same way Hades was doing with my mother.

"You always were much more of romantic than anyone has given you credit for," my mother said, and Hades smiled and took her hand. Their fingers entwined, and my mom looked at me. "Hello, my beautiful girl "

"Hi mom," I said, trying to fight back tears of relief.

She released my father's hand and took mine. "Thank you, my love. You didn't have to do that. I knew what I was doing."

"Why on earth did you do it?" I asked her.

She smiled. "You are eternal, Mollis. You never, ever would have forgiven yourself if Nether had killed the shifter. I am made of stronger stuff than he is. And I was fine with dying if it meant saving you from that."

"I don't love you any less than I loved him," I said.

"I know that. And, as I said, I figured I had a better chance of surviving than he would." She shrugged a thin shoulder. "You certainly pack a punch, kiddo," she said, grinning.

"I'm sorry, mom," I said again, and she let out a weak laugh.

"Considering what you went through to save me, and that it wasn't your fault in the first place, you have absolutely nothing to apologize for. I love you, my darling girl. I am more proud of you every single day. Do you know that?"

I blinked tears back from my eyes. "Thank you."

She squeezed my hand again, then pulled it back, and Hades held it in his.

"I'll take a look at the gateway and see if anything had changed," I said to them, and Hades nodded. "And then I'm going to hunt down Strife and Nether."

"Nether will be impossible to find until she generates a body. She is nothing more than energy now, floating around in the world," Hades said. "That takes several weeks in mortal time."

I nodded. "Strife will be easy," I said.

My mom watched me. "How do you figure that? She's been eluding you for months."

"Thanks for that vote of confidence, mom," I said, and she laughed. "That last moment, before she killed me, she looked into my eyes and was talking to Nether. She told her to come and find her when she was ready. And she was excited, and the dumb bitch projected exactly where she'd be. Good thing I have a decent memory," I finished, and I could feel my energy rising, my lust for battle, for the blood of my enemy, making it soar. And now, I felt stronger, more in control than I ever had been.

"She is wily, daughter. Be careful. She will be surrounded by her minions. You know this."

"Oh, I know," I said. "I just don't care."

They both watched me.

"She is a thing of beauty, isn't she?" Hades finally said to my mom.

My mom smiled, nodded in agreement.

I shook my head, couldn't help the smile that spread across my face. "I should go. I'm glad you guys are staying with us."

My mom nodded. "The demon figured you would feel better if we were here. Though I think at least part of his intent was to have your father here in case you needed more rage to complete your recovery.'

I smiled. "I'm sure it was. He's very practical, my husband."

"And devoted. And possessive," my father said, agreeing.

"And absolutely in love with you. But you already know that," my mom said.

I nodded. "Yes. I do."

I leaned down and kissed my mom's cheek, patted my father's shoulder, then I showed myself out of their room. I made my way through the loft and into Nain's office. I found the loose floorboard, opened the safe. There it was, wrapped in dark fabric. I could feel its power and I took a deep breath, slid it up over my arm. I still hated the way it felt. Still hated the angry, vicious feeling that emanated from it. But I also felt my power increase even more, and that was what mattered.

I pulled my sleeve back down, put everything back the way it was, then I stood still and focused. I closed my eyes, and envisioned the yard outside my house.

When I rematerialized in my yard, the first thing I saw was the black SUV parked on the otherwise-empty street. I leaned against the trunk of one of the few remaining trees and watched the SUV. There were three Normals inside. They were nervous. Afraid. Also determined.

A few seconds later, the doors opened and they climbed out. Three men, all dressed in dark suits, ties. One was probably in his forties, dark hair graying at the temples, laugh lines around his eyes. Not especially tall, but sturdy looking. The second one was black, hair cut close to his scalp, a neat beard. He watched me, watched everything, as if he was ready to strike if he had to. The third man was the youngest. Blonde hair, blue eyes. He was mostly nervous.

The three men reached me, stood about four feet away from me, and we sized each other up.

"Angel," the youngest one said, and I nodded. They screamed "government" and Jones had told me they knew about me. About us. And they all had decent mental shields, which means they'd trained to face me. They hadn't come unprepared.

"I'm agent Ross, these are agents Monroe," he said, gesturing to the older man, "and Dyson," he said, gesturing to the younger.

"Pleasure," I said, keeping my arms folded across my chest.

"We lost a good man in Chief Jones," Ross said. "I am sorry. I know you were friends."

"Thank you. We were."

"He thought very highly of you, even though you scared the hell out of him," Ross continued.

"I thought very highly of him, too. He was strong. And he gave everything he had to try to keep this city safe."

"He did," Ross agreed. "I know he told you that we wanted to meet with you. That we wanted you to help calm everyone down."

"Yes."

"We've known about you, about supernaturals, I mean, for a long time. We are also smart enough to know that we don't stand a chance in hell against you. We did try, back in the seventies. We had people rounding up shifters, vampires. That never worked out well for us, no matter how outnumbered the supernaturals were."

"I'm sure," I said, feeling more than a little pride on the behalf of my supernatural brethren.

"So we decided to take a different approach. We'd watch. We'd monitor. We'd ally with high-powered supers like Jones to keep an eye on things. We did try to ally with your demon friend, but he wasn't exactly welcoming toward us."

"That does not surprise me," I said, hiding a smile, trying to imagine these men trying to work with Nain. Recipe for disaster, that.

"We're here to ask for your help, Angel. People are terrified. It's chaos out here, and no one knows how to handle this. People are organizing hunts for supers, and that's not going well for them. And we can't even arrest the supers who retaliate, because it's mostly impossible to catch them and even if we did send some men in to do it, they'd never make it out alive."

He took a breath. "We all know that mortals messing with supers is a bad thing. And we also know that out of all the supers, you are the one the mortals know. They trust you. They never knew what you were, only that they suspected you weren't entirely human."

"So what do you want from me?"

"Cooperation. That's all. Work with us. Advise us. Maybe try to reassure everyone. We don't even know. We thought we were ready for this. We're not."

"It's a mess," Dyson said, and Monroe nodded.

I shook my head. "I'm not a diplomat, Agent Ross. I don't do well with people in general. I work best in the shadows. If everyone knows what I am, my job will be harder. And I'm sorry, but saving people beats reassuring them, every time."

"And how many might you save by warning them against hunting supers?" Dyson asked.

"And how much might it incite the crazies more if I start making speeches and shit?" I shot back at him. "They already fear us. Do you really think it's not going to freak a certain segment out more if they think the government has supernaturals at their disposal? The conspiracy theorists will just love that."

"What else can we do?" Ross asked, frustrated.

"You can stay out of my way, and let me do my job," I told him. "The answer is no. I would be very unhappy to see any of you around my homes, friends, or allies again. Do you understand?"

"We're already there. We've had one of our people in the Nain Rouge's team for the past fifteen years," Ross responded. "How do you think we know so much about you?"

And I felt it. An energy signature I knew all too well. I stared past the three agents at the man walking toward us. A man whose every line, every feature I'd memorized once upon a time.

"You son of a bitch," I whispered, feeling as if I'd been punched in the gut.

Brennan stopped a few feet away from me, and the three agents backed away.

"Oh, you goddamn son of a bitch," I said again, putting my hands over my mouth.

"Molly," he said.

"I can't believe this. Oh my god," I said, backing away from him.

"Molly. Stop it. I've always been on your side. Always. I'm on Nain's side."

"You've been telling them about me? About Nain?"

"About everyone," he said quietly.

"Why?"

"My parents died trying to protect people. I'm doing the same thing in a different way," he said.

I stared at him. I couldn't even process it.

"My role was to share information. My loyalty hasn't changed." Then he glanced at the other three agents. "Give us a minute."

They walked back toward the SUV, stood there watching us.

"Did Nain know?" I asked quietly, wanting to hit him, wanting to hurt him so much it scared me.

He smirked. "This is Nain we're talking about. Do you seriously think he didn't know?"

"And he was just okay with that?"

He shrugged. "We never talked about it. I really don't think he cared all that much. He knew the team was being watched. He knew there was a government agency that deals with supernaturals. They approached my parents when they were part of his team."

"Did they join?"

"No."

"I don't see how anyone could be okay with this. You lied. You told them things about us—"

"Listen to me," he said, raising his eyebrows, and I got the drift.

I never told them anything that would put you in danger. I am on your side, on Nain's side, first.

"You told them about me," I said aloud.

You know what I didn't tell them? I didn't tell them about us. I didn't tell them how amazing it felt to be loved by you. I didn't tell them about how the night you walked out on me, I was pretty sure my life was over. That's none of their business. Okay?

Aloud, he said, "I believe working with them will save people. The secret's out about supernaturals and now nothing is going to be the same."

I stayed there, staring at him, wondering if Nether had fried my brain when she'd been in there. This couldn't be happening. The three agents were staying back, surveying the destruction around my house, and Brennan wouldn't stop looking at me.

"It was all a lie," I said softly. "All of it."

He reached toward me, and I held my hands up, used a force of my power to shove him back. "Do not touch me," I growled.

He held his hands up, then glanced at the other three agents, who had all gone for their guns. "Stand down," he shouted, and they did. He looked back at me.

What we had wasn't a lie. I love you, he thought at me.

"And I'm sure part of the allure wasn't that you'd learn a whole lot about me," I muttered.

"Emotions don't lie. You know that," he said quietly.

"Maybe they do." I looked down, not able to look at him, not able to look at those slate blue eyes that I'd found myself falling into too many times. "You used me."

"It was both," he admitted. "I got close to you to learn more about what you are. That was my assignment. And the closer I got..." he trailed off, shrugging.

"That shit about imprinting on me as your mate," I whispered.

"That was true. It made my job a lot easier," he said whispered, looking in the opposite direction of the agents, hiding his mouth from them. "And a lot harder."

I shook my head. "I guess you didn't just spend those years away 'traveling,' huh? Not the way you said you did."

"Yeah. They approached me when I was twenty, and after a year or so of thinking about it, I took them up on it. I told Nain and the team I needed time, that I was going to use the money my parents had left me to see the world. And I did see the world, just not in the way I'd said."

"Must feel good to have lied to everyone who's ever loved you," I said.

He just watched me. "I know you're pissed. I get it. I understand. And I'm sorry. Hurting you was the last thing I wanted. We need to work together, Molly. You know that what Ross was saying is true. You can save lives by talking to people. Calming them down. Putting a face to supernaturals. Jones knew it."

"He knew about you?"

"No. And we didn't approach him until it was clear that supernaturals wouldn't be a secret anymore. We watched him, same as we watched everybody else." By now, the other agents had rejoined Brennan and I, sure that any dramatics had passed. I felt numb. And the laughable thing was that this particular little revelation wasn't even in my top five things I had to worry about just then.

Brennan watched me. "Jones agreed to ask that of you because he believed it was the only way to calm everyone down. Because he believed you were a living, breathing superhero. Because he had faith in you. And so do I."

"I'm not a politician. Or a liar."

"And we don't want you to be. We want you to be a hero."

I shook my head. I couldn't look at him any longer. I clenched my fists at my sides. "Time to go before I hurt you. Stay the hell away from me," I snarled. "I have shit to do that has nothing to do with making speeches and pretending to be something I'm not."

They were annoyed. Dyson was flat-out angry. Brennan was irritated, guilty. But they left, each nodding respectfully to me as they walked away. Before he went with them, Brennan met my eyes. "I will be around. I hope you can try to understand why I did things the way I did them. You save the world your way, and I save it mine."

"Fuck off, Brennan."

He shook his head and turned and walked away. I watched him climb into the SUV and drive away, my mind spinning with the things he'd just revealed.

It explained so many things. Why he'd tried so hard. Why he'd been so frustrated with me when I left him behind. His training, his aptitude for organizing things and commanding teams. A freaking secret agent. And he wanted me to be some kind of superhero.

"Superhero, my ass," I muttered.

"Well, they weren't wrong," a smooth voice said behind me. "Why are you the only one who can't see it, little Fury?"

Power roared over me, around me, at the appearance of the immortal. It was like nothing I'd ever felt before. Ancient yet timeless. Expansive. Suffocating. And my power recognized it. Leapt in excitement.

I turned, and the being standing before me smiled. "I thought they'd never leave. It's an honor to meet you, granddaughter."

CHAPTER TWENTY

The being standing in my yard looked like me in every way. Same small stature, same pale skin, white glowing eyes. Dark hair, huge black wings. I'd thought I was powerful until that moment, until I understood what true power felt like. Power older than anything in existence. Power older than time and space itself.

This was the being who'd created the Nether and the Aether. She'd created the Furies, the Fates, the Guardians, mostly in her own image. She was darkness.

My grandmother, Nyx.

I did the only thing that made any sense. I bowed my head to her, went down on one knee. The urge to pray, to beg her blessings, was almost impossible to ignore.

This was a god. This was what I didn't feel with any of the other immortals. It was beautiful and terrifying, and I was crying before I even realized it.

"Rise, darling," she said, and her voice was strong, quiet. Warm.

I rose, and watched my grandmother as she studied me.

"I am so grateful your mother and Hades had it in them to ignore that stupid prophecy."

"Where did the prophecy come from?" I asked, hating to speak.

She smiled, and it was nearly too beautiful to handle. "From me. But, as the Fates so often do, they got it wrong. I love my daughters, but the egos of those three knows no bounds."

"Maybe you should have spelled it out better," I said, and she laughed.

"I said that the child of the lord of the Nether and the avenging Fury would turn the world of the gods on its head. That her coming would change everything, that the world of the immortals would cease to exist as they had known it. That she would raise an army and defend her homeland against all threats. I should have remembered that most beings, no matter how powerful, see change as something worth fearing." She shrugged, and it was quite possibly the most graceful shrug I'd ever seen.

She smiled again. "But things that are meant to be will find a way, won't they? And you are here, and you are an honor to behold, my dear."

I bowed my head again, overwhelmed. "Thank you," I said.

She came over to me and took my hand. She was warm to the touch, hot, really, almost uncomfortable to be in contact with. "I am guessing you have questions," she said, and she led me over to one of the trees I'd knocked down, and we sat on the trunk. It had started to snow, fluffy flakes falling everywhere, except on us. I shook my head.

"They said you wouldn't help, that you slept," I said, looking at her.

"They were right, for the most part. Things are best when I sleep. I have done my part here. I created the beings I wanted to create, the realms of the immortals. A few other things as well," she said, smiling a little. "I sleep, and things stay in balance. But I am needed now, and I wanted to see you."

I nodded, not knowing what to say.

"You are here to check on the gateway," she said.

"My parents said it wouldn't let them through," I explained.

"And it won't, ever again," she said. "The immortals will have to live in your world now. Their homelands are lost to them with the weakening of the Nether. I cannot allow what is imprisoned there to run rampant in this world, and a few too many monsters have already gotten through. You will have to hunt them, but the rest will remain locked away from your world."

"Thank you," I said, breathing a sigh of relief, and she smiled.

"Don't thank me yet. The immortals will not be happy about this."

"They are rarely happy in general," I said, and she laughed.

"So why can't they go back?"

"After I have finished speaking with you, I will retire to the Nether to sleep. Before my slumber, I will destroy the gateway between the worlds. It will never exist again. The things that reside in the realms of the immortals will stay there, as they should. The monsters we've imprisoned there. The Titans, minus two who escaped into your realm And I am sorry for that, dear girl. Nightmares, angry souls. Those shall remain locked away. With Tartarus failing due to Nether's loss, the realms themselves will have to serve as prisons for what gets loose. I can easily cut those realms off from your world, but the immortals would be in constant danger. I am not willing to see constant slaughter and torture of them, no matter how prideful and ignorant they can be."

"How will Hades and the Furies do their jobs, then?"

She smiled. "They will always be what they are. They will always judge and punish those who have done wrong.

They will just do it in new ways now, by your side. It was time. I will deal with the souls of the dead now, in my own way." She stopped talking, looked around. "One thing I did not foresee was you destroying the Nether, my girl."

"Well I really didn't mean to," I said, and she smiled.

"I know. I have to give her credit. She is much more cunning than even I knew. She was patient, and the second she had a chance to free herself, she did." Her gaze sought mine. "She hates us, granddaughter. Every single one of those I created. She was insane before she was imprisoned, and she is even more so now, after eons of being both prison and prisoner. She will stop at nothing to destroy you and everything you hold dear. Know that."

I clasped my hands together. "Is it true she knows what I know? She can do what I can do?"

"Yes. It is. Your first steps should be moving anyone you love. She'll attack their homes first, trying to hurt you."

"She can kill immortals?"

"Yes."

"Can she kill me?"

She took a breath. "That, we don't know. I have no idea." Frustration rolled off of her. "I just don't know how it will work when you two face each other. Assume she can."

"Well, if she can't necessarily kill me, and we have the same powers, then that means we're not sure I can kill her either."

"I know," Nyx said.

"So what am I supposed to do?"

"You will figure it out," she said, and I nearly growled in frustration. "I do have a few last words of advice for you before I go." She stood, and I stood with her.

"What can you tell me, grandmother?" I asked, and she smiled and clasped my hands in hers again.

"I can tell you that you need to start trusting yourself more. This final betrayal has rocked you to the core. Do not let it. Have faith in yourself. Stop doubting what you are. I know you feel the darkness in you sometimes, the temptation to be an absolute terror. I know that you fight against that."

I nodded.

She gripped my hands tighter. "Stop fighting it. Be what you are. All of it."

I just stared at her.

"Your power lies in your unending dedication to saving innocents. Your power is terrifying, as it should be. But you are my granddaughter. You are strong. Fearing yourself weakens you." Then she smiled. "Remember, my love, that darkness is not merely the absence of light. In truth, light can only be born from darkness. And I would know, wouldn't I?"

I watched her, and she leaned forward and pressed a kiss to each cheek. "I am proud of you, Mollis Eth-Hades."

And she let me go, and I watched my grandmother, this ethereal, powerful goddess, walk toward the gateway. When she reached it, she turned and smiled, and brought her fist to her chest, using the same gesture my imps did, and I mimicked her. She gave me a slow nod, then stepped through the gateway and was gone.

I stared after her, and a few seconds later, I felt the gateway cease to be. I hadn't even realized I'd been crying, but I felt tears rolling down my face. I stood in my former yard, looking at the gateway's former place, and my mind was a mess. As afraid as I was, I vowed to remember my grandmother's words.

I had a big fight ahead of me, sometime in the future. I would put everything I am into making sure I came out victorious, because the alternative was not acceptable.

"Mistress." A low, scratchy voice behind me. I spun and saw my imps there, all of them, Bashiok and Dahael standing at the front of the group. Their heads were bowed, their ears drooping. Their postures were defeated.

Sadness, anger rolled off of them. I crouched in front of Dahael.

"What is it, my friends?" I asked, and Dahael started sobbing. She tried to pull herself together to speak, and she couldn't do it. Bash took her hand. Angry tears shone in his eyes as well.

"Have to leave you, Mistress," he croaked, and I stared at him.

"What? Where are you going?"

"Stronger being pulls on us. Have to serve another," he said, a growl in his voice. Dahael started crying.

"Who?"

He just looked at me helplessly, and it hit me. The enchantment on them that kept their current master safe had already taken effect. They couldn't tell me who, because they were already in their new master's service.

And their new master had to be stronger than me.

"Nether," I said, and Dahael just cried harder.

"Kill us, Mistress," she managed, even thought it seemed to cause her pain. "Won't go back. Won't hurt innocents. Won't do it," she wailed, and collapsed on the ground, her agony and helplessness rolling over me. "Please," she begged, her face still in the grass.

I went over to her and helped her sit up. "I will not kill you, Dahael," I said, and she looked at me, begging. "I will get you back. I swear it to you."

She still pleaded with me and I knew it was the idea of harming innocents more than leaving me.

"Showed us a different way, Mistress," Bash said, giving words to her anguish, and the rest of the imps nodded. "Can't go back now."

I looked at him, glanced at every one of my over two dozen imps. "I will get you back. I know you can't disobey her. Do not blame yourselves. Believe in me," I said.

At my words, every single one of them bowed their head and put a fist to their chest.

"Only thing we believe in, Mistress," Falrog said, and Dahael started crying harder.

"Have to go. Can feel her pull," Bash said, and I nodded, swiping tears away from my eyes.

"Believe," I reminded them, and then I watched my imps walk away from me. When I couldn't see them anymore, I roared in rage, released my anger, knocking down what was left of my house as my power exploded around me.

Once I settled down, I started thinking. So she was stronger than me. I'd have to figure out how that was possible later on. I'd have to prepare myself to destroy the bitch. I'd have to find new places for everyone I loved to live. I'd have to find a place for the immortals to live now. I'd have to deal with Brennan's lies and how they'd affect us from here on out.

I gritted my teeth as my power rose in response to my anger and stress.

At least I didn't hurt anymore when I used it.

And then I smiled. I had an overload of power built up.

And I knew exactly how to use it.

I took one last look at my backyard, then I kicked and rose into the air, heading toward the river, toward Belle Isle.

Toward Strife.

When the river, and Belle Isle, came into view, I steeled myself for the upcoming battle. I was grateful that no one had tried to fight me on the fact that I was coming alone. I couldn't stand to have to worry about Strife killing anyone else I cared about.

By now, I think they knew I could take care of myself. And Nain had been too out of it to even argue. He'd be irritated with me later.

That was fine. Strife would be gone and maybe the loss of her influence would help calm things down. It wouldn't end the mess we had now; the cat was out of the bag regarding supernaturals, and panic wouldn't abate any time soon. But it would only be worse with her here, spurring it on.

She'd caused too many deaths. I blamed her personally for Levitt. Jones. The eleven allies besides them who had died in battle, mostly shifters and vampires.

Who knows how many Normals caught up in the crossfire.

She would pay for every single one of them.

I flew around until I found the abandoned zoo. I'd been there once when I was a kid. My foster family at the time hadn't been too bad, and I'd actually liked them. They'd brought the three kids they were fostering out to the island for the day. We'd gone to the zoo and had a picnic on the beach.

The zoo had been sitting empty now for over ten years. It looked like one of those features in *National Geographic*, when they find deserted villages. The zoo had been a series of wooden bridges, and you'd look down into the pits below to see the animals. Along the boardwalk were cedar-shingled pavilions that had offered shade to zoo visitors, as well as several buildings, one that used to house reptiles, one that had housed insects. I landed near one of these and looked around.

The zoo was eerie. Vines had grown along and across the wooden walkways, and the pits that had been dirt or grass were now overgrown with trees and brush. The small building near where I'd landed was nearly covered with vines.

And amid all of it, I could feel power. I took a deep breath. If I could feel her, she could feel me, too.

It wasn't just Strife. There were demons there. Shifters. Witches and warlocks. I'd never thought to look for her there. The idea of anyone using any part of the island as their base of operations wasn't something I'd ever even considered. The zoo was one of those places so-called "urban explorers" sometimes toured, snapping photos to post on Instagram. I wondered how many of them had ended up falling at the hands of Strife's people.

I walked along the boardwalk, through one of the pavilions. I focused, trying to sense where Strife and her people were. In the end, I didn't have to find Strife at all.

She found me.

I was walking, nearing another pavilion, and she appeared about fifteen feet in front of me. I stopped, and we stood and watched one another.

"So, the little hero has recovered," she sneered. "How fares mommy dearest?"

I didn't answer.

"I suppose you feel like I played dirty at the end there," she said. "And I did. It's what I do. Chaos isn't caused by following the rules."

"You know you can't beat me, Strife," I said, and she laughed.

"It was never about beating you, Fury. It was about making you suffer. Hurting you. Making you pay for Enyo and Ares. And then you killed Terror. That one hurt."

And then she smiled. "And, just as I can't destroy you, you can't destroy me, either. Oh, I'll end at your hands. I don't doubt that. This avatar will fall, and I'll go on. I'll forget you and everything that happened here." She stopped, laughed. "But you won't. You'll live with it forever. You'll replay watching your demon friend die, seeing your mother near death. It will haunt you, every single day of your miserable existence. You will know that you failed as Nether's prison. Maybe she will succeed where so many others have failed."

"Don't hold your breath," I said, still watching her. I could feel what was happening. As she talked to me, doing the stereotypical super-villain monologue thing, her demons and shifters had started approaching me from behind. There were around twenty of them back there. I tried to pretend I couldn't feel them. They were creeping silently along the boardwalk, excitement and nervousness flooding from them. Love and desire. Not for me. For Strife.

"How did you know Nether was in me?" I asked her, trying to make it seem like I was clueless.

She smiled. She really was insanely beautiful. Perfect. I almost wanted to believe she wasn't a monster based on that one smile. It was easy to see how she'd convinced so many to die for her.

"Elsoloth brought me your daddy's helmet. Fun little thing to play with. You have no idea how many times I was in your home. How many times I stood and watched as your friends relaxed, as you and your demon lover shared moments you thought were private. It was easy to share that knowledge with Aphrodite. She had just as much reason to hate you as I did. She was supposed to go for the little vampire first. I would have loved watching you mourn her after you saved her from death once already."

Rage coursed through me and I felt dizzy with it. Nauseous.

"I am the most powerful I've been in years," Strife said, laughing. "The last time I felt this good, I was standing in London during the second World War."

Her people were right behind me and I could feel her glee at the idea that she'd pulled one over on me.

I smiled at her and the air around me exploded in white flames. I heard the screams of her little army as they fell, and I walked forward out of the flames.

She tried to take off, and I rematerialized behind her before she could disappear.

"Fine, you Fury bitch. Just kill me. I've done everything I wanted to do."

I watched her, keeping a strong grip on her arm.

She was stronger than she'd been in a very long time.

I could feel it, how much power coursed through her.

I yanked my sleeve up, revealing the stone containing the souls of Ares and Dionysus.

"Oh, I'm not going to kill you," I said softly.

She did try to fight her way away from me then, but I kept a grip on her. She tried to rematerialize and I refused to let her go anywhere.

"Eris, spirit of chaos," I began, and she started screaming, panicking. The wooden boardwalk behind us burned, creaking with the damage. It would all fall soon.

"For your crimes, for the deaths of countless mortals, as well as the deaths of two of my friends and eleven of my allies, I sentence you to spend eternity trapped in a prison made entirely of the Nether," I continued, and she continued shrieking, the fear coming off of her feeding me, strengthening me, and I didn't even need it. I smiled.

"It will be so."

As I said the words, she gave a higher-pitched shriek, and I watched as she dissolved into a silvery mist, just as Ares and Dionysus had. She wailed, and the mist hung in the air above me. Within moments, it spiraled toward the stone in my armband and then there was nothing left of the spirit of chaos.

I could feel her in the stone, raging, her power strengthening me further, making me so strong I felt practically drunk with it. That would be the last time I'd be able to play that particular trick. The stone could only hold three souls, based on what Nether had shown me when I was trapped in my grave and she was showing me how to strengthen myself.

Good thing she hadn't known that my life and the powers she'd given me would spell her end someday. I hated doing this. I hated the way it felt to have these angry souls imprisoned, to gain strength from them.

But Nether would be nothing but ruthless when she struck me. And I would have to be as well.

I looked around. The wet vines growing on the boardwalk had ended up making the fire fizzle out, and smoke still rose into the air from the burnt bodies of Strife's army.

I walked along the boardwalk. I hadn't even gotten a chance to throw a punch, I thought to myself.

Sometimes, it's not all about smashing, I guess.

I looked around through the former reptile house, looking for the only thing Strife had that I'd ever wanted, and I found it, stuffed into one of the empty tanks, wrapped in a white cloth.

My father's helmet. I ran my fingers along Hephaestus's fine, detailed work. No one would sneak up on my family that way again.

No one would watch us without our knowledge.

I took a deep breath. Nain and I had some things to talk about, and I wasn't looking forward to it.

I rose into the air, clutching my father's helmet in my hand, and flew away from the island.

I flew over the city, back home toward the loft. I could have just rematerialized, but I needed the time to think. So much had happened since I'd left the loft that morning. Brennan's little revelation. The loss of my imps. Meeting my grandmother. Strife.

How was I going to keep everyone safe?

We had immortals in our world now who were openly against us. Two Titans who'd escaped from the Nether.

And then we had Nether herself, who would come after everything I held dear as soon as she'd generated a body.

The loft came into view, and I could see Nain on the roof. Along with Artemis. They both saw me, watched as I landed on the roof a few feet away from them.

"Hey babe," Nain said, looking me over.

"Hey."

"Anything new?" he asked.

"Oh, a thing or two," I said, my eyes on Artemis, who was watching me just as closely.

"Fury, relax," she said, "I'd rather not die today."

"Did you know?" I asked, and she nodded.

"Molls," Nain said, and I turned to him. "We were just talking about Brennan. He talked to you?"

I nodded, not able to trust my voice, still not quite able to believe what Brennan had told me.

"I knew, baby," he said. "I knew."

"And you didn't think to share that with me?" I asked him. "You didn't think to step in and say 'hey, Molly. The whole reason he wants you is so he can tell his little government buddies all about you?'"

"Yeah, except that that wasn't why he wanted you and everybody including you knows that," he said. "I knew they were watching. It didn't matter. And when was I supposed to tell you that? When you were already in love with him and I thought you maybe had a chance at being happy? Or maybe when I wanted you back so bad I could have killed him? It was his place to tell you or whoever else he's been watching, not mine. I wasn't going to come running to you telling you something he should have been man enough to tell you in the first place." He paused. "And I know him. He did it to protect us."

"Right. He was all about protecting us," I said, rolling my eyes.

"Do you really think he told them everything? That him agreeing to work with them wasn't as much about controlling the flow of information as anything else? Having one of our own in there, deciding how much they are allowed to know just makes sense," he said. "Give the man a little credit." He paused. "I can't fucking believe I just said that."

Artemis laughed, then she looked at me. "He loved you. He still does. He's just trying to learn how to love you in a different way. Do not think for a second that he didn't."

275

"So, what? Everything is just fine between all of you?"

"I knew we were being watched. He told them what he thought they needed to know. Not everything," Nain said, and Artemis nodded.

"He wanted to tell you," Artemis said. "He knew you would hate him once you found out. We all know how private you are. By the time he wanted to, you were together and he knew it would end you."

"Right. Had to keep me close to keep spying on me," I said. "I guess I can see how you could be okay with this," I said to Nain. "This is what you do. This is the game you all play. But I can't be okay with it. It's just a little too personal. Don't expect me to work with him." I paused, and they both watched me. I closed my eyes, fought back a wave of exhaustion. Time to change the subject.

"Strife is gone. We need to move everyone before Nether regenerates." I took a breath. "How are things?"

"They're okay, somewhat," Nain said. "Still fighting in the streets. Mobs of dumbass Normals organizing to try to hunt down supernaturals. That's not working out very well for them," he finished. I could sense what he wanted from me.

"You think Jones and Brennan are right," I said softly, meeting his eyes. "That shit they're asking me to do."

He reached out and took my hands. "I think you need to do what you think is right. And whatever you decide, I'm with you."

I glanced at Artemis. "Can you excuse us?"

"Sure. I will see you, Mollis," she said, and I nodded, my eyes on Nain.

When she was gone, I set my dad's helmet down. I went to Nain, let him fold me in his arms.

"I'm sorry I didn't tell you about Brennan," he murmured, his deep voice vibrating through me. "It wasn't my place. Besides that, it was just something I was used to, and I figured it might never have to come out at all. I didn't want you to think I was trying to use what I knew about him to win you back or some shit like that. I wanted you to come to me because you wanted me, not because you were pissed at him."

"I know. It's fine," I said, resting my face against his chest. Tired of fighting and emotional bullshit. I breathed him in, let his touch soothe my frazzled nerves.

"Did you really kill Strife?" he asked.

"I didn't kill her. Ares and Dionysus have company now," I said.

He stood and held me in silence. "Why?"

"Because I need to be stronger." I told him about my imps. About my grandmother and what she'd said, and when I was done, he just stood and held me. Anger, protectiveness, concern washed over me. Love, desire. I let myself feel it. All of it.

Then I pulled back and looked up at him. "So. Given what I just told you, are you sure you don't wanna run?"

He smiled. "There is nothing that is going to make me leave your side, Molls."

"Ready to put that in blood, demon?"

I felt a leap of happiness, possessiveness from him. "You already know the answer to that."

I smiled and pulled my knife, the brown ribbon from his dresser drawer, the one we'd originally used when we'd bonded, out of my pocket.

"You came prepared. Eager, are we?" he asked, smirking.

"Just a little," I told him, and he reached down and squeezed my waist. "We're doing this, and a little more."

"A whole lot more," he said, and I laughed.

"I'm going to claim you," I said, meeting his eyes.

"What does that mean?"

"It means you're mine. I claim you, and I'm a powerful goddamn immortal, and you'll be even stronger than you already are once I make you mine. You get a little of my power, and I can always, always find my way back to you."

He watched me, need and possessiveness roaring over me. He gave me a nod, eyes locked on mine.

The evening air was cool around us; the sky clear. The nearly-full moon shone bright in the darkness. We stood on the roof, the city twinkling around us, night noises comforting in the distance.

He slit his wrist, and passed the knife to me. I slit mine as well, and we pressed them together. Nain wound the ribbon around our wrists, and we stood, my hands in his, fingers entwined. His lips were on mine, devouring me, and I felt the moment the bonding began, the moment his blood flowed into my body again, and I gasped, shivered at the sensation. He groaned, satisfaction rolling off of him, and he was completely open to me in that moment. Love, desire, possessiveness. Determination to do better this time around, to be the man I deserved. I closed my eyes, and smiled against his lips. Time for a little something extra.

Mine, I thought, focusing my powers, the ones I had as an immortal child of the Nether. I thought the word over and over and over again, putting my power behind it, claiming my husband.

"Holy shit," he rasped, feeling it the second my bond took hold, as it wrapped itself around the bond we'd already been making. His heart was pounding, and the raw desire coming from him was enough to make me blush, even as I knew he was feeling the same from me. He'd know, now, what I was feeling. Physically, at least. Just as he had for a little while the first time we'd bonded. We stood there until our wounds healed, and he slowly unwound the ribbon.

His eyes were glowing, the effect of our bonding making itself evident. We might make it to the bed. Maybe.

"That was... wow," he said, his voice rough.

"I'm not losing you again. Ever," I said as he put his arms around my body.

"This is forever, Molly. Whatever comes next, we're facing it together."

"I love you, my husband," I whispered.

"Come and show me how much, wife," he said, his voice a low growl in the night.

And I did.

EPILOGUE

I stood in the lobby of the Fisher Building, podium full of mics in front of me, the mayor of Detroit, the new chief of police, the head of homeland security, and Brennan (dressed in a dark suit and tie, which looked both weird and oddly right) standing behind me. I tried to focus on not turning around and strangling my former boyfriend.

There were rows of folding chairs full of reporters in front of me, others standing around watching. Lights glaring at me from every direction. Nain stood near the back of the crowd, along with Heph. Watching me. Watching for threats.

I took a deep breath. Looked directly into the nearest camera. I couldn't bring Jones back, but I could grant the last favor he'd ever asked of me, no matter how badly I wanted to tell this particular little task force to go fuck themselves. There was no way to avoid it now, anyway. And if I could save lives, it was worth it.

"The citizens of Detroit know me as the Angel," I

began, and I could hear my voice wavering. Nerves. "For years, I have saved those who were believed lost. I have protected the innocent from the nightmares that walk among us. Countless women, girls, boys, and men have made it back to their loved ones because I or my friends interceded." I paused, swallowed. This was more terrifying than just about anything else I'd done recently.

"You've seen the news reports. You've seen unbelievable things these past few weeks. And so, I'm here today to tell you what you already know: supernatural beings exist. We walk among you. We always have. We are your neighbors, your co-workers. Many of us are just like you, trying to raise our families and live a content life."

"And there are others. There are those who believe our powers make us superior. There are those who crave power. Control. And there are those, like me, who have made it their life's mission to fight against those who would harm you. Just as there are noble humans and evil humans, there are noble supernaturals and evil supernaturals, and everything in between. You cannot know, from looking at most of us, what we are."

I took another breath, glanced toward Nain, whose eyes were on me. *You're doing good, Molls.*

"And here's where I make my plea to you. If you know of me, you know that I have always been on your side. You have prayed to me, when all other hope was lost. You know I have been this city's guardian for years. So when I ask this of you, I hope you'll listen. Trying to hunt supernaturals, trying to hunt us down, believing you'll keep the world safe from us, is a fool's notion. The strongest among you is nothing compared to the weakest supernatural. And yes, there are supernaturals out there causing trouble. Leave them to me. I will take care of them. You can't hope to do anything against them."

"I have come out of the shadows. I have made myself known, so you know that there is someone out there protecting you. I'm one of many, but I'm the one you know. I'm here, on behalf of myself, my friends and allies, and our government to tell you that yes, we exist. And that when one of us steps out of line, I will be there to protect you. I swear it on everything I am. I am supernatural. I am on your side. And I will protect you until I take my final breath."

"Thank you."

THE END

Keep reading for a sneak peek
at the final book in the Hidden series

NETHER: HIDDEN, BOOK FIVE

NETHER: CHAPTER ONE

My name is Molly Brooks.
Mollis Eth-Hades, if we're being fancy.
Telepath.
Godslayer.
Smasher of all kinds of things.
Protector of the city of Detroit.

And not just that.
I'm a daughter.
A friend.
A wife.

Good thing I'm as scary as I am. It is going to take every bit of my insane amount of power to keep the people in my life safe. For the first time in a very long time, I am facing something stronger than me.
Crazier than me.
Meaner than me.

Nether.

But if she comes after the people I love?

I will do whatever it takes to keep them safe. And all that darkness I've been holding back? All that power I've been afraid of using?

Well. I guess we'll see what I'm really capable of. With two Titans, an insane primordial spirit, and a handful of pissed off gods free in my world, I've got my work cut out for me.

Nain and I walked through the huge arched front door of Assumption Grotto just as the church's bells started ringing. I glanced over at him for about the millionth time since he'd come out of our room that morning.

"Stop gawking at me, woman," he muttered, even as a smile quirked at the corners of his mouth.

"You are wearing the hell out of that tux, babe," I said, and he laughed. "Damn." He pulled his hand out of mine and put it around my waist, pulled me close. The wedding party was already assembled in the foyer, minus the bride, of course. I glanced around and had to smile. Nain, Brennan, and one of Stone's best friends, a shifter from the Hamtramck pack, all stood there in their tuxes. The three bridesmaids were three of Ada's best friends, fellow witches she'd known her entire life. We all greeted one another, and Eunomia and Heph walked in.

"A dress, Mollis? Will wonders never cease?" E asked, hugging me. I looked down at the pale purple long-sleeved dress I was wearing. Matching heels and everything, which had nearly killed me at least a dozen times. Screw Titans or insane immortals; it was the heels that would be the end of me.

"Ada picked this out. Can you believe she didn't trust my fashion sense?" I asked, and she laughed. We all chatted for a few minutes as guests filed in, the priest came out of a little side room and smiled at all of us.

"Father Balester," I said respectfully when he came over and shook my hand.

"Angel. It is an absolute pleasure to see you under happier circumstances," he said, smiling.

"Definitely," I agreed.

Father Balester wasn't your average Catholic priest. His flock was not exactly normal, either. Father Balester was one of us.

Supernatural.

The man could turn into a tree. Not even kidding. He was an Earth guardian. His kind were rare, and their job was to try to keep the natural world in some kind of balance. He had his work cut out for him, working in an industrial city like Detroit. But he loved the city, and he went into the priesthood because he could sense that there was a need for someone like him for our kind to turn to.

In the past three weeks, he'd had his hands full presiding over supernatural funerals. Levitt. Chief Jones. Three vampires from Queen Rayna's family. Five shifters from various packs. Two witches and a warlock who were allied with us. Things had been grim, and Ada and Stone had considered calling off the wedding they'd started planning before the world went insane.

As I stood there with my friends, I was even happier they'd decided to go ahead. Life was insane, and ours was even crazier. You had to grab happiness the second you had a chance at it, because it could be taken from you at any time. We knew that all too well.

"Shall we head in, then?" Father Balester asked, and the groomsmen all headed up the aisle toward the front of the church, where Stone was already waiting, looking more nervous than I'd ever seen him, his white handlebar mustache impeccably trimmed and combed. I smiled as I watched him pull yet again at the sleeves of his jacket. Nain kissed me before heading in, and Father Balester gave me another small smile. E took my hand, and we walked into the church together, heading for one of the front pews reserved for the bride and groom's family. I spotted Shanti and Zero sitting with the rest of Rayna's family, and waved at both of them.

One of the pews on the right side of the church could easily have been dubbed "immortal section." Heph, Athena, my aunt Meg, my mother, my father, Persephone (who had struck up a fast friendship with Ada over witchy stuff after the battle downtown), Asclepias, and Artemis were all sitting there, and E and I joined them. I sat between E and Artemis, who had Sean on her lap.

I greeted everyone, then glanced at Sean, who looked pretty dapper in his tiny suit. He was almost a year old, and had just started walking. "Hey kiddo," I said. My glowing eyes didn't impress him anymore the way they had when he was an infant. Too many supernaturals around, all of us with varying colors of glowing, freaky eyes, and I was nothing special.

"This child is a nightmare," Artemis said, a small smile on her face. She adored her great times about a hundred grandson. "I am starting to miss the playpen days."

I smiled. "He's keeping you in shape, old woman," I said, and she smacked my arm lightly, laughing.

I looked down the row. The immortals weren't here because they were particularly close to Ada (though some of them were). They were here for security. One reason we'd even considered holding off on the wedding was because things were still crazy among supernaturals, and a big gathering of our allies all in one place seemed like just asking for trouble. Ada and her witch friends and Persephone had worked a whole lot of magic to shield and protect the church and its grounds, and it was unlikely anything that wasn't supposed to be there could get in.

But if they did, they'd have ten immortals ready to kick their ass. Nothing was going to mess up Stone and Ada's day.

I glanced toward the front of the church to see Nain watching me. I gave him a tiny smile, then the organ music started, and the bridesmaids started making their way down the aisle. I turned with everyone else to watch them, and as I did, I surveyed the room. We were doing a good job working together. It was strange to see demons, immortals, shifters, werewolves, vampires, witches, and warlocks all in one place. It was even stranger to see them sitting, not solely in groups of their own kind, but all mixed up together. The battle for Detroit (as some in the media had started calling it) had brought us together, made us interact with one another in a way we never had.

I turned my attention back to the bridesmaids, and once the final one reached the altar, the music changed, the wedding march started, and everyone rose and turned toward the back of the church.

When Ada walked through, tears came to my eyes. She was radiant, her silver hair intricately braided around her head, her face glowing with happiness. She wore a long cream dress that trailed behind her, lace everywhere. I could see the silver pentacle she always wore, still around her throat. No veil, and I was glad. The look in her eyes, the happiness there, was absolutely breathtaking. She glanced toward me as she made her way up the aisle, and smiled. I smiled back and watched her continue up to the altar.

We all sat, and I dabbed at my eyes.

"I never would have taken you for the type to cry at weddings," E whispered, leaning toward me.

"Shut up," I said. "I'm not crying."

"Of course not," Artemis whispered on my other side, rolling her eyes.

I shushed them both and focused on the group at the front of the church. Father Balester started talking, and my attention went back to my husband.

Damn.

As crazy and sad as the last few weeks had been, between the continued fighting and all of the funerals we'd attended, it had been a happy time for the two of us. We were having that goofy, happy newlywed period we'd never had before. We were all over one another, and it still wasn't enough. Every day I learned something about him that I loved. And every day, he did at least one thing that made me want to kick his ass.

He's a demon, after all.

I watched him, smiled to myself.

I can't wait to tear that off of you later, I thought at him.

You are insatiable. Quiet, woman.

Though maybe you could keep the tie on.

I watched as he tried to keep a straight face.

You are gonna get it later.

Promise?

His eyes met mine, and I could see that he was trying not to laugh. And then I turned my attention back to Ada and Stone as they started saying their vows.

They were beautiful. That was all I could think as I watched them say their vows, exchange golden bands as if they were the only two people in existence. The way they focused on one another. The love between them was strong, warm. I wiped at my eyes again, and E passed me a tissue, right before she dabbed at her own eyes.

When it ended, everyone milled around taking photos, and then we all slowly but surely made our way back to the loft for the reception.

The loft was empty of all of our usual furniture. That was all sitting in moving vans down in the garage, waiting for us to move the rest of the stuff out. Nain had found us two duplexes, side by side in Harper Woods. Between the four units, there would be enough room for everyone who currently lived at the loft.

I hated that we had to move.

But now that Nether was free, it was just a matter of time before she finished generating a body. And once that happened, she would come after me.

Which meant that she would come after everyone I loved. And she knew everything I knew from sharing soulspace with me for so long. From sharing my mind and body. She knew who I loved. Where to find those people. Who my friends and allies were and where they lived.

Everyone was moving. Shifter packs. Rayna had already relocated her people to a house in Indian Village. We were almost done packing, and then we'd be moving on from the loft, too. But it was the perfect place to host this little get-together, now that the main part was empty. Long tables had been set up, each covered with a white tablecloth, with wooden folding chairs along all of them. The reception, like the wedding, would be fairly small, but we hadn't cut any corners. There was a towering white wedding cake on the kitchen island, where everyone could see it, and the former training floor was now a dance floor. Near that, one of the vampires was setting up his system. Yep, a vampire DJ, one of Rayna's people.

Rayna had brought us plenty of connections. She was a shrewd business woman, and it was becoming clear how she made her money. She had several small businesses, including a restaurant and catering company. So we used them, and even got a discount because she likes us. The vampire servers were setting the food up on a long table along one wall, and I could smell it. I was starving.

Everyone milled around, talking and eating, congratulating the bride and groom. The cake was cut, and then the DJ started doing his thing and we watched Stone and Ada have their first dance. Nain stood beside me, huge hand on my hip, and I could feel his happiness for his two oldest friends.

"They look so happy," I said to him.

"They do."

I glanced up at him. "We should try to get them to retire. Move them to Florida or something," I said quietly.

He nodded. "We'll see. You know they won't take us up on that."

"We should still try."

He squeezed my waist, then took my hand and led me to the dance floor, where other couples were starting to sway to the music as well. I danced with him, loving the feel of being in his arms, his strong shoulder under my hand, his fingers twining with those of my other hand. I loved the way he leaned down and nuzzled the side of my neck.

"If you don't stop that I'm going to drag you into our room one last time," I whispered.

"We should have another go on the roof before we move out, too," he murmured, and I blushed. Our roof had seen more than a little action in the past couple of weeks. We'd broken the glider, and Nain promised me he'd get it fixed.

I kissed his throat as the song ended, and then we both started trying to be good hosts, talking to the people who had come to Ada and Stone's reception. Of course, any gathering of supernaturals is an opportunity for politics, and this was no different. Shifters and witches who were maybe not as high up in our hierarchy as Nain, Brennan, Rayna, Jamie, and I seemed, already, to always be trying to work their way up, as if leadership of Detroit's supernatural community was something to aspire to. I spent the next hour and a half listening to people complain. I promised meetings. I answered questions. When I finally freed myself from an especially irritating conversation with an older warlock, I looked for a quiet corner to hide in.

Ugh. Socializing. This so wasn't my thing.

I looked toward the living room, which was quieter than the dance floor and where the tables were set up. There were folding chairs there, too, arranged in small groups for conversation. Brennan sat in the corner, Sean on his lap. I glanced toward the dance floor, where Nain was dancing with Ada. I caught his eyes and glanced toward Brennan, and he nodded.

I walked over to Brennan and Sean and sat down in the chair next to him. I kicked the torturous heels off and tucked my feet under the chair, barely suppressing a sigh.

"It was a nice wedding, huh? I've never been to one before," I said. Sean dozed against Brennan's chest.

"It was nice. They looked happy," he said. I sensed for him. Nervousness. Sadness. Guilt.

"No date?" I asked him, and he shook his head, met my eyes.

"I'm taking a break. I think that's for the best," he said, and I didn't know how to respond to that.

We sat in awkward silence for a few minutes. "I'm surprised you're talking to me," he said finally.

I glanced over at him. "Did you think I would give you the silent treatment forever?" I asked him.

"I wouldn't have blamed you if you did."

I sighed. "I have a hard time being mad at you. I mean, maybe someone saner than I am would look at everything that's happened and wonder why I haven't killed you yet."

"I have wondered that myself," he said, and I was happy to see a little bit of a smile on his lips.

"I can't hate you, Bren. Not for the witch, not for Sean. Not even for telling Ross and his guys about me." Agent Ross, who headed a special division of the Department of Homeland Security that was specifically tasked with watching supernaturals and responding to the chaos that had erupted because of Strife. Brennan's boss. "Like you said: I save the world my way, and you save it yours."

He was quiet for a minute. "So you get that none of what we had was a lie, right?"

I nodded. "I know."

He took a deep breath, and I felt relief roll off of him. "Good."

"Why did that relieve you so much?" I asked him.

He shook his head. "Because if you actually believed that I didn't really love you, that would only make you doubt yourself more, and that's the last thing you should do. And I was crazy in love with you and it matters that you know that."

"I do."

"Why the change of heart?" he asked me.

I shrugged. "Look how crazy everything has been. How many we've lost." I shook my head, ended up looking over at him and meeting his eyes. "Life is too short and too insane to stay mad at the people you care about. And no matter what else happened, you were there for me when no one else was. I mean, I'm not ready to start hanging out or anything like that, but I'm sick of losing people. And I'm sure the hell not going to lose someone who's still alive and well."

He just stared at me. "Who are you and what have you done with Molly?"

I laughed, and after a couple of seconds, he joined in.

I glanced around, saw that Nain was on his phone. He hung up and started walking toward me and Brennan. He leaned down.

"We have to take off, baby," he said.

"What's going on?" I asked, standing up. Brennan stood up too, shifting his hold on Sean.

"That was one of the Delray shifters. Apparently the whole fucking neighborhood just disappeared."

"What do you mean, disappeared?" I asked him.

"I mean it's gone. Nothing there, like the Earth just swallowed it up. That's what he says, anyway.'

I watched as Brennan and Nain exchanged a glance. "Hopefully he's been hitting the bottle again," Brennan said, and Nain let out a grunt of agreement.

"That's what I'm hoping. With all the other weird shit going on, I doubt it, though," Nain said.

Brennan gestured to Artemis, and she walked over, took Sean. "I'm coming too. Can you watch him, Artemis?" he asked, and the immortal nodded and took Sean from him.

Within a few minutes, we were heading out of the loft, still dressed in our wedding clothes, heading for a neighborhood that no longer existed.

READ MORE IN
HIDDEN BOOK FIVE:
NETHER
COMING IN FALL 2014

Visit http://www.colleenvanderlinden.com/hidden
for news, updates, and more

Never Miss an Update!

Sign up for the Hidden Newsletter.
http://bit.ly/hiddennewsletter

For backstory material, news, and upcoming
events be sure to check out
http://www.colleenvanderlinden.com/hidden

ABOUT THE AUTHOR

Colleen Vanderlinden is the author and publisher of the *Hidden* series, which currently includes *Lost Girl*, *Broken*, and *Home*. She lives in the Detroit area with her husband, children, and two lazy cats. She enjoys reading, obsessing over comic book characters, gardening, and playing World of Warcraft.

Website: http://www.colleenvanderlinden.com
Facebook: facebook.com/colleenvanderlinden
Twitter: @C_Vanderlinden

The Hidden Series

Book One: Lost Girl
Book Two: Broken
Book Three: Home
Book 3.5: Forever Night
Book Four: Strife
Book Five: Nether - Available Fall 2014

www.ingramcontent.com/pod-product-compliance
Lightning Source LLC
Chambersburg PA
CBHW071253170626
46809CB00001B/202